"I NOTICE EVERYTHING ABOUT YOU."

Alyse tensed as Rand cradled her jaw with the heels of his thumbs. While she stared uncertainly into the dark shadows of his face, he slowly bent and pressed his lips to hers.

Rand groaned, and Alyse flowed into his arms. His hands moved down, and then under her top, settling hotly into the bare hollow of her waist as he pulled her tightly against him.

The fragrance of plumeria blossoms drifted on the gentle night breeze. The slow, rhythmic pounding of the surf seemed to grow disant.

"Rand," she sighed as his lips moved over her hair, then down to the lobe of her ear and the curve of her neck.

They stood there for a long time, locked in an exploratory embrace. Their kisses grew intense, demanding, until Rand suddenly drew back, tucking her head tightly against his shoulder. He held her like that for a moment, struggling to regain control of himself, then took an uneven breath.

"Do you want me to take you back to the cottage?" he asked hoarsely.

Alyse shook her head, not trusting her voice. She had never felt this way with a man before — so totally, unequivocally *right*. Love, and being loved, made all the difference.

KAREN RHODES

Shining Tide

ZEBRA BOOKS
KENSINGTON PUBLISHING CORP.

ZEBRA BOOKS

are published by

Kensington Publishing Corp.
475 Park Avenue South
New York, NY 10016

Photo Credit: Helen Duchon

First printing: October, 1992

Printed in the United States of America

*With love to Marshall Carnell
and Hayashi "Donald" Tokunaga — the real
hunters of the dragonfly.*

Prologue

As the driver whipped the cab into a no parking zone, Alyse Marlowe jammed a twenty-dollar bill into the money slot and threw open the door. Forfeiting at least seven dollars in change, she leaped out and sprinted madly up the crowded sidewalk, her tawny curls swirling in the gusty autumn breeze.

It wasn't her fault that an idiot had chosen this of all mornings to drive a balky truck tractor through bumper-to-bumper traffic on Madison Avenue. Even so, if she missed the bidding on the lacquered box, Conrad Brace would have a fit. She was too deeply in his debt to risk incurring his wrath.

She almost lost a shoe when she skidded to a halt on the damp pavement in front of Bundys. Alyse hauled open the heavy brass-and-plate glass door and reeled into the baize-walled lobby of the New York art auction house. Before she could get her bearings, she ran headlong into a swarthy, muscular man in a gray business suit and an incongruously bright coral shirt.

"Sorry," she gasped, as he threw his arms around her to keep her from falling.

"My pleasure," he laughed, flashing even, white teeth. "Where's the fire?"

"Traffic jam," she panted. "I'm late."

Alyse disengaged herself. She took a quick step to one side and almost collided with a tall, stern-faced but strikingly handsome man. He was carrying a large wrapped package under one arm, and had a small, sad-eyed boy in tow. The child, who appeared to be about six years old, looked back at her as they pushed through the front door onto the sidewalk.

She froze for an instant, mesmerized by the odd, aching expression in the boy's soft brown eyes. A powerful longing that was almost like grief welled up inside her. Alyse shuddered, and thrust the feeling aside.

"Late for what?" asked the swarthy man, regaining her attention.

"The Tokugawa Shogun tea box," she said. "I'm from the Brace Gallery."

His smile faltered. He looked at her carefully.

"Bad news, miss," he said, nodding toward the front door. "That fellow just bought it."

Alyse spun back toward the door with a plaintive groan.

"Wait!" she cried.

Too late. The door had swung shut. She raced out onto the sidewalk, glancing frantically in both directions. The man had been tall enough to stand out in any crowd. But he and the child had already disappeared.

* * *

The boy skipped at his side to keep up as Rand Turnbull strode purposefully across the intersection. He had saved a bundle on the Tokugawa box by bidding on it himself, rather than purchasing it from a dealer. Rand made a mental note to send a token of his appreciation to the Bundy brothers for letting him know the box would be on the auction block that morning.

"Not now, Tommy," he said, tugging the boy's hand as the youngster paused to ogle a toy store window.

"Yes, Uncle Rand," Tommy said, the words soft and practiced, as if they had been firmly drilled into his copper-blond head.

Rand shifted the package under his arm, still preoccupied as they headed up Park Avenue toward his apartment. The Tokugawa box would make an impressive gift to present to his new Japanese clients at the luau next week. The presentation of gifts was a traditional part of the Japanese business culture, and he wanted to make sure their relationship got off on the right footing.

Years of experience as a contract negotiator had left Rand closely attuned to the sometimes intricate customs of his international clientele. Still, he thought it was odd—but shrewd—that the Japanese real estate investment group had actually hinted for the antique through their American partner, Lyle Eason.

"Uncle Rand?" Tommy sounded out of breath.

Rand slowed, feeling a twinge as he glanced

down at his brother's orphan. The kid was Chris's duplicate, right down to the dimple in the left cheek. Every time Rand looked at Tommy, he could almost picture Chris and Pat drowning in that damnable accident. After ten months, the pain still gnawed in his chest.

"Does Moowy smell bad?" Tommy asked as they passed a reeking hedgerow of garbage bags, thanks to the latest sanitation workers strike.

"Maui," Rand corrected, concerned that Tommy had lapsed into baby talk — among other things — since being orphaned. "No. Maui doesn't stink."

The boy was quiet as a monk most of the time, which also worried Rand. As much as he loved Tommy, he didn't have the remotest idea how to go about raising a kid, particularly a prodigy. They had been together for two months now, and yet they were still awkward around each other.

Tommy was Chris's legacy and Rand was determined to adopt the boy. In spite of the obstacles Chris's industrial-strength mother-in-law tried to throw in the way. Elaine Fielding had already done Tommy enough harm for a lifetime. Her recent hiring of a private detective was a new and unexpected low blow.

"Will we live in Maui forever and ever?" Tommy asked.

"*On* Maui," Rand corrected. "It's an island. We'll be there just until the luau a week from tomorrow."

"What's a luau?"

Rand stopped and looked down at the boy. "It's a

big party," he said, struggling for a child-friendly tone of voice and failing miserably. "With roast pig and pineapples."

Tommy lowered his button chin as if he'd been scolded. Rand sighed. He was never going to get the hang of this, he thought, as he reached down and scooped the boy into his arm.

"How could you have done this to me, Alyse?" Conrad Brace stormed, his pale face flushed with anger.

Alyse had expected her employer to blow a fuse when he learned she had arrived at Bundys too late to bid on the Tokugawa box. She just hadn't anticipated his taking it so personally.

"I told you this morning that I'd already promised the box to a valued customer," Brace continued, without giving her a chance to speak.

Not that she had anything to say. In the past ten minutes, Conrad had pretty well covered all the bases. In essence, he had let her know loud and clear that she had let him down big-time.

"Now, I want you to hightail it back to Bundys and find out who stole the box out from under me," Brace said, jabbing a finger in front of her face. "Get it back at any price, do you understand? I don't care if you have to sell your body for it."

Alyse's eyebrows shot up. They stared at each other for a long moment, contemplating what he had just said. Then Brace's round shoulders seemed to slump inside his Irish tweed suit. He sighed, forced an apologetic smile, and raised a hand to her cheek.

"You know what I mean," he said.

"I'll do my best, Conrad," Alyse promised, feeling a tremor in his fingers. She sensed something beneath the heat of his anger. Something cold— *frightened?*

"Of course, you will."

His hand fell to his side. Brace fidgeted, working the knot in his wool tie higher against his thick neck. He seemed on the verge of saying something more. Suspecting that he was about to shift gears and make yet another clumsy effort to insinuate himself into her personal life, Alyse quickly bailed out of the conversation.

"I'll get right on it, Conrad," she said, and beat a hasty retreat to her tiny office.

The day had certainly taken a depressing turn, she thought. Alyse glumly scanned the clutter of notes thumb-tacked to the cork board over her desk, searching for the scribbled phone number of her contact at Bundys. Her gaze snagged on a six-month-old bulletin from the U.S. Customs Service. It reported the theft of an item known as the dragonfly pendant, stolen from a Japanese imperial exhibit in Kyoto. The Japanese government was offering a staggering reward for information leading to the return of the national treasure.

Alyse took a deep breath and let it out slowly, her mood sliding down yet another rung. Rob had died of a sudden heart attack in Kyoto last spring. Had she really been a widow that long? His death had been so shockingly unexpected, considering his mania for physical fitness.

Rob had been chief overseas buyer for the Brace Gallery, a job that had kept him traveling most of the time during the four years of their dismal marriage. They had grown so far apart that his sudden death still had an aura of unreality about it.

She unconsciously rubbed the naked ring finger of her left hand. Those months had been unbelievably lonely. But she was no lonelier, she realized, than she had been before becoming a widow. The elusive Tokugawa box seemed to have made her unlucky in life in general.

Alyse continued shuffling through papers in search of the contact's phone number. She wasn't sure why she had stayed on at the Brace Gallery. She had received her art appraiser's certification two years ago. Even Conrad knew she would someday strike out on her own. But she kept putting off that day, perhaps because he had been so good to her these past months.

Besides, Rob hadn't exactly left her financially secure. She couldn't afford to open a curbside hot dog stand, let alone her own gallery.

Every few months, she would sit herself down and calculate how much it would cost to launch her own business — just to prove to herself how far out of reach her dream remained. The result of that little exercise was always disheartening. At her current salary, Alyse figured she'd have enough saved to open her own gallery just about in time to retire to an old folks' home. And yet, her dream somehow lived on as if it possessed a heart and soul of its own.

Shaking herself, Alyse snatched a business card from the cork board and sank onto her swivel desk chair. This was no time to stand around feeling sorry for herself. Not while she had a two-hundred-year-old lacquered tea box to track down.

Chapter One

Alyse walked along the edge of the foaming surf, carrying her shoes, her bare toes digging into the warm wet sand of Waikiki Beach. A brisk sea breeze fanned the skirt of her cotton dress, wrinkled from the long flight from New York. One glance at the beach from the balcony of her room at the Beachcomber Hotel had thoroughly seduced her. She hadn't even bothered to change clothes.

She still couldn't believe the quest for the Tokugawa box had so swiftly catapulted her into paradise. By the time she had tracked down the buyer, Rand Turnbull had already left for the islands. To her surprise, Conrad Brace hadn't so much as blinked at the expense of sending Alyse after the globe-trotting lawyer. Whoever Conrad had promised the box to, she concluded, must be loaded to the gills.

The breeze whipped her skirt. She batted the hem down and gathered a wad of fabric in one hand to protect her modesty. The beach was crowded with sunbathers scattered on towels and sporting varying degrees of first-degree burns. Only a few swimmers bobbed in the water near shore. Farther out a lone adventurer crouched on his surfboard, preparing to catch an incoming wave.

Alyse stopped to watch a small boy wading alone a dozen yards up the beach. His pale skin was reddening in the brilliant tropical sun. There was something vaguely familiar about his thatch of copper-blond hair and the somber expression on his face as he picked his way along the surf line. As he drew nearer, she found that she was smiling.

A thin cry carried on the breeze and she glanced out to sea. The surfer had risen on his board, deftly skimming along the edge of an enormous swell. Alyse watched, spellbound, as the swell grew, grew to a towering height. The surfer yelped again, slicing in along the bore as the wave peaked out and toppled forward in a gargantuan curl into which the board and rider disappeared.

The wave crashed down in a thunderous roar, and the surfer emerged from the foaming rubble of saltwater, miraculously still standing, bellowing in exhilaration. Alyse laughed, vicariously sharing the joy of his adventure. Then she turned back toward the wading boy—and froze.

The child had vanished.

The breaker charged far onto shore, grabbing hungrily at her ankles and rapidly climbing to mid-calf. Alyse searched the momentarily inundated stretch of beach for any sign of the boy. Farther out, movement caught her eye. Shading her eyes against the sun-glare, she peered into the receding surf and spotted a small, flailing figure being dragged swiftly away from shore.

Alyse dropped her shoes and took off running into the water. A second wave thundered in just as she dove forward, and drove her deep into the swirling surf. Surfacing, she spotted the boy thrashing wildly not ten feet away, his eyes wide with panic. She called to him, and struck out in his direction in a strong crawl.

She reached him in seconds and tried to time her final stroke. But his movements were erratic, and he caught her under the eye with a hard fist just as she reached for him. The blow jarred her, but she grabbed him anyway, lifting his head out of the water.

"Hold your breath," she shouted, tightening her grip. "Here comes another one."

A third wave crashed down, tumbling them head over heels and driving them bodily against the sandy bottom. Alyse kicked and struggled against the vicious undertow, feeling it sucking them toward deeper water like some horrific, voracious monster.

Her skirt wrapped around her legs, impeding her movements. But she couldn't shed her clothes and maintain her grip on the boy, while battling the deadly undertow. She grabbed a handful of his thick hair, giving herself more freedom with her feet in the side kick. She began to make progress, praying that the child was managing to get enough air.

The final wave caught Alyse totally by surprise.

17

Its impact knocked the breath from her. She gulped sea water as she flipped, still hanging onto the boy's hair, and completely lost her bearings. He became dead weight — an anchor to her drowning struggles. Her lungs screamed for air as white-hot panic flared within her.

Suddenly, Alyse felt her knees and thighs grind punishingly into the sandy bottom. She rolled over and rode the surf into shallower water. Weak, battered, and still disoriented, she managed to shove the child onto the beach. She lay in the shallows for a moment, coughing and gagging on saltwater, before crawling on all fours to his side.

He was choking. Alyse gave him a couple of sharp whacks between the shoulder blades. When he started sobbing, she lifted him into her arms and sat in the wet sand, rocking him. To her surprise, he flung his thin arms around her neck, clinging desperately to her with an iron embrace. She hugged him back possessively as tears stung her eyes.

"You'll be all right," she murmured, stroking his shivering body. "It was just a nasty scare."

He nodded vigorously. His sobs began to break up into irregular hitches and coughs as a crowd began to gather around them. Alyse looked down at herself, increasingly aware of how the wet cotton dress had plastered itself against her body. She tugged at it self-consciously, feeling naked.

A stocky teenager wearing fluorescent-green jams stepped forward. "Hey, lady," he said, scratching his bony chest. "Didn't you see the warning flag?"

Alyse peered up at him, blank-faced. The kid jabbed a thumb over his shoulder toward a bright pennant fluttering over a building set back from the beach.

"That means the riptide is too dangerous for swimming," he said.

The child abruptly stopped crying and looked up at the youth, his chin still puckered. "We wasn't swimming," he declared in a high, clear voice with just a hint of a lisp. "We was *drowning*."

A smattering of tension-breaking laughter rippled through the crowd, and the sunbathers began to disperse. Alyse rose, shook the worst of the wet sand from her dress, and helped the boy to his feet.

"I'm Alyse Marlowe," she said, fingering his fair hair away from soft brown eyes that looked much too old for his face. She experienced another twitch of recognition.

"I'm Tommy Turnbull," he offered, sliding his hand into hers.

Alyse smiled and at the same time realized why Tommy looked so familiar. She had seen him before.

"Why, Tommy, I saw you at Bundys in New York, last Friday."

Tommy blinked, then smiled. "You was prettier in New York."

She grinned, amused by his pint-size candor, and a little puzzled at the contrast between his too-young speech and his too-old face. She gave his hand an affectionate squeeze. His gaze shifted past her, and the guileless smile wilted.

19

"Here comes Mrs. Saunders," he said, in a downcast undertone. "My governess." The last word came out sounding like a disease.

Alyse turned as a big, heavy-limbed woman with a suitcase-size purse flopping against her vast flank steamed toward them across the beach. She held an ice cream cone in one fist as if it were an Olympic torch, the green pistachio melting over her chunky fingers.

"Thomas!" she boomed, as soon as she was within shouting distance. "I expressly forbade you to wade in past your ankles while I was gone."

Alyse felt her hackles rise. "He didn't *wade* in," she said curtly. "A giant wave pulled him in kicking and screaming."

Mrs. Saunders hove to in front of them, glaring alternately at Tommy and Alyse. "Just wait until Mr. Turnbull hears about this," she snapped, as if she hadn't heard a word of Alyse's explanation.

The woman thrust out a hand, her hard eyes daring Tommy not to take it. He sighed, and released his grip from Alyse. Mrs. Saunders snatched up his wrist and jerked him to her side.

Alyse clenched both fists at her waist, watching them trudge off across the beach toward the hotel. She could barely restrain herself from running after them and chewing out the witch.

Tommy glanced back at her once, earning himself another testy jerk of his arm. Seconds later, when Mrs. Saunders wasn't looking, he surreptitiously waved at Alyse over his shoulder, sending tears coursing down her cheeks.

"Punkin'," she murmured in disgust, "your daddy must be a turkey of the highest order."

When the mismatched pair was gone, Alyse discovered to her dismay that the giant wave had snatched more than just Tommy Turnbull from the beach. It had also swallowed up her shoes. Two hundred bucks down the oceanic drain, she thought dismally, staring out toward the sun-dazzled horizon.

She felt the loss dearly, wishing she had listened to her usually frugal inner voice and not splurged on the pricey pumps. At the time, they had seemed necessary. After all, Conrad expected her to dress appropriately when dealing with the Brace Gallery's affluent clientele.

Now that her investment was gone, however, Alyse deeply regretted not having added the money to the painfully small savings account that might someday grow into a down payment for her own Marlowe Gallery. Two hundred dollars would have bought — what? — a display easel, or a strip of track lighting. Paradise was definitely losing some of its shine.

Dripping and dejected, Alyse headed toward the hotel. She had almost reached the beach entrance when she noticed a handsome, swarthy man. He was in a bright Hawaiian luau shirt and lounging in the shade of a striped patio umbrella. For an instant, she felt the same sense of déjà vu that she had experienced earlier with Tommy.

Alyse slowed, trying not to stare, wondering what seemed so remarkable about the man. He was obviously Hawaiian. Under the circumstances, though, that didn't exactly set him apart from the crowd.

Then it hit her in a rush—he and Tommy were a joint remembrance. She had first encountered both of them in the lobby at Bundys, having plowed headlong into the man's bright coral shirtfront as she raced into the auction house.

Running across Tommy again wasn't really much of a coincidence. After all, she had chased his father across an entire continent and half the Pacific Ocean to the islands—to this very hotel. But crossing paths with the Hawaiian a second time was a horse of a different color. In fact, finding him seated there under the patio umbrella seemed almost bizarre. Alyse frowned uneasily as she hurried inside.

The rap on the door came just as Alyse was toweling down from the shower. She glanced at herself in the full-length mirror on the bathroom door. With the sand rinsed out of her hair, she felt almost restored, but she didn't look it. Her knees and elbows were scratched and abraded, and a small purple bruise had blossomed under her left eye where Tommy had accidentally clobbered her in his panic.

It was her eyes themselves, however, that gave her pause. She had experienced real fear of the water for the first time in her life today . . . and it showed.

Another knock on the door, louder this time.

Alyse grabbed an enormous white body towel from the rack over the tub, wrapped it around herself, and tucked the corner into the cleavage between her breasts. Turbanning a smaller towel around her soaking hair, she padded barefoot into the adjoining room. Standing to one side, she opened the hallway door on its safety chain.

"Tommy!" She stared down at the small boy, clad in crisp khaki shorts and a seersucker sport coat.

He smiled up at her, both arms held behind his back. Alyse closed the door, released the safety chain, and then edged back to open it a little wider. Tommy stepped just inside the doorway. To her astonishment, Rand Turnbull followed him in.

"Sorry," the elder Turnbull said, eyeing her makeshift attire. "We should have called you first, but Tommy couldn't wait."

Alyse clutched the top folds of the towel, feeling her bare shoulders and arms go crimson. She tried to tell herself that she was far more covered than she would have been in the bikini she'd brought in her suitcase. The rationale didn't work. A bath towel was a bath towel, even if it was the size of a bed sheet.

"I'm Rand Turnbull, Miss Marlowe," he said, extending a hand as his expression shifted from mere studied politeness. He seemed to be having trouble prying his gaze off her towel. "Tommy's uncle."

She glanced back and forth between the two Turnbulls, thrown off balance by the news that they weren't father and son. Still holding onto the towel with one hand, she offered the other to the attorney.

His grasp was firm and businesslike. Hers was damp.

Alyse had been anxious to meet Rand Turnbull, attorney at law. But this was hardly the scenario she'd had in mind.

"The boy told me how you saved his life." His gaze took in the scratches on her arms and the tiny bruise under her eye. "We're in your debt."

"Don't be silly," Alyse said, feeling pretty ridiculous herself, standing there in a towel. "Anyone would have done the same thing."

"Oh?" Rand's eyebrows shot up and he smiled humorlessly. "The beach was crawling with people. I understand nobody else even tried to help."

Tommy stood wriggling self-consciously between them, his hands still behind his back. His eyes glowed with anticipation. "I have a present for you, Miss Marlowe."

"Call me Alyse," she said, smiling down at the boy. He glanced up at his uncle, who nodded.

Alyse knelt in front of Tommy, securing her towel with both hands. The boy pulled a small paper sack from behind his back and held it out to her. She stared at the crudely shaped bright paper hearts glued all over the sack, and a lump rose unexpectedly into her throat.

"For me?" she said softly.

"Yes," Tommy said soberly. "For not letting me drown like Mommy and Daddy."

Rand Turnbull's stomach muscles clenched as if he'd just taken a sharp blow in the solar plexus. His

24

expression remained impassive, however, as he met Alyse Marlowe's startled glance.

Alyse accepted the sack and carefully unfolded the top to peer inside.

"Oh, Tommy," she said in a tone of wonder, reaching in to draw out the ugliest necklace she had ever set eyes on in her life. "This is gorgeous."

Fake rubies and emeralds of stupendous dimensions alternated with garishly painted plaster beads. A hideous facsimile of an oversized sand dollar hung in the middle. If Alyse had seen the thing lying on the street, she wouldn't have bent down to pick it up. So, why was she kneeling there about to burst out bawling at Tommy's generosity?

She leaned over and wrapped an arm around the child, sniffling as he hugged her back. As they parted, he startled her again by planting a wet kiss on her cheek. Then he turned and darted past his uncle and out the door toward the elevators.

Rand looked at the necklace, shaking his head. "That boy," he sighed. He suspected that Tommy had blown a month's allowance on the blasted piece of junk.

"What's that supposed to mean?" Alyse demanded, holding the necklace defensively against her breast.

"If he had asked," Rand said, wondering what had suddenly gotten her dander up, "I could have helped him pick out something decent." Rand would even have enjoyed the chore, he thought, considering what they both owed Tommy's courageous rescuer.

Alyse glared at him. The man obviously knew nothing about children. "As a matter of fact, this is quite possibly the most delightful present anyone has ever given me," she said, emphasizing the point by slipping the gift over her head. It settled around her shoulders with a clatter, the sharp-edged beads digging into her bare flesh.

"Come on, it's hideous," Rand countered.

"It has *heart,*" she said, her temper flaring. "But if you're the one who hired that storm trooper he calls his governess, I can see how you might not understand that."

Alyse bit her tongue. The words had just tumbled out before she'd had time to think. The attorney's gaze slowly took her in again, head to toe.

"Mrs. Saunders is competent," he responded evenly. But Alyse had hit a winner.

When Rand began the adoption proceedings, he had figured that Tommy needed a woman's influence. Hiring a governess had seemed like a good idea at the time. But what did he know about that sort of thing?

"Mrs. Saunders left him alone on the beach," Alyse said, measuring out each word. "And as far as I could tell, Tommy can't swim a stroke."

They faced off for an eternity of seconds. Rand didn't like arguing a case when he sensed he was on shaky ground. Finally, he took a step back toward the door. Right or wrong, there was no point in turning this into a bad scene.

"I just wanted you to know how much I appreciated what you did. Forgive the intrusion."

"Wait," Alyse called, realizing she was on the verge of blowing the entire trip.

Rand hesitated. Alyse searched madly for words that would smooth over their rough beginning. Finding none, she decided her best bet was to simply lay her cards on the table.

"I work for Conrad Brace, of the Brace Gallery in New York," she said, talking fast. "I was late arriving at Bundys to bid on the Tokugawa Shogun tea box. Mr. Brace is prepared to purchase it from you—at any price."

Alyse got it all out in one breath, then winced, grateful that Conrad wasn't there to witness her pathetic lack of negotiating skills. She told herself that Turnbull had two definite advantages—one professional and the other psychological. He was a highly respected contract negotiator in both government and corporate circles. And he was wearing clothes.

"Sorry," Rand said. "Not interested."

She stiffened. "At least do me the courtesy of considering the offer." She tried not to sound desperate.

Rand put a hand on the door jamb, counted slowly to ten, and shook his head. "The answer's still no."

He wished he could hang around and find out why the Brace Gallery was so all-fired anxious to get its hands on the Tokugawa box. But he had a conference call with the Japanese investment group coming in from Yokusaka in fifteen minutes. Lyle Eason, their partner, would be splicing in from San

27

Francisco. So, Rand nodded a polite farewell to the lovely young lady in the gross necklace and the devastatingly tempting attire, and stepped out into the hallway.

"Mr. Turnbull—"

"Rand," he interrupted, ready to fend off another offer.

"I don't intend to give up this easily," Alyse said, with more determination than she felt.

He backed away a couple of steps, flashing an astonishingly boyish smile. "Fair enough," he said and, looking quizzically distracted, turned to stride down the wide corridor toward the elevators.

Alyse sighed in annoyance, watching his straight back and springy, athletic gait. She had lost the first round. She desperately hoped there would be others.

As she started to close the door, a man in a gaudy Hawaiian shirt swung into view around the distant corner of the hallway. Before he caught sight of her, Alyse ducked back into her room, unsure why she had a sudden urge to hide.

She left the door open a crack, watching as the thick-muscled man approached the door across the hallway and entered. The same man she had seen outside the hotel earlier. The same one she had run into at Bundys.

Alyse eased her door shut, and secured the night lock, her skin prickling.

Chapter Two

Alyse leaned close to the bathroom mirror that evening, dabbing another layer of makeup base over the small bruise under her eye. Then she stood back and examined her handiwork, pleased. The baby shiner was all but undetectable. At least, she wouldn't look like a clown when she went down to dinner.

The garish necklace that Tommy Turnbull had given her lay on the lavatory counter. She smiled and held it up against her blue dress. The colors clashed. She suspected the necklace would clash with just about anything, but was sentimental enough to wear it anyway.

Her smile faded as she fingered the glass and plaster beads. Sentimentality was her downfall. Sometimes she even used it as an excuse for cowardice. Settling for the status quo was so much less painful than making the necessary moves to take control of her life. Being a master of the universe wasn't one of her driving ambitions. But being mistress of her own destiny would be nice.

Since receiving her appraiser's certification a

couple of years ago, however, Alyse had been spinning her wheels at the Brace Gallery. True, Conrad had taught her a lot about antiques and objets d'art. But she had begun developing a healthy reputation of her own in the art dealing community.

Still, the thought of opening her own business gave Alyse the jitters, thanks only in part to the enormous financial obstacle that lay in her path. The fact was, she had never been completely on her own before. And unless she was able to retrieve the blasted tea box for Conrad, she couldn't be sure that she was cut out to run her own company. On the other hand, if she could somehow manage to pry the antique from Rand Turnbull, she might take that as a kind of omen.

Alyse toyed with the idea of stopping off on the West Coast during her return trip to New York, if everything worked out all right. She could take an extra day to nose around for a possible gallery site — perhaps someplace near the shore. Of course, she wouldn't be able to afford it, but having a place picked out would add one more link to her chain of dreams. Her smile returned.

She draped the heavy necklace around her throat and reached back to fasten the clasp, her concentration drifting. The hook snagged on her dress and, as she worked to free it, the entire necklace suddenly slipped from her grasp. Alyse made a mad grab for it, but the fake sand dollar struck the ceramic tile floor with a surprisingly solid cracking sound.

With a distraught moan, she reached down and

picked it up. The front of the sand dollar was intact, but a piece of plaster the size of her thumbnail had chipped from the back. She brushed away the plaster chips — and then blinked.

A gossamer-thin pattern of inlaid jade and mother-of-pearl shone beneath the plaster dust on the back. Alyse flaked away a little more of the coating with her fingernail, and sucked in her breath. Inside the clunky fake sand dollar, she could just make out the delicate tip of what appeared to be an inlaid jade and mother-of-pearl dragonfly wing.

"What on earth?" she whispered in confusion. Mentally she matched the intricate wingtip with the drawing on the U.S. Customs Bureau "wanted" poster that had hung over her desk back in New York for the past six months. "It *can't* be."

A sharp thump sounded in the next room. Alyse started with a gasp, and then held her breath, listening. After a moment, she relaxed, nervously laughing at herself.

"It's the maid, dummy," she muttered, clutching the chipped necklace to her breast.

She glanced at her watch, thinking the housekeeping service was jumping the gun a little. It was barely dark. But then, they probably had to start early if they were going to turn down beds in all the rooms.

She opened the door . . . and blinked. The bedroom was pitch dark. Alyse was certain she had left the bedside lamp on.

Stretching one hand in front of her, she groped

31

toward the bed. As she stepped out of the bright shaft of light from the bathroom, she could see a faint, grayish glow through the window curtains across the room.

Halfway to her goal, she thought she detected a movement nearby. She hesitated, her senses snapping to attention as icy fear slithered down her back.

"Is somebody here?" she asked in a weak voice.

Dead silence. But Alyse had a crawly feeling that she wasn't the only person holding her breath in that room. Her heart pounded, then skipped a beat as the air seemed to shift very close to her.

Suddenly she was lifted bodily by powerful hands and tossed aside. Alyse yelped as she hit the bed facedown, arms flailing, and bounced on the firm mattress. Scrambling to all fours, she was almost blinded by light as the hallway door was flung open. She just managed to glimpse a bright floral shirt as the intruder dashed from the room and the door swung shut.

Darkness returned. Shaken, Alyse fumbled for the switch on the bedside lamp. The light came on. She bolted from the bed to the door, slipping the security chain into place with trembling fingers. She stood with her back against the door, knees rubbery, her heart still triphammering wildly.

Across the room, a dresser drawer had been pulled open. Her nightgown hung out of the drawer and several items of clothing lay strewn on the floor. She had obviously interrupted the intruder in mid-snoop.

After a while, she cleared her throat.

"Birdbrain," she said, purely to test her voice. "Didn't living in New York all these years teach you to use *all* the locks?"

Satisfied that she wouldn't come off sounding like a hysterical mouse, Alyse crossed the carpet to the phone. Her hands still trembled as she dialed the hotel management.

As she hung up a minute later, her gaze drifted to the necklace, where she had dropped it on the bed. Tiny flecks of jade and mother-of-pearl glinted from the back. She stared at it for some time.

Her gaze drifted to the double-locked door, her mind replaying the pell-mell flight of the bright Hawaiian shirt. A random hotel burglary attempt? she wondered. Or, a thief with a specific goal?

Slowly, feeling a little dizzy, Alyse pulled the telephone directory from the drawer in the bedside table. When she found the number she was looking for, she sat down on the edge of the bed, picked up the phone again, and dialed the Japanese consulate.

Rand Turnbull paced restlessly. The walls of the spacious executive suite seemed to draw inward with each circuit. The shower in the bathroom off Mrs. Saunders's room had been running for more than twenty minutes now as the woman underwent her endless ablutions. She spent an hour barricaded in there each evening, only to emerge swaddled in a flannel robe, smelling of camphor and cold cream.

Across the sitting area, another door stood slightly ajar, the room beyond softly illuminated by a night light. Tommy was afraid to sleep in the dark—afraid that monsters somehow lurked in the shadows, eager to turn his terrors into reality.

Rand paced another circuit and stopped at the doorway, frowning. He had let the boy down by hiring a so-called governess who seemed to know as little as he did about the needs of a child. If it hadn't been for Alyse Marlowe, Tommy would have drowned, a cruel footnote to the boating accident that had taken Chris and Pat.

He shuddered. The thought of how close he'd come to losing the boy—Rand's last fragile link to his older brother—made him break out in a cold sweat. And yet, there were times when the burden of responsibility for that small, precious life threatened to crush him. Acting as a parent far outweighed anything Rand had ever encountered in his law practice.

Easing the door open wider, he crept in to the boy's bedside. Tommy lay clutching a small, worn teddy bear that he'd outgrown a year or so ago, then gone back to within days of being orphaned. He scowled in his sleep, his pale, copper-fringed eyelids fluttering fitfully. No sweet dreams for the little trooper.

Rand leaned over and brushed a lock of soft hair from his nephew's face, the familiar ache rising in his chest. Tommy's coloring and facial structure were so much like Chris's that sometimes Rand could hardly bear to look at his nephew.

Rand turned away, suddenly too overwhelmed by lingering grief to remain in the room. As much as it hurt to have Tommy near, it would hurt a lot worse to abandon him to the clutches of Elaine Fielding. Neither Chris nor Pat would have forgiven him for that.

The shower was still running when Rand returned to the sitting room. He glowered in the direction of the bathroom. Making mistakes wasn't one of his favorite pastimes, but he wasn't shy about admitting his errors. He had made up his mind that Mrs. Saunders was a doozer. Back in New York, he had been too busy to notice the glare of her shortcomings. Nobody had expected her to be Mary Poppins, but this was ridiculous. The boy deserved better.

Rand sank into one of the deep cushioned chairs facing the window and stared out at the moonlit outline of Diamond Head in the distance. Since Chris and Pat's boating accident off the New England coast, some of the magic seemed to have gone out of Rand's lifelong love affair with the sea. He wondered distractedly if it would ever return, or if he would end up turning his back on the ocean altogether and selling his cottage on Maui.

The Tokugawa box sat on the end table beside him. He picked it up and turned it over on his lap, caressing the smoothly lacquered surface. A rampant dragon writhed across the lid, looking almost three-dimensional against a dark vermillion background. The antique was in magnificent condition, considering its age.

35

He shouldn't have been surprised that he had already received two unsolicited offers for it since making the purchase at Bundys—but he was. The first had come early this morning from a respected dealer in Oriental artifacts representing an anonymous private collector in Honolulu. Rand hadn't given that offer any more consideration than he'd given Alyse Marlowe's later in the day.

Indeed, the fact that word of his acquisition had gotten around so fast convinced him more than ever that his new clients had been shrewd. Not only did they let him know what they wanted, they saved face by having Lyle Eason make the suggestion.

Even though gift-giving was a time-honored tradition in Japanese business dealings, the "arranged" element of this particular gift struck Rand as being a shade mercenary. Considering the fee he was charging the real estate investment group, however, he wasn't about to squawk.

Still, he half wished he could sell the Tokugawa box to Alyse as a small token of his appreciation for saving Tommy's life. True, her pithy remarks about Mrs. Saunders had stung. But then, he'd had that coming, hadn't he?

Rand could still hear the shower running as he carefully returned the tea box to the end table. His jaw muscles bunched. Rand shoved himself out of the deep chair and went to the window. He stood close to the glass, staring blindly at his ghostly reflection, his shoulders sagging beneath the emotional burden that never let up, day or night.

Tommy was a good kid, dammit—the best. But

having the boy was like living with an alien under his roof. How the devil was Rand supposed to cope with a blasted prodigy?

He sighed, raking a hand through his hair. It was just like Chris—the artistic Turnbull brother—to have a kid who would rather play the piano than shag flies. As if that weren't bad enough, Tommy hadn't even touched the keyboard since Rand had finally rescued him from Mrs. Fielding. What that woman had done to her only grandson ought to be a crime.

Rand cursed under his breath. The shower pattered on and on. If he didn't get out of there for a little while, he told himself, he'd end up putting a fist through the window. He grabbed his sport coat off the back of a chair and headed downstairs for a drink.

Chapter Three

The lobby was crowded with guests just returning from dinner, or heading out on the town for the evening. Alyse stepped warily out of the elevator and edged her way toward the cocktail lounge. The frightening encounter with the intruder still had her jumpy. As bad as that had been, it didn't compare at all with the perilously exposed feeling that came with knowing that she wore the dragonfly pendant around her neck.

Alyse fingered the fake sand dollar, just to reassure herself that it was still there—as if the sharp beads digging into her bare neck weren't proof enough. She had anticipated being rid of it by now. But she had hit a sizeable glitch. Her plan had been to turn in the necklace to local representatives of the Japanese government, but the consulate had already closed for the night by the time she made her call. She wouldn't be able to inform them of her incredible find until tomorrow morning.

Meanwhile, Alyse wasn't about to let the garishly camouflaged artifact out of her sight. She was elated at having found the priceless treasure. But even greater was her fear that she might somehow lose the pendant.

Alyse was still too shaken to think straight. She couldn't begin to imagine how the dragonfly had come to be encased in cheap plaster, or what wild quirk of fate had ordained that it should find its way to her.

Through the fog of dismay, she realized that the answer was held by Tommy Turnbull. For her own peace of mind, she would have to find out where he had bought the gaudy plaster-and-paste necklace that he had so lovingly presented to her.

After opting for a room service supper that she barely touched, Alyse had calmed down sufficiently to turn restless. Between the would-be burglar and her anticipated leap into instant riches, events seemed to be whirling out of control. She needed to get out of her room and make physical contact with the rest of the planet. Just to make sure it was still there and that she wasn't trapped in some kind of crazy, cosmic dream.

In the lobby, Alyse stopped, her attention caught by a poster on an easel immediately outside the wide double doorway to the lounge. She gaped at the large, four-color advertisement of the night's live entertainment, taking in the dark, familiar face beneath the broad banner proclaiming "Eddie Komake — in Person!" Two couples nudged her from behind, but she held her ground, unable to wrench her gaze from the poster.

"You!" she murmured under her breath, recognizing the man whom she had run into at Bundys.

After spotting him twice more since arriving in Hawaii that afternoon, Alyse had almost begun to believe that he had followed her from New York. Now, she felt silly.

A hand touched her arm.

"Alyse?"

She turned and looked up into Rand Turnbull's warm smile. The smile didn't quite reach his eyes, which looked tired and strained. Her hand automatically flew to her necklace. Her curiosity almost caused Alyse to burst right out and ask where Tommy had found it, but she bit her tongue and remained silent. She didn't want to draw any more attention to the pendant than necessary before she had an opportunity to notify the proper authorities.

"May I impose on your evening plans?" he asked, noting the way her blue silk dress clung to her curves. With her thick, tawny curls pulled up on top of her head, she looked striking enough to be a model.

The picture was marred somewhat by the hideous junk jewelry that Tommy had given her. Oddly, Rand thought more of her for choosing to wear the tacky thing. The lady clearly wasn't hung up on superficial values.

"Impose away," Alyse said, delighted by this unexpected opportunity to discuss the Tokugawa box. She still felt responsible for letting the tea box slip through Conrad Brace's fingers at the Bundys auction. She was just as determined to retrieve the box for Conrad as she was to see that the dragonfly pendant was returned to its rightful owner. She owed Conrad that much. "I was just on the trail of a Mai Tai to calm my nerves."

Rand raised an eyebrow and inclined his head toward her questioningly. Unlike too many men, he had an openly expressive face. Alyse was surprised by how much that appealed to her. Although she hadn't intended to mention it, she quickly told him about the intruder.

He whistled softly through his teeth. "This just hasn't been your day, has it?"

Alyse allowed herself to be ushered into the dimly lighted lounge, where Rand found them a table in a quiet corner. As she slid into a chair against the wall, Alyse noticed a man in a tropical beige linen sport coat and colorful print shirt watching them from the bar. He quickly averted his gaze when she glanced his way. As far as she could tell, he seemed to be drinking alone. The fellow was probably sitting there idly ogling everyone who came into the lounge, she decided. This was no time for her to develop a paranoia of Hawaiian shirts.

She sat toying with a monkey-pod bowl filled with bar nuts as she and Rand waited for their drinks. The cozy table with its flickering candle centerpiece was a more intimate setting than she would have liked for their discussion of the Tokugawa box. So much so that Alyse couldn't bring herself to broach the subject right away. Not with Rand's knees brushing hers beneath the tiny table.

They sat quietly until the waitress returned with their drinks. Rand removed the swizzle stick from his scotch-on-the-rocks, leaving the glass otherwise untouched. Ignoring the paper parasol in her Mai Tai, Alyse barely sipped the deceptively fruity drink, anxious to maintain a clear head.

"Married?" Rand asked, nodding at her unadorned ring finger.

Some women didn't wear wedding rings, these days. The only way to be sure was to come right out and ask. Still, he couldn't say why he suddenly thought he had to know about this particular woman's status.

"Widowed," she said, wishing too late that she had just said no. When Rand cocked his head, she reluctantly added, "Rob died of a heart attack in Kyoto last spring."

"Sorry."

That was all he said. Alyse was grateful that he didn't belabor the subject.

"Speaking of the deceased," she said, hoping she wasn't trampling all over something with hobnailed boots, "what happened to Tommy's parents?"

Rand's cheek twitched grimly. He raised the glass to his lips, took a long swig, and stared out across the room while she mentally kicked herself for flogging what was obviously still an open wound.

"Chris and Pat went down in a sailboat off Martha's Vineyard last year," he said in a barely audible voice. "A sudden storm. No warning."

He raised the glass again, stared down into the dark liquid for a long moment, then placed the glass carefully on the table without drinking. He knew better than to get that started.

"Was Pat your sister?" Alyse asked when the silence dragged on.

"In-law. She was a peach. Chris really lucked out."

"With Tommy, too."

Rand nodded. His pained expression was replaced by one of worry. "I'm adopting him."

"Really?" Alyse straightened, intrigued.

"Chris and Pat had asked me to, if anything ever happened to them." He sighed, shaking his head. "Funny thing is, none of us ever really expected this."

"No, I suppose not." Alyse took another sip of her Mai Tai. "Tommy's grandparents aren't living?"

"Just Pat's mother," he said with a dry, mirthless laugh. "Old lady Fielding disowned Pat when she married my brother. She didn't want her daughter hooking up with an artist, even if he was damned good and on the brink of being wildly successful."

Alyse plucked the parasol from her drink and twirled it between her fingertips. "I take it the grandmother doesn't want Tommy." She found the thought appalling.

Rand laughed again, grimly. "She'd never set eyes on him until he was an orphan. Then she suddenly got all hot and bothered about preserving the precious Fielding bloodline, or some such crap. Just before the custody hearing, she had Tommy stolen from his playschool. It was kidnapping, pure and simple, but it still took me four months of court proceedings to get him back."

He didn't mention that Elaine Fielding hadn't let

43

it end there. She had hired a detective to follow Rand, tracking his every movement, maliciously searching for evidence of any kind that might prove him an unfit guardian and interfere with the adoption process. For the last two months, he'd felt as if he were on display in a glass specimen jar.

Alyse fingered her necklace, saddened to learn that Tommy Turnbull was the subject of a bitter custody battle. She could understand Rand's powerful desire to carry out his brother's wishes. But she couldn't help wondering if Tommy had become an emotional football between Rand and the boy's grandmother. It was all too possible that both adults had lost sight of the six-year-old's needs.

"People can change," she observed. "Maybe his grandmother really made a connection with Tommy while he was with her."

"She made a connection, all right," Rand noted bitterly. "Tommy has this . . . ability . . . with the piano. He can actually play Rachmaninoff and Bach — hard stuff. She held weekly recitals for all her society friends — had the kid playing for them like some kind of trained carnival monkey."

"How did Tommy feel about being exploited?"

"Pretty miserable, I imagine," Rand said candidly. "He doesn't play at all now. He's mixed up. I've had some problems with him, since getting him back from Elaine."

"Such as?"

"Well, he takes things," he admitted reluctantly. He didn't add that Tommy sometimes lied, as well. And Alyse wasn't deaf. She must have noticed the boy's lapse into near baby talk. "He never did that before."

"That's understandable."

"Oh?"

"Sure. Everything has been taken from him—his parents, his home. He's probably just acting that out himself. Taking things, I mean. He just needs reassurance." And affection, she thought, which Tommy wasn't likely to get from a man as standoffish as his uncle.

Rand gazed at her intently. The lady had insight, as well as physical courage—all wrapped up in a very attractive package. He was impressed.

"What about you, Alyse? Do you have kids?"

"No." She felt the old ache surface once again, thinking *almost*. Rob had left her with nothing to show for their four years of marriage.

"Ah!" Rand nodded. "You're wedded to your job."

She laughed. The gray shadow that had hung over their conversation began to lift.

"Not really. I enjoy working for the Brace Gallery most of the time. You can't buy that kind of education. But working for another person isn't something I can live and breathe."

Her hand drifted up to the clunky paste beads draped around her slender neck, and her stomach fluttered nervously. Alyse wanted to tell Rand about her discovery. She was dying to tell *someone*. But she couldn't bring herself to breathe a word about the dragonfly pendant until after she contacted the Japanese consulate in the morning.

45

"I would be pleased if you'd let me swap that for a more suitable expression of Turnbull gratitude," Rand said, eyeing the ugly necklace. "There's a quite respectable jewelry store up the street, if you—"

"No!" Alyse said too sharply.

Her response clearly startled Rand. She reddened, and lowered her voice. "No, Rand. I appreciate your thoughtfulness, but this means more to me than you know."

Rand pressed his lips together, then shook his head. "Suit yourself." His tone implied that he seriously questioned her judgment.

They sat quietly for a while, pretending interest in what was going on at neighboring tables. In spite of the hidden treasure about her neck, Alyse found their silence oddly relaxing. She hadn't expected Rand Turnbull to be so comfortable to be with.

"So, you aren't going to keep hounding me about the Tokugawa box?"

Alyse returned his smile, pleased that Rand had been the one to toss the subject onto the table.

"Wrong. I'm afraid I solemnly promised Conrad that I would bring it back."

Rand's smile faded. "And I'm afraid you're out of luck. You see, *I* have already solemnly promised the box to my newest clients. They're a mostly Japanese real estate investment group—very big on ceremonial gifts. In fact, I'll be presenting it at a luau I'm throwing for them on Maui this coming Saturday."

Alyse tried not to show her frustration. After

46

muffing her assignment at Bundys last Friday, she wouldn't be able to face Conrad Brace if she failed again. She was dead determined to somehow persuade Rand to cough up the Tokugawa box. She only hoped, for the sake of her expense account, that it didn't take her all week to find a way to talk him around.

"I noticed you eyeballing Eddie Komake's poster in the lobby," he said, shifting gears as he glanced at his watch. "Would you like to see his performance?"

"I'd love to."

Rand rose and held out a hand to her. As they wound their way through the obstacle course of lounge tables, Alyse was intensely aware of his gentle touch on her bare upper arm.

"Komake has become immensely popular on the islands these past few months," Rand told her, as they crossed the lobby to the dining room. He resisted the urge to stroke her tantalizingly soft flesh, acutely conscious of how appealing he found this small, determined woman. "He and his back-up group will perform at the luau on Saturday."

The dinner hour had passed. Most of the tables were occupied by patrons nursing after-dinner drinks. Alyse waited just inside the doorway while Rand held a brief, whispered conversation with the maître d'. She thought she glimpsed a discreet pass of money as the two men shook hands. That was confirmed when the smiling maître d' escorted them to a choice table near the stage, where musicians were tuning instruments and making little adjustments in the amplifiers.

"I'm impressed," she said, after Rand had ordered another round of drinks.

"I aim to please." Rand toasted her across the table, glad that he had finally done something right, from Alyse Marlowe's standpoint. He was enjoying her company.

A musician played a riff on a steel guitar. A ukelele joined in, and the audience grew quiet at the first chords of distinctive island rhythm. The house lights dimmed, the stage lights came up, and Eddie Komake swept on stage, riding a wave of welcoming applause. Alyse gazed up at the entertainer, suddenly enthralled by his exotic presence. After their repeated encounters this past week, she felt almost as if she knew him personally.

The singer launched into his latest hit, a lilting song made blatantly sensuous by his mellow baritone. The steel guitar that now was his only accompaniment sounded far away — a soulful cry of heartstrings being stretched to their limit. Komake's gaze drifted slowly around the audience, as if he could pick out each of them in the dark shadows beyond the glare of the stage lights. Finally, he looked directly at Alyse, seated at the very edge of the halo of light.

Rand folded his arms across his chest and watched, thinking Komake was exhibiting inexcusably poor taste in singling out Alyse. He was singing almost suggestively to her, as if she were the only woman in the room. Rand frowned, realizing with some discomfort that he was actually jealous.

The song ended with a surge of applause from

the audience, and Komake's velvet voice drifted smoothly into "Sweet Lailani." Alyse blushed when she saw that Komake intended to focus entirely on her through yet another haunting Hawaiian melody.

She felt herself falling under the entertainer's spell. No wonder Komake had become so popular. He had a way of making a woman feel unique, special. But as the music wove into and through her, transporting Alyse into a dreamlike world of island colors and exotic scents, Komake's face blurred. In its place, she saw Rand Turnbull's strong, angular features—a transformation that produced a disturbingly physical response in her.

Eddie Komake devoted nearly his entire set to Alyse. Rand was forced to sit there like a bump on a log through the hour-long show, as if he were merely chaperoning Komake's date. By the time Rand rode up on the elevator with Alyse later that evening, he had about had his fill of island ambience.

"Komake really is good, isn't he?" Alyse said, a wistful look in her blue-green eyes.

"You'd be a better judge of that than I am," Rand responded stiffly.

Alyse looked up at him curiously. But Rand kept his gaze focused on the floor buttons, his jaw muscles knotted. The elevator stopped and the doors whooshed open onto Alyse's room level.

"Thanks for a pleasant evening," she said tonelessly, wondering what in the world had gotten the man's goat. "Perhaps I'll see you tomorrow."

He could bet on that, she thought, stepping off the elevator. With the Tokugawa box hanging in the balance, she was prepared to become the plague of Rand Turnbull's life, if that's what it took.

"Alyse . . ."

She stopped and turned. He had stepped off the elevator behind her, leaving one hand on the rubber bumper to keep the door from closing. His jaw remained set, but the expression in his eyes had softened. Alyse swallowed dryly, astonished by the ease with which her own gaze met and held his.

She hadn't seen such naked need in a man's eyes for a long time. But she wasn't entirely sure that what she was seeing wasn't her own need reflected back at her.

She waited for Rand to say something more. Their probing eye contact continued for an eternity of seconds, until her expectation became anticipation. Alyse mentally braced herself for his touch.

The elevator door started to close, checked itself against Rand's hand, and retreated. He blinked, snapping out of the adrenaline-charged fog that seemed to have enveloped them.

What the hell were you about to do, Turnbull? he thought, getting a grip on himself. He'd been on the verge of exploring the flavor of Alyse Marlowe's lipstick, that's what.

Rand glanced around nervously at the deserted corridor. There was no sign of a lurking spy taking lurid notes for Her Ladyship Fielding. Not that there would be anything to report — unless the detective happened to be clairvoyant enough to read Rand's decidedly warm-blooded thoughts about Conrad Brace's enticing little agent.

"Goodnight," he said hoarsely, and stepped inside the elevator.

The door slid closed, leaving Alyse alone in the hallway. She stood there for a moment, blank-faced, feeling as if she'd just reached the end of a gripping suspense novel and discovered the last pages were missing. Finally, she cleared her dry throat and continued on down the strip of carpet to her room.

Alyse unlocked her door, flipped on the light, and headed for the bathroom, kicking out of her shoes as she went. Once there she stopped suddenly, sensing . . . something.

Her makeup case lay open on the counter where she had left it. Hadn't she? She couldn't quite remember. Alyse stared at it for a moment, then backed out of the bathroom and moved slowly to the closet. Her dresses were undisturbed. Weren't they? Had she really left her white linen blazer so askew on its hanger? Across the room, the top dresser drawer stood slightly open. She frowned at it pensively.

The spread had been removed from the bed, and the crisp sheets neatly turned back. A single foil-wrapped chocolate mint lay on one of the pillows.

The maid had come and gone. But Alyse had a vague, undefined feeling that someone other than the hotel's housekeeping staff had been in the room during her absence. Someone who didn't have her

51

comfort in mind. She shuddered, fingering her necklace uneasily.

"Get hold of yourself," she muttered snatching her hand away from the beads.

By chance, she had uncovered a stolen treasure of incalculable value. Perhaps because of that, her room already had been broken into once. But if she didn't stop looking for bogeymen at every turn, she was going to turn herself into a basket case before the Japanese consulate even knew she existed.

Alyse took a deep breath and let it out slowly. The knot refused to leave her stomach. She went over to the door and set all the locks, but the tension wouldn't disappear. She wondered how she had made it through the evening without coming apart like a two-dollar suitcase.

Rand Turnbull is how, she thought. Rand Turnbull, a powerful dose of hypnotic music, and two deceptively punch-flavored Mai Tais had floated her dangerously out of her depth. For a while, that evening, Alyse had forgotten what was at stake.

She was scared. She was also angry. There was no point in calling the hotel management and demanding that she be given other accommodations, when she couldn't prove even to herself that someone had broken in a second time. Besides, a different location wouldn't necessarily be more secure than her present one. Not as long as she had the dragonfly pendant in her possession.

Her chin stiffened. She wore her dream around her neck, and she wasn't about to permit anyone to snatch it from her grasp. Alyse dragged a straight-back chair over from the desk and jammed it under the doorknob.

"Try getting past that, you sleaze," she muttered.

Chapter Four

Bright sunlight poured through the wide window, warming Alyse's skin. The door opened and closed softly behind her and she was once again alone. But she hugged herself, feeling cold and abandoned. She had expected her early-morning call to the Japanese consulate to end it all, relieving her of the enormous responsibility of protecting the precious dragonfly pendant. Instead, she knew now that this frightening episode in her life was only beginning.

A man carrying a thin briefcase had arrived at her door within twenty minutes of her call to the consulate. He spent a long time examining the chipped area of the necklace with a jeweler's loupe, handling the beads with profound reverence. Finally, he lowered the eye piece and told her that the plaster sand dollar did, indeed, contain the jeweled dragonfly. To Alyse's surprise, he then handed the necklace back to her.

When Alyse stammered in confusion, the Japanese official graciously assured her that the reward for finding the dragonfly treasure would be transferred to her bank account in New York the next day. When he said the amount right out loud, she had to sit down. He went on to request a favor — one that Alyse still couldn't believe she had agreed to.

In strictest confidence, he revealed that the dragonfly pendant represented only one of several recent thefts of national treasures. An international investigation was on the verge of cracking the case and, if Alyse cooperated, her reward would be twofold.

In addition to the monetary compensation, she could count on formal, public recognition of her help by the Japanese government. In the meantime, to insure her safety, she would be kept under constant surveillance.

Alyse made some quick mental calculations. There was no doubt the reward would enable her to open the art gallery that she so desperately wanted. But public recognition for helping to recover an important piece of art would provide the kind of international publicity that no amount of money could buy. In two words, cooperation could bring her *instant success*. And all she had to do was pretend that she hadn't discovered the dragonfly pendant sealed within the fake plaster necklace.

With rubbery knees and a chalk-dry mouth, she had refastened the treasure around her neck. Smiling for the first time, the official had produced a thin microcassette recorder from his briefcase and taken her lengthy statement as to how she had come into possession of the stolen item.

She stroked the nubby contours of the beads,

now deeply troubled by the vision of little Tommy so proudly and lovingly presenting her with the gift. How could a work of such magnitude have been inadvertently sold to a six-year-old child? It didn't make sense.

The knot in her stomach twisted tighter, this time reminding her that she hadn't eaten breakfast. Alyse started to phone room service. But she decided that nothing was to be gained by remaining holed up indoors. Besides, the dragonfly pendant wasn't her only concern. She still had the Tokugawa box to retrieve for Conrad. Sucking up her nerve, she grabbed her straw purse and headed downstairs.

The Beachcomber lobby was practically empty as Alyse stepped off the escalator and headed toward the coffee shop, hoping she wasn't too late for a quick Continental breakfast. The necklace made her feel blatantly conspicuous, as if she were wearing a neon sign flashing *Rob me! Rob me!* But nobody seemed to notice. She finally had to admit that the gaudy bauble did not look out of place with her brightly flowered shirt and shorts.

Halfway across the lobby, Alyse drew up short as she spotted Eddie Komake emerging from the coffee shop alcove. He caught sight of her at the same instant, and the exotic contours of his face broke into a disarming smile. Komake strode toward her, both hands extended, his face glowing with pleasure. A lush lei of plumeria blossoms hung about his neck.

"*Aloha,*" he cried, clearly delighted with their

chance encounter. "Did you enjoy the show last night?"

"Actually, I found it a little overwhelming," she confessed, as he clasped her hand in his two big fists. "I'm not accustomed to being singled out that way."

Komake threw back his head and laughed—a tumbling cascade of bass notes that shook his barrel chest—and flashed a set of straight white teeth. Alyse found his good humor infectious, and grinned back.

"Really, Miss Marlowe. Do you expect me to believe that a woman of your rare beauty isn't singled out at every turn?"

Alyse politely withdrew her hand, automatically reaching for her necklace. "I can see why you're so popular on the islands. But, how do you know my name?"

The singer's expression altered slightly. His smile remained, but it suddenly seemed plastic, posed.

"Hotel security called on me last night," he explained. "It seems that you and I are staying on the same floor. They told me you'd had an intruder, and they were checking out neighboring guests just to make sure it was an isolated case."

"And was it?"

He chuckled, and then his smile died away. "I should hope so," he said seriously. "I wouldn't want you to get a bad impression of paradise, *wahini u'i*—beautiful lady."

Alyse flushed. His warm gaze continually flitted over her face like a feathery touch. She was enticed by his bold familiarity, until his gaze drifted down to her jewelry.

"What brings you to the islands?" he asked, his languid smile returning.

"Business." She was beginning to grow suspicious of Komake's smoothness.

He looked disappointed. "Ah. I had hoped you were here for pleasure . . . and that I might assist you in that endeavor. What type of business?"

"Dull business, I'm afraid," she said evasively, trying to keep her tone casual.

Komake's dark eyes narrowed slightly. He cocked his head, looking amused. "How mysterious." He chuckled. "A secret mission, perhaps?"

Alyse began to feel cornered. His smile, his smooth tone, the warmth of his eyes—none of those could conceal his insistent probing. She couldn't imagine why a near stranger would be so interested in her. He couldn't possibly think she was some airhead groupie. Could he?

"I represent a New York art dealer," she said, deciding to grease her way out of the conversation with a healthy slathering of truth. "I'm here to—"

"Yes!" Komake suddenly pointed a finger at her nose. "I met you at Bundys last week!"

"I believe we did run into each other there," Alyse smiled. For some reason, she hadn't really expected him to make that connection.

"I *knew* you looked familiar when I spotted you in the audience last night. I've been going out of my mind trying to figure you out."

Komake impulsively removed his plumeria lei

58

and gently settled it around her neck, then gave her the traditional Hawaiian embrace. Alyse had no choice but to submit to being momentarily smothered with fragrance and attention.

"Welcome to paradise, *wahini*."

"Thank you, Mr. Komake."

"Please — Eddie," he insisted.

Alyse smiled and stepped back out of his arms. "I hope to see you perform again sometime soon," she said politely. "But for now, I'm afraid I'm on my way to an important meeting."

Komake glanced down at her hot pink shorts. Alyse reddened, wishing she'd taken her attire into account before tossing out such an obvious fabrication. But Eddie had the good grace to not call her bluff. Instead, he grinned, and winked rakishly.

"I'll be sure to reserve a stage-side table for you."

Then he was gone, leaving her feeling flattered and confused.

Alyse sat in the hotel coffee shop for an hour, picking at a chilled pineapple croissant and sipping papaya juice. By the time the early lunch crowd began trickling in, she was convinced that she had spotted the watchers from the Japanese consulate — ten of them. By her count, exactly half the customers in the restaurant were studiously watching her necklace without having once glanced her way.

Disgusted with her paranoia, Alyse realized that constantly looking over her shoulder would eventually drive her insane with worry and suspicion. She would just have to accept that she was being protected, and go on about her business.

Just then a familiar figure joined the lobby crowd outside the coffee shop entrance. Alyse perked up, her gaze following a distinct thatch of dark blond hair moving purposefully toward the elevator bank. At the moment, she told herself as she quickly shouldered her purse, her business was Conrad's business.

She caught up with Rand on the far side of the lobby. Alyse called his name over the hum of the crowd. He turned. When he saw her, his face didn't light up like a Christmas tree the way Eddie Komake's had. But he raised his finely carved chin, and something in his dark eyes sparkled, sending a ripple of warmth through her body.

"I called your room earlier," he said. "I had hoped you weren't on your way back to the mainland."

"Not without Conrad's tea box." Alyse was more than a little surprised that Rand had been trying to contact her.

He rolled his eyes toward the ceiling. "Alyse, you aren't still harping on *that* lost cause are you?" he said through his teeth. But then, he smiled as if he really didn't mind.

"Till the bitter end. If you give the box to your clients Saturday, you'll have to pry my hands off the lid first."

He laughed outright. "We'll cross that rickety bridge when we come to it." Rand took her arm and ushered her over next to the wall, out of flow of the foot traffic.

Alyse waited for him to mention why he had called her room. When he didn't, she asked, "How's Tommy?"

"Fine. I'm on my way up to our suite now. I don't like to leave him alone for long."

"Alone? Isn't Mrs. Saunders with him?"

Rand winced and shook his head. "I just got back from taking the battle-ax to the airport. You were right about her, of course. Unfortunately, I didn't realize just how right until I overheard her threaten to wash Tommy's mouth out with soap if he didn't stop lisping."

"You aren't serious."

Rand looked embarrassed. "Sometimes, it's hardest to see what's staring you point-blank in the face."

Alyse put her hand on his forearm, and felt the muscles twitch beneath the sleeve of his sport coat. A small answering electric response sang up her own arm all the way to her shoulder. She drew her hand away.

"Don't be so hard on yourself, Rand. There are two or three billion people on this planet, and not one perfect parent among them."

He mustered a grateful, lopsided smile. "I see you're still wearing that exquisitely tasteful accessory item Tommy gave you."

She glanced down. The gaudy necklace peeked out from under Eddie's fragrant plumeria lei.

"Since you refuse to let me replace it with something suitable," Rand went on, "how about at least permitting me to express my appreciation for your lifesaving feat by showing you a bit of Maui. We'll be flying over there within the hour."

"For the day?" Alyse bit the inside of her lip, her mind racing. This might present her with an excellent opportunity to press her case.

"Well, Tommy and I will be staying there. I have a small cottage on the beach near Lahaina. But you can return to Oahu on the evening shuttle." Rand rubbed his neck. "I imagine all the hotels over there will be full up, this being the height of the convention season."

Alyse took two more seconds to make up her mind. "Do I have time to change clothes?"

His gaze floated down to her bare legs. "If you insist. But frankly, I don't see the need."

Rand's gaze lingered just long enough to make her skin prickle. Recalling the look in his eyes when they parted last night, Alyse wondered about his uncanny ability to touch her without physically laying a finger on her.

They rode the elevator up together. Alyse got off first, leaving Rand to continue on up to his floor. She ran down the corridor to her room, where she breathlessly swapped her shorts for a flowered wrap skirt. As an afterthought, she stuffed her bikini into a big straw shoulder bag, just in case.

On her way back down to the lobby, Alyse took several deep, calming breaths. She told herself repeatedly that she was keyed up over the opportunity to advance her campaign to retrieve the tea box. But she knew it was more than that. She was excited about being with Rand.

Her excitement bogged down in disappointment when they reached the airport and discovered that the flight to Maui was overbooked. Again, she watched Rand take an official aside for a quiet discussion. Twice, he gestured toward Alyse and Tommy, where they stood staring at a neat, masculine pile of leather luggage bearing the initials RWT. In a moment, the uniformed clerk nodded and gave Rand a discreet thumbs-up.

Ten minutes later, the three of them filed onto the interisland DC-6 along with a horde of Hawaiians and tourists. Alyse was too relieved to mind that Tommy and Rand were seated three rows away. She strapped herself into her window seat, listening to the happy chatter of a Japanese child in the row ahead.

At least a dozen Japanese customers had done business with Brace Gallery in recent years. Out of necessity Alyse had taken a beginner's course in the language. She leaned forward now, listening intently, trying to find out if she knew as much Japanese as she thought she did. To her delight, she discovered that she grasped at least the gist of nearly everything the child said. She barely noticed a late passenger take the aisle seat next to her.

"Well, well. If it isn't the beautiful Miss Marlowe."

Alyse turned at the familiar voice and looked straight into Eddie Komake's grinning face. She leaned back slowly in her seat as the boarding

63

hatch thumped shut and the plane began taxiing.

"Are you following me, Eddie?" Alyse asked the question with a smile to hide a deeper and growing concern. Komake seemed to be everywhere.

"I assure you, I would if I had the time," he said, chuckling. "I have a gig at a big luau on Maui Saturday. I'm hopping over there to check out the sound system."

"Would that be Rand Turnbull's luau by any chance?"

"It would." Komake glanced up the aisle toward where Rand and Tommy were seated. "I noticed you were with Turnbull at my performance last night. You two are pretty good friends, are you?"

Sensing another interrogation coming on, Alyse opened her straw bag and dug inside for the paperback she had started on the flight from the mainland only yesterday. "We're business acquaintances," she murmured, and buried her nose in the novel.

Komake took the hint and left her alone. After a while, he seemed to doze. Alyse kept the book open on her lap, reading the same page over and over, too distracted by Komake's inexplicable appearances to concentrate. She was beginning to feel tethered to him with invisible handcuffs.

Sooner than she had expected, the aircraft began its descent, circling in over the deep water port of Kahului. Alyse shifted her attention from her book to the view out the window, enthralled by the lush green vegetation shouldering down to the sandy beach rimming the harbor.

"How long will you be visiting Maui?" Komake asked as the plane dropped in for a smooth landing.

"Only for the day," Alyse said, gathering her bag onto her lap. "I'll fly back to Oahu this evening."

"So will I. Perhaps we'll see each other on the shuttle."

Alyse was pretty sure that she could bank on running across Komake yet again. She found that prospect strangely unnerving. She glanced at him as the plane taxied in to the terminal. Was he just an incorrigible skirt chaser? Or, was it something else?

She was still wondering about the singer as they disembarked. It was difficult not to. Komake followed her closely down the narrow aisle and out into the brilliant tropical sunlight. Alyse was glad to see Rand and Tommy waiting for her on the tarmac. As they approached, Rand shifted his suit bag to his other arm, and extended a hand to Eddie.

"I'm looking forward to your big bash" Komake said, pumping Rand's hand.

Rand nodded, his gaze shifting intently between Komake and Alyse as if he were trying to figure out why they were standing so close together. Alyse was wondering the same thing.

"I don't suppose I could bum a ride into town with you folks?" Komake suggested breezily.

Alyse gaped at him, astounded that the intrusive entertainer actually intended to tag along with them. In spite of herself, she found that his bold tactic bordered on the comical. Rand, too, appeared taken aback . . . but far from amused. Unlike Alyse, he deftly countered Komake's brazen gameplan.

"We'd love to help you out," Rand said with well-feigned regret. "But you know how cramped cars are these days. By the time we get our luggage stowed, we'll be lucky if we all fit inside. Sorry."

Komake shrugged, unconcerned. "No problem," he drawled. He bade them good-by, and strolled off toward the car rental office.

Minutes later, Alyse was settled next to Tommy in the front of Rand's roomy sedan at a nearby vehicle storage lot. Rand slammed the trunk lid. As he climbed in behind the steering wheel, she glanced back at the empty rear seat. He caught her looking at it and shook his head, frowning.

"I've always had trouble with spatial concepts. I was convinced we wouldn't have room for an extra passenger."

Alyse smiled, then laughed out loud.

"Komake's a major heartthrob, these days," Rand said, glumly recalling the way the singer had focused on Alyse during his performance last night. "You aren't teed off at me for nudging him out of our day?"

"I couldn't be happier."

Rand glanced down at Tommy, who was craning his neck to see over the padded dashboard. "Do you mind if Tommy sits by the window? He gets carsick when he can't see out."

Alyse swapped places with the boy. As she helped him with his seatbelt, she noticed the way he kept eyeing her sand dollar necklace, obviously pleased that she was wearing his gift. She was dying to ask him where he'd bought it—and to tell him and Rand of the secret she had unlocked when she dropped it on the bathroom tile.

Thoughts of incredible riches flew from her mind, however, as Alyse found herself pressed snugly against Rand's bicep. Her pulse quickened at the physical contact. She turned her face away to look out Tommy's side window, so Rand couldn't see her nervous smile.

"Where are we off to?" she asked as they pulled out onto the highway.

"My cottage." Rand gripped the steering wheel with both hands, resisting the urge to stretch his right arm across the back of the seat behind Alyse's shoulders. Feeling ridiculously like a teenager on a first date, he was half-afraid of getting his knuckles rapped. "Kiku is expecting us."

"Kiku?" Alyse looked into Rand's face. He seemed tense. The terrible thought flashed into her head that he might be living with someone, and that he was regretting having invited her along.

"My housekeeper." Rand glanced past Alyse at Tommy. "You'll like her, spud. Wait till you taste her home-cooked seaweed."

Tommy's eyes widened in horror. He made a face, and clapped a hand over his mouth.

Alyse laughed and hugged the boy's hunched shoulders. "I'm with you, Tommy."

Rand grunted in mock disgust and turned onto the inland highway that cut south across the narrow isthmus that connected the two huge sleeping volca-

67

noes that made up the island. Beyond Waikapu, nestled near the base of the mountains of West Maui, the verdant valley opened onto a majestic view of the sparkling waters of Ma'alaea Bay.

They took the coast highway along the south shore. After passing through the tunnel west of McGregor Point, Rand drove on for a few miles and then pulled the car onto the shoulder and stopped. He pointed toward a grove of monkey-pod trees off to the right. "There are ancient rock carvings on that hill. Above the petroglyphs there's an old Hawaiian temple called the Kaiwaloa Heiau, where human sacrifices were carried out centuries ago."

"Nice," Alyse said dryly.

"Creepy," Tommy said appreciatively, his face plastered against the window.

"I thought you'd like that," Rand noted, pulling back onto the highway.

The scenery gave way to lush sugar cane fields, the green leaves gently undulating in the mild sea breeze. Drawing from a seemingly limitless supply of local lore, Rand informed them that the original plantation had been founded by King Kamehameha back in the 1870's. Alyse rubbernecked constantly, taking in the sights, wishing she had brought along a camera.

"Too bad we didn't have time to take the long way around by way of Hana. I'd like you to see Haleakala."

"What's that?" Tommy asked.

"She's supposed to be the largest dormant volcano in the world," Rand said.

"She?" Alyse smiled.

Rand nodded. "At sunset, Haleakala rivals the grandeur of the Grand Canyon. I've always felt that anything that spectacular has to be a woman."

Alyse met his warm gaze. She flushed, unsure if he intended for her to take his comment as a personal compliment. Her growing physical attraction to him aside, she still found the man to be an enigma in many ways.

Rand braked suddenly as a small animal emerged from the cane field bordering the highway and streaked across the pavement in front of the car.

"Look fast, Tommy!" he barked, pointing at the blur of shiny fur just before it disappeared into the tall grass along the roadside.

"What was *that?*" Tommy asked in awe, his face again pressed to the window glass.

"A mongoose. They were imported to the islands from India, years ago, to help control the rats that came here on whaling ships. Big mistake."

"How come?" Tommy wondered.

"As it turned out, the rats prowled at night and slept by day, and mongooses did just the opposite. Their paths seldom crossed. So now, the mongoose has become as much of a pest as the rat."

"Wow!" Tommy breathed, fogging the window glass.

They entered the historic old waterfront town of Lahaina, the original capital of the Hawaiian Kingdom, where Rand continued to play guide. Right or wrong, Alyse had the distinct impression that Rand was trying extra hard to please her, as well as Tommy.

She expected him to stop the car and insist that they get out and nose around the shops. Instead, he merely whetted her appetite before leaving Lahaina behind and driving north.

"We'll be at the cottage in two shakes."

Tommy surprised Alyse by slipping his hand into hers, tension drawing his peachy cheeks. She squeezed him reassuringly, guessing what his problem was. For his sake, she fervently hoped Rand's housekeeper didn't turn out to be another Mrs. Saunders.

The low cottage hugged a sandy crescent of beach. Rand pulled into the driveway and parked in the shade of a tall angel trumpet tree with large white blossoms cascading downward from the heavy, dark green foliage. Alyse waited for Tommy to get out, then slid across the seat after him.

A gentle breeze fanned her cotton skirt as she pitched in with Tommy to help Rand unload the luggage from the trunk. They rounded the corner of the house to a lattice-covered walkway, where a petite, moon-faced woman of about sixty met them at the side door.

"Alyse, Tommy," Rand said, pausing in the doorway, "this is Kiku, my favorite person in all of Hawaii."

The housekeeper swatted playfully at Rand with the dish towel she held, and then turned to bow formally to Alyse and Tommy. Alyse felt instantly drawn to the tiny Japanese woman, whose gentle

70

smile was warm and welcoming. Even Tommy seemed to relax as Kiku beckoned them inside.

They trooped into a cool, airy living room filled with overstuffed couches and big rattan papasan chairs overflowing with floral-print cushions. Woven rice straw mats covered the floor. A baby grand piano filled one corner, next to a solid glass wall that looked out onto a pristine stretch of beach and the mesmerizing expanse of ocean beyond.

"This is heaven!" Alyse said in a half whisper, as though speaking too loudly might break the spell and she would wake up in her dull, cramped studio apartment back in New York.

She turned to find herself alone in the room with Rand, who apparently had been watching her. He looked away quickly. In the hallway angled from the far wall, she could hear Kiku talking softly to Tommy in strongly accented English, the sound of her voice receding as they moved into another room.

Rand opened double French doors leading onto the beachside lanai and ushered Alyse outside. A heavy scent of tropical flowers rode the salt sea breeze that stirred scattered leaves across the damp flagstones underfoot. Colorful orchids draped woven fernwood baskets hanging from the rafters.

Alyse settled onto the plump cushion of a rattan settee. She was surprised when Rand sank down beside her, rather than taking one of the matching chairs. He clasped both hands behind his head and stretched, then leaned back and casually looped an arm across the back of the settee.

71

"That's Molokai," he said, pointing off to the right toward a distant land mass. "It's called the Friendly Isle."

"As far as I'm concerned, this is the garden of the gods." Alyse made a sweeping gesture that took in the sea view, the comfortable lanai, and, off to one side, a gracefully arched wooden bridge crossing a small pool filled with water hyacinths and lilies.

"You really like it?"

She glanced over to find him looking at her again, a soft light in his dark brown eyes. Their gazes locked, and it was Alyse who pulled hers away first, her heart pounding. She stared off to the Pacific for a moment, her lips clamped between her teeth to quell a disconcerting tingling sensation.

Rand was so close, his arm almost touching her back, her shoulder just inches from the swell of his thick chest. Alyse was more than a little dismayed at how much she wanted him closer even than that. From the look in his eyes, the feeling seemed to be mutual.

All she had to do was glance at him again, and he would kiss her. She considered the risk that Tommy might wander out onto the lanai and catch them in an embrace. But she could hear the boy's piping voice — and Kiku's — neither sounding anywhere near the living room. So, why was she holding back?

You're here to talk Rand into selling Conrad the Tokugawa box, an inner voice warned her.

The longer she looked out to sea, the fainter that inner voice grew. Rand's fingers moved to her shoulder, his touch as ethereal as a shadow on the soft cotton of her blouse. Alyse almost stopped breathing, her gaze fixed blindly on the orange-and-red sail of a catamaran that came skimming into view fifty yards off the beach.

Rand tensed.

Alyse started to turn toward him—half curiosity, half desire—when he suddenly bolted to his feet.

He took two quick steps away from the settee and stood with his fists knotted at his sides, his gaze riveted on the boat. The small craft's sole occupant leaned out from the far side, barely visible as he worked the billowing sail.

"Is something wrong?" Alyse asked.

Rand watched the catamaran a moment longer, then seemed to shake himself. "No, of course not." But when he turned back toward her, he looked worried and distracted.

"Maybe we should go inside," he suggested with with sudden crispness, avoiding her curiosity. "Kiku has an early supper planned, so we'll have time to eat before I take you back to the airport."

He held out his hand and Alyse took it, feeling vaguely whiplashed by his abrupt transformation. Why did she sense that food was the farthest thing from Rand's mind—that his actual objective was to get her into the cottage and out of sight as fast as possible?

73

Chapter Five

The last coral-and-tangerine tints of the sunset had faded into star-studded darkness. Off to the south, intermittent lightning danced through an approaching bank of blue-black clouds.

Rand bore down harder on the accelerator, speeding toward the airport at Kahului. Every few minutes, he glanced at the digital clock on the dashboard, hoping against hope that they could still make it.

This is what he got for not allowing extra time for emergencies. The fates couldn't resist throwing him a bum break. In this case, a flat tire on the highway between Lahaina and Kahului.

He should have left earlier. He shouldn't have invited Alyse to Maui in the first place. Should have. Shouldn't have. All of a sudden, he felt as if he were being torn in a dozen different directions, all because of old lady Fielding's detective.

The catamaran had sailed back and forth along the beach all afternoon, making half a dozen passes offshore from his cottage. Rand was as certain as he could be without proof that the monotonous sailor was watching him.

He couldn't even go out onto his own lanai, not in the company of Alyse, anyway. It wouldn't do for the detective to be able to run back to Mrs. Fielding with a report that he had a beautiful woman with him. Even if Alyse was there just for the afternoon, with Kiku as chaperon.

Damn! he thought. *Has the old witch reduced me to hiding out in my own house?*

Up ahead, flashing lights rose suddenly into the night sky. Rand slammed a fist hard against the steering wheel and pulled over onto the shoulder.

"What is it?" Alyse cried.

He pointed up at the lights climbing steadily into the black night. "The flight to Oahu."

"Oops."

"Sorry. I really blew it."

Alyse spread both hands, trying to shrug off the let-down feeling that their mad dash had gained them nothing. "Hey, this isn't your fault. I'm the one who misplaced the lug nut from the wheel."

They sat silently for a few minutes, watching the plane's lights dwindle in the velvet-black distance until they were indistinguishable from the stars.

"You're taking this very well," he said finally.

"It comes from having no choice." Alyse laughed resignedly.

In truth, she was relieved that she would miss Conrad Brace's late-night call. She could put off for one more day the necessity of informing him that

75

she'd had no luck at all in persuading Rand to sell.

Her unexpected reluctance to put up with Conrad's badgering surprised Alyse. She fingered the chipped necklace pensively. The reward for finding the stolen dragonfly pendant was already giving her a heady, unaccustomed sense of independence, and she didn't even have her hands on the money yet.

Still, Alyse felt an obligation to retrieve the Tokugawa box for Conrad. Perhaps the unanticipated overnight layover on Maui would give her one more opportunity to break down Rand's resistance. So far, her best efforts had accomplished little more than to further harden his already firm resolve to present the box to his Japanese clients on Saturday.

"I suppose we'd better find a phone and see if I can scrounge a room at an inn," she said.

"Forget that." Rand pulled onto the highway and headed back in the direction from which they had just come, this time at a less breakneck speed. "As I said before, the hotels will be packed. I had to book accommodations months ahead for my luau guests. I'm afraid you're stuck with spending the night at the cottage."

Something in his tone caused Alyse to glance sharply at Rand. His face looked grim in the greenish glow from the dashboard.

Lightning flickered in the distance. The storm was going to break before they reached home, Rand thought. Considering the way the rest of the evening had gone, he could hardly expect anything less.

He navigated the dark, winding road with more

caution during the return to Lahaina. The urgency was gone now that Alyse had missed her flight. There was no sense in risking a wreck. Besides, he had his mind on more than just what lay ahead.

Rand tensely checked the rearview mirror again. Only one car had shared the highway with them for a couple of miles now. The headlights were still back there. He spotted them every now and then on the straightaways. His lips tightened into a hard, bitter line and he ground his teeth together audibly.

"Is something wrong?" Alyse asked, nervous.

Rand jerked his gaze off the mirror and started to shake his head. Then he changed his mind and wiped a hand across his face. He had brashly invited Alyse to accompany him to the island, and then failed in his promise to get her on the return shuttle back to the big island. Because of that, she was having to spend the night at his place—the worst possible scenario. Since none of this was any fault of hers, he figured the least he could do was lay his cards on the table.

"Something is lousy, Alyse." The digital speedometer readout began to rise steadily. "Tommy's grandmother hired a private detective to prove that I'd make an unfit father figure. I think the jerk is following us right now."

Alyse spun around to look out the rear window as big raindrops began plopping against the roof. She saw nothing at first in the pitch darkness of the cloud-cloaked night. Then, perhaps a quarter of a mile back, a quick flash of high beams. She settled back in the seat, her stomach fluttering uneasily as several very large pieces of puzzle dropped into place.

"The catamaran that kept sailing past your cottage all afternoon," she said, recalling how Rand had watched it through the window wall in the living room. "That was the detective?"

"Possibly."

Alyse sagged, and pressed her fingertips to her lips. "Oh, Rand." She shook her head. "I shouldn't have come. And I can't possibly spend the night at your place. How would that look? If you lost Tommy because of me, I'd never forgive myself."

Rand glanced at Alyse. Some of his anger and tension evaporated, replaced by a floating sensation in his chest as he realized that her concern extended to him, as well as to Tommy. He reached out and covered her hand with his. Her skin felt cool and disturbingly soft against the feverish heat of his.

"It'll be all right." His conviction sounded strained. "I don't intend to let that evil old hag run my life — or Tommy's. As far as I'm concerned, Elaine Fielding trashed her rights to grandmotherhood when she disowned her own daughter for marrying my brother. That's ignoring the little fact that she coldly kidnapped Tommy for her own selfish purposes while he was still in shock over being orphaned."

The sky suddenly opened, spilling a torrent of rain. Rand glanced at the rearview mirror again and smiled grimly, releasing Alyse's hand.

"Hang on," he said with icy calmness. "We're about to find out who knows this road better."

78

Startled, Alyse grabbed the handle on the passenger door with one hand and braced herself on the padded dashboard with the other as Rand floored the accelerator. The transmission kicked down with a roar, the rapid acceleration pressing her back in her seat as the car leaped forward into the storm. She realized that Rand was, indeed, familiar with every twist and turn of the darkened highway as he maneuvered easily around one bend after another.

She said a prayer under her breath as the tires squealed into a sharp curve on the wet pavement. The sedan rocked slightly from side to side as it came out the other end and settled into a long straightaway. The straining engine responded smoothly to Rand's smooth, skillful manipulation of the clutch and gear stick. He suddenly laughed — a mirthless bark of triumph as he checked the mirror once more. Alyse glanced over her shoulder in time to see the following headlights buck wildly into the low night sky before going out. She felt a sense of shared elation with Rand — along with a deep chill.

"Lost him," Rand said, slowing.

He glanced at Alyse and suddenly braked. By the time he had the car stopped on the shoulder, she was shaking uncontrollably. Rand set the brake and slid across the seat to take her in his arms.

"Damnit, Alyse," he said, stroking her hair as she huddled against his chest. "How could I have been so stupid? I didn't mean to scare you."

Alyse shook her head, her throat too constricted with hot, dry fear to permit speech. Nestled in his protective embrace, she had neither the power nor the will to tell Rand that her trembling had nothing to do with his flight from an old woman's hired detective. Nor could she bring herself to say that she didn't believe the other car had anything to do with Tommy's grandmother.

As she had glanced back at the crashing pursuit vehicle, she'd suddenly felt a withering stab of personal fear—as though *she* were the stalker's prey. The sand dollar concealing the precious dragonfly pressed against her breast like a lead weight.

For the first time, Alyse realized the treacherous depth of the quagmire she had waded into by agreeing to wear the treasure while authorities sought to uncover the theft ring.

She had become bait.

Alyse closed her eyes, shivering against Rand. He stroked her hair, her cheek, the quivering pulse point at the side of her neck. She listened to his soothing voice, barely audible above the patter of rain on the car roof, without hearing the words.

Gradually, the tremors subsided. She slowly relaxed, becoming aware of the musky scent of Rand's cologne and the steady, calming rhythm of his heartbeat against her cheek.

The clunky necklace dug into her flesh, but Alyse didn't dare to move. She was afraid that if she shifted even a fraction of an inch, Rand would release her. And at the moment that was the last thing in the world she wanted.

Never, not even with Rob, had Alyse felt such a comforting sense of rightness. Cradled in the warm, nurturing hollow of Rand's arms, she was absolutely certain now that the Shogun tea box wasn't the only thing that had lured her to Maui.

The cottage was silent when they entered through the side door. Alyse followed Rand's stealthy footsteps as he led the way into the living room. A single lamp burned on an end table on which a small plate of rice cookies waited. Rand scooped up the dish, doled out half of the prize to Alyse, and grinned.

"Kiku doesn't like anybody to go to bed hungry," he whispered.

Alyse popped a cookie into her mouth, surprised that after what they had just been through, she actually was hungry. She trailed Rand down the hallway to an open doorway through which a nightlight shone dimly and peeked past his shoulder as he leaned inside.

Tommy lay sleeping with his face to the light, curled around a ragged teddy bear, one fist pressed tightly against his mouth. Alyse sighed, feeling a powerful urge to go in and cuddle the little fellow into her arms. Instead, she followed Rand across the narrow hallway to a closed door.

He paused, pointed to a third room at the end of the hallway, and whispered, "Kiku."

Alyse nodded. He quietly opened the door to the room across from Tommy's and they stepped inside.

It was as cozy and welcoming as the rest of the snug cottage. The thick, bamboo-print comforter on the brass bed had been turned back. A novel lay on the teakwood night stand. On a matching dresser nearby, Alyse noticed a framed photograph of a handsome young couple holding a baby.

"I think you'll be comfortable here, tonight," Rand said in a low voice.

While he crossed to a wide double window on the far wall and closed the wooden plantation shutters, Alyse took a closer look at the picture. The baby, probably less than a year old, was clearly Tommy.

"Chris and Pat," Rand said, appearing at her side. He touched the frame tenderly, then quickly turned toward the closet.

Alyse took another quick look around as it dawned on her where she was. "This is your room!" she whispered. "I can't crowd you out."

"No problem." He pulled a blanket and pillow off the closet shelf. "Besides, Kiku would have kittens if she found you sleeping on the couch in the morning. Then she'd murder me. She has a remarkably powerful sense of hospitality."

"What about you?"

He chuckled. "I'm not a guest. I suppose that makes me expendable in Kiku's eyes." He smiled wryly at Alyse, and then his expression softened. "In this case, I happen to agree with her."

Alyse flushed, suddenly feeling awkward. As if sensing her discomfort, Rand cleared his throat and moved toward the door. Halfway there, he stopped and looked her up and down.

"Uh—I don't suppose you brought a nightie in that bag." He nodded at her big straw purse.

She shook her head. "I wasn't counting on needing one." Alyse pulled out the bikini that she'd worn only once, for five minutes, back at Macy's in New York.

Rand eyed the minimal patches of fabric until Alyse blushed again and stuffed the flimsy garment back out of sight. Then he seemed to rouse himself, and crossed over to the dresser. From the bottom drawer, he produced a set of neatly pressed men's tartan cotton pajamas.

"I'll tell you what," he said, flipping the pajama bottoms over one shoulder and tossing the top to Alyse. "We'll share."

Alyse held the top up to her. The bottom hem came almost to her knees. She bit her lip, suppressing a childish giggle. But when she looked up into Rand's eyes, the mirth died away, drowned in a flood of feelings that she was ill-prepared to hold at bay.

He stared down at her, his lips parted slightly. They each moved a step closer, as if caught in a powerful magnetic field. His hand came up in a slow motion to cradle her jaw and raise her face to his, one thumb tracing the outline of her lips like a feather—or a dream. Alyse held her breath, waiting—wanting—the warm blossoming of her desire driving every thought from her mind.

Rand suddenly snapped his hand from her face as if he had been scalded. His head jerked to one side, and she followed his gaze to the photograph of his dead brother and sister-in-law . . . and Tommy. Alyse watched, powerless, as Rand's features settled into an expression of pure anguish and dread.

In a flash of prescience that startled her, she knew he was thinking about the detective that Tommy's grandmother had hired to haunt his every move.

"It's very late," he said hoarsely. "You'd better get some sleep."

Alyse nodded. Understanding did little to ease the tension of desire left over from their aborted move toward a kiss. As she watched Rand leave, pulling the door softly closed between them, she felt as if a part of her were being torn away.

She dropped her straw bag on the floor where she stood, stepped back, and sagged onto the edge of the bed. She'd come to Maui on business — she thought. But there was nothing businesslike about the way Rand had touched her, just moments ago. And there darn sure wasn't anything even remotely businesslike about how that touch, along with the deep yearning in his eyes, had made her feel.

Between the blasted box and the pendant, her life was becoming a sticky spider's web of complications. Her rapidly deepening attraction to Rand — a man she barely knew, but whom she felt she had known all her life — was only making her situation less bearable.

Alyse spread her arms wide and plopped down on the mattress with a heavy sigh. She was getting in way over her head. The dragonfly had been found. The reward was hers . . . and Tommy's. Why didn't she just pick up the phone, call the authorities, and tell them they could jolly well forget about using her as their bait?

Next, she could get in touch with Conrad and tell

him that, if the Tokugawa Shogun tea box was all that important to him, he could come out to Hawaii and arm-wrestle Rand for it himself. Then, she could disappear from Rand's life before she caused real problems that might result in his losing Tommy, thanks to the nosey detective.

She closed her eyes and went limp, wanting nothing more than to roll over on the pillowy comforter and scream her frustration into its fluffy folds. But she couldn't succumb to those emotions, any more than she could bug out on the commitments she had made. She was a vital link for both the Japanese and Conrad. However much she was coming to hate the idea, Alyse felt it was her duty to follow through on her responsibilities to those two separate causes.

In spite of her fatigue, Alyse sensed her resolve hardening into a call for action that she couldn't ignore. She forced herself to get up, finger-comb her tousled hair, and shake out her wrinkled skirt. Rand was bound to be equally as tired as she was. If he hadn't already turned in, this might be the perfect time to catch him with his guard down and persuade him to give up the Tokugawa box.

The door opened soundlessly. She stepped out into the hallway, glanced across to Tommy's open room . . . and stopped.

In the dim glow of the nightlight, she could see Rand was sitting slumped on the edge of Tommy's bed, the child cradled against his chest. The boy's arms were draped limply around his uncle's neck. Both Turnbulls appeared to be half-asleep.

85

A knot rose in Alyse's throat as she studied the touching tableau. She squeezed her eyelids shut to clear a sudden stinging mist. After watching them for a while, she slipped quietly back into her room and closed the door.

Alyse removed the sand dollar and placed it carefully on the nightstand. As she changed quickly into the baggy pajama top and crawled into Rand's bed, she was surprised to find herself comparing him with her late husband.

Rob had been openly affectionate, and yet so coldly deceptive that in retrospect she felt she never really knew him. Rand Turnbull represented the opposite side of the coin. He seemed to hold himself in tight reserve — and yet, Alyse sensed an almost subliminal kinship with his hidden tenderness.

After four years, Rob had left her practically destitute, both financially and emotionally. How strange, Alyse thought, that she was already having such vivid premonitions of a greater and more painful loss to be suffered when she left Maui tomorrow.

A clap of thunder awakened Alyse from a fitful sleep. She lay perfectly still for a minute or two, disoriented, listening to the rain sheet off the roof outside the shuttered bedroom window. When she finally figured out where she was, she rolled over to squint at the clock on the nightstand.

Three A.M. She groaned groggily, writhed into a slow, feline stretch, and sank her head into the pillow as thunder once again rattled the window.

Within seconds, she was well on her way back to sleep.

Suddenly the bedroom door sailed open, bumping against the wall, and a small figure streaked across the darkened room toward the bed. Alyse barely had time to register his whimper of distress before Tommy hiked a knee onto the edge of the mattress . . . and froze.

"It's okay, Tommy," she whispered, realizing that he must have expected to find Rand. "It's me—Alyse."

Tommy remained as motionless as stone, one knee half on, half off the bed. A brilliant, strobe-like flash of lightning illuminated the shutters, followed immediately by a deafening crash of thunder that vibrated through the house in a diminishing succession of thuds and shudders. The child flinched. Alyse could hear his ragged breathing even above the steady rumble of rain on the roof.

"Are you afraid of storms?" she asked.

He nodded vigorously.

Alyse threw back the covers and held out her arms. He barely hesitated before scooting into bed and burrowing against her side. She settled his head on her shoulder and gently dabbed the tears from his cheeks with the hem of the sheet.

With the incredible resilience that nature seems to reserve only for children, Tommy promptly dropped off to sleep. Alyse lay awake much longer, hardly able to believe that she was actually in Rand's bed, her chin resting in the sweet-smelling wilderness of Tommy's tangled mop.

In less than forty-eight hours, she seemed to have become firmly implanted in the Turnbull family's scheme of things. How would she ever extricate herself?

Chapter Six

Alyse awoke with a sense of unease. She started to roll over, and bumped into something. When she opened her eyes, she found herself staring straight into Tommy Turnbull's face. He lay with one fist pressed against his cheek, slumbering peacefully.

She studied his small, handsome features. For a moment, her heart seemed to swell. She could learn to love this little boy heart and soul, Alyse thought, as her untested mothering instincts welled to the surface. Something about him spoke to a part of her that she'd tried to keep buried for almost two years now.

The thought of what might have been caused its usual ache of grief. But the pain was stronger this time, because of the warm, trusting body nestled against her. Without thinking, Alyse leaned over and pressed her lips lightly against Tommy's pale forehead. He murmured softly in his sleep and smiled.

A tear meandered down her cheek onto the pillow. The boy didn't know it, but they shared a common bond. He had lost his parents. Alyse had lost someone equally dear — someone she'd never had a chance to get to know. And although she didn't like to admit it even now, she'd always suspected deep down that Rob had been just a little relieved by that loss.

The feeling of unease returned. Alyse focused on it, trying to find the source. Finally, she raised her head, her attention drawn to the open bedroom door.

Rand stood in the doorway, his fingers tucked into the pockets of faded cut-off jeans. Muscles bunched tensely beneath his sky blue *Maui* T-shirt as his gaze shifted back and forth from Tommy to Alyse. His stony frown confused her.

She raised up on one elbow. Her first impression was that Rand disapproved of Tommy being in bed with her. Then it occurred to Alyse that, more likely, he was stung because the boy appeared to have turned to her during the night, instead of to him. She found that she could empathize with that.

Of course, Rand didn't know that the storm had frightened Tommy out of his wits, sending him fleeing to adult protection. Nor had Rand seen the the boy's startled expression when Tommy discovered Alyse occupying his uncle's bed. As much as she might wish otherwise, Alyse knew she had been nothing more than a willing substitute for the child's first choice.

She waved one hand placatingly, anxious to set the record straight. After his generous hospitality,

90

Alyse definitely didn't want Rand to think she was intentionally horning in on his already complicated domestic situation.

Careful not to awaken Tommy, she eased to the far side of the bed and dropped her feet to the floor. But Rand didn't give her a chance to slip across the room and explain.

"Kiku will have breakfast ready in twenty minutes," he said curtly.

Although he kept his voice quite low, with the obvious intent of not disturbing his sleeping nephew, the words carried across the room with penetrating clarity. Just the right kind of galvanizing quality for either intimidating a witness or influencing a jury, Alyse thought. She could almost feel the heat of his displeasure.

And then, he was gone.

Alyse stood hugging herself, unsure whether she should be embarrassed or angry. Glancing down at the baggy pajama top that Rand had loaned her, she settled on anger—at herself.

She had barged into this man's life with the expressed purpose of wheedling him out of a piece of property that he had bought at auction fair and square. In light of that, Rand had every right to be suspicious of her motives where Tommy was concerned.

"Wonderful," she murmured dismally, scuffing around the end of the bed. "Just terrific."

Okay, she thought, so she found Rand immensely attractive—and his nephew profoundly endearing. Alyse went a step further. She conceded that, however incredible it might seem in such a brief period of time, she was coming dangerously close to falling irretrievably in love with both of them. But that didn't give her license to take up squatter's rights in their personal lives.

Alyse closed the door before padding over to the nightstand, where the sand dollar necklace lay coiled atop the spy novel that Rand was reading. She picked it up and fingered the thumbnail-size chip on the back that revealed the delicately inlaid jade and mother-of-pearl wing of the dragonfly pendant.

The Japanese consulate official had solemnly promised that the reward would be transferred to her New York bank today. Her morning had taken a rocky turn. Yet she couldn't help smiling now at the thought of the flurry of interest the interbank wire transfer would cause when it hit her heretofore anemic checking account.

Alyse pressed the dragonfly wing to her lips. She was still having trouble believing that such a small object had brought her dream of owning her own gallery so quickly within reach. For the first time ever, she was gaining control of her destiny. That was going to take some getting used to.

Her life had been an unbroken parade of demeaning compromises, all the way back to Rob and beyond. Alyse was sick of them. They left a thick, unpleasant taste in her mouth, like a hangover from bad wine. The reward would buy her freedom from compromise forever.

Her gaze drifted back toward the doorway where

Rand had stood, and her smile faded into a pensive expression. A strangely hollow but entirely familiar sense of loneliness settled to the floor of her stomach. Alyse suddenly had a painful, all-too-vivid picture of exactly what money could not buy.

As she fastened the necklace around her neck, she chewed her lip, mentally adding yet another layer of imaginary bricks along the top of the high wall that she had begun building around her heart two years ago, on the bleak day when she had lost her first flesh-and-blood dream. Gradually, as though succumbing to a powerful numbing agent, the pain in her chest subsided.

Alyse looked at Tommy through the renewed inner barrier. She felt like a destitute child staring longingly through a candy store window.

In this case, the protective wall was a necessary precaution—she might even go so far as to call it Rob Marlowe's legacy. Because the simple fact was that, with or without the Tokugawa box, she would be departing Maui later today. And after just one night, she already knew that leaving was going to be like walking away from a part of herself.

Squaring her chin, Alyse considered the prospect of saying good-by to the Turnbulls—Great and Small—and tried to put it all in perspective. In terms of emotional lacerations, she thought, we're talking about a first-class paper cut. The pain likely will be far out of proportion to the apparent wound, but you'll get over it with Band-Aid therapy.

That was today.

At the rate she was going, however, she sensed that she couldn't afford to hang around to make another damage assessment tomorrow. One more day, and Alyse had a sneaking suspicion that she'd be lucky to survive without a full-scale heart transplant.

Kiku served breakfast on the lanai, a slightly odd combination of toasted cinnamon bagels with peanut butter and fresh island fruits. From the good-natured way Kiku scolded Rand, it was obvious to Alyse that the tiny woman was in the habit of indulging his tastes, regardless of how much they went against her own.

Alyse sipped her coffee and stared out at the gentle surf, thinking the setting should have made the meal pleasurable and relaxing. It didn't. An invisible cloud of tension hung in the air, not at all diluted by Rand's rigidly polite conversation.

"You have most of the day before your flight back to Oahu," he said, slathering a bagel half with peanut butter and topping it with a pineapple ring. "Would you care to go into town for some shopping?"

She hesitated, trying to square his suggestion with his apparent displeasure at finding her snuggled up with Tommy earlier. Was he hoping to send her into town alone in order to get her out of his house?

Alyse brushed at the wrinkles in her cotton skirt. She hadn't brought a change of clothes. Although she had showered that morning, she still felt less than clean in yesterday's skirt and blouse. If Rand was intent on getting rid of her, she could do worse than a shopping excursion in Lahaina.

Now that she could afford to spend all she wanted in the town's pricey tourist shops, she could even see how a shopping spree might be just the ticket to lift her spirits. Anything would beat straining the outer limits of Rand's hospitality, which seemed to be all she was accomplishing at the moment.

"I'd love to go shopping," she said, exaggerating.

What she would *love* to do was go for a long walk on the beach with Rand, preferably hand in hand, and most certainly alone. But that was precisely the sort of rose-colored fantasy that she didn't dare allow herself to dwell upon.

"Good," Rand said. "We'll make a day of it — as soon as Tommy wakes up."

Alyse smiled, surprised that she had so badly misjudged Rand. He apparently wasn't trying to pawn her off on the local shopkeepers, after all. His generosity caused her to approach her next thought with more than a little guilt. She fully intended to boost the gross sales of Lahaina's retail shops. However, she still felt duty-bound to spend at least part of her remaining time on Maui lobbying for the tea box.

"I guess the sprout's going to sleep all morning," Rand remarked. He poured them both a third cup of coffee from the insulated carafe that Kiku had left on the glass-topped table.

"He's had a couple of eventful days." Alyse watched a desolate, five-mile stare come and go from Rand's expression as he doctored his coffee with cream. After a while, she added, "Did you know Tommy is afraid of storms?"

Rand's eyes snapped up from his coffee. "No."

"The thunder scared the willies out of him, last night," she said. "He came running into your room looking for comfort . . . from you."

Rand looked at her for a moment, his gaze turned inward. Finally, he pushed his cup aside and rubbed both hands down his face.

"Damn," he muttered through his hands. "I feel like such an idiot. I've tried so blasted hard to be a father to Tommy these past months. Tried, and failed miserably. Then along you come and— wham— you have him wrapped around your finger. When I found him with you this morning, I just assumed—"

"Don't assume anything, where Tommy is concerned," Alyse said. "Least of all, that you've failed. You can't replace what he's lost— what you've both lost. But that doesn't mean he doesn't love you a great deal more than you probably imagine."

She smiled. "And as far as having Tommy wrapped around my finger is concerned, I have to tell you it's the other way around."

Rand looked searchingly at her across the tops of his hands. He wanted to believe her assessment of how he was doing with his nephew. He desperately needed all the reassurance he could get that he wasn't making completely wrong moves where the boy was concerned. And he especially wanted to hear it from Alyse.

After all, she had been dead right about Mrs. Saunders. Alyse seemed to have excellent instincts when it came to childrearing in general, and Tommy in particular. Rand had seen for himself how natural they looked cuddled together in their sleep. Natural enough to make him green with envy. Standing there in the bedroom doorway watching them, he hadn't been able to decide of whom he was more jealous—Alyse or Tommy.

Rand rubbed his face again. While holding Alyse in his arms in the car last night, he had felt as if some sort of emotional scar tissue were tearing loose inside him. He suddenly found himself standing in a minefield of reawakened needs and feelings, trying to decide where to make his next step.

But how did you tell that to an intelligent, attractive woman you've known less than forty-eight hours, Rand wondered, without scaring her out of your life? *And* without scaring the hell out of yourself?

He was trying to figure out some way to let Alyse know just how much she was beginning to mean to him, when she abruptly veered in a different direction.

"I'll tell you what," she said, trying too hard to make a joke of it, "I'll put in a good word for you with Tommy if you'll change your mind and sell the Tokugawa box to Conrad Brace."

Rand's expression abruptly hardened. He stared

97

at her as if he didn't want to believe what he had just heard. Alyse wiped the playfully cunning smile off her face. She had a panicky feeling that she had made a huge mistake, only she wasn't sure where or how.

He rose slowly, his wrought iron chair scraping loudly across the flagstone paving, and went to stand at the edge of the lanai with his back to her. She wondered why he was so sensitive about her bringing up the tea box. He had brought it up himself yesterday, and they both knew it was her reason for being there.

"I expected better of you than that, Alyse," he said in a constricted, confused voice. He turned to face her. "I didn't think you'd stoop to using Tommy to manipulate me."

"Using Tommy!" Alyse looked up at him, stunned that he had actually taken her joke seriously. She had to remind herself that they were still near strangers. Because of that, occasional misreadings were all but inevitable. "Rand, I can assure you—"

"No." He cut her off with a shake of his head. "I'm afraid you can't."

"Now, wait just one minute!"

Alyse shot to her feet, the color rising in her cheeks. She stalked around the table, the heels of her sandals clacking harshly on the flagstones.

"At this point, I would cheerfully walk through fire to get that box," she admitted, her voice rising. "But if you think I would even consider using Tommy as a pawn, you had jolly well better wake up

98

and smell the coffee, counselor. I hold children far too dearly for that."

"Since when?" Rand immediately regretted his words, wondering how on earth he could have forgotten for even one second that Alyse had risked her life to save Tommy's.

"Since I miscarried my own, two years ago," Alyse said in a hoarse, anguished whisper.

Alyse tottered, dizzy with shock that she had let down her guard and revealed so much. Rand's face went totally blank. They stared at each other in a fragile, deafening silence. And then suddenly she was in his arms, being crushed against his powerful chest.

"I'm sorry, Alyse," he murmured into her hair. "Please forgive me."

Too choked to speak, she shook her head, meaning there was nothing to forgive. Rand took it to mean the opposite. He silently cursed himself.

"Then let me make it up to you," he said, raging inside at his blunder.

Grief had made him so damned self-centered, these past ten months. It simply had never occurred to him that someone as warm and giving as Alyse could be hiding a painful open wound of her own. Rand was suddenly obsessed with the need to make it right with her. He couldn't let her walk out of his house and fly back to New York before he'd even had a chance.

Rand held her out so he could see her face. Her enchanting blue-green eyes glistened with pent-up tears. The color had risen into the soft contours of her cheeks, like the fine blush on a peach. Her lips parted and before he knew what he was doing, Rand was kissing her.

Alyse tried to draw back, but could not. He held her too tightly and his lips were far too tender — as if he were kissing a soulmate. He cradled her to him, and she trembled slightly, her hands moving tentatively to his sides.

"Oh, Alyse," he breathed, his fingers in her tawny curls. "Do you have any idea . . ."

His words were drowned in another kiss. This time, Alyse didn't even try to fight it. She took a deep breath — and let go. Rand's lips became demanding, his breath growing ragged. Alyse dug her fingers into his broad back, feeling his muscles respond to her touch — feeling her own rising desire break free to soar alongside his.

Finally, Rand tore his lips from hers and drew back. He shot a quick glance toward the door leading off the lanai, as if to make sure Kiku wasn't watching. Then he looked down at Alyse, his thumb gently tracing the outline of her full lower lip, his eyes wide with a wonderment identical to her own.

She had never felt such sudden and unreserved passion. It left her shaken and giddy. Judging from the deep glimmer in his dark eyes, Rand clearly shared her feeling that something almost magical had just transpired between them. Something far more important than mere passion alone.

Rand took a long, deep breath and gazed past Alyse toward the sunny beach. Everything out there looked different—brighter, richer. He had a weird feeling that his whole life had tilted on its axis. It was a good feeling, he decided. A little scary, but most definitely good.

Out beyond the foaming surf, an orange-and-red catamaran skimmed across the bright, sun-glittered sea. A frown line appeared between Rand's eyes. A half smile died on his lips. All the air seemed to rush from his lungs and his arms dropped away from Alyse.

She said his name, questioningly. Rand barely heard. He stared intently at the boat, trying to determine if it was the same one that had sailed back and forth under his nose yesterday afternoon. The pattern of orange-and-red stripes on the sail appeared to be the same, but he couldn't be certain.

The catamaran. The car that had followed them from the airport, last night. Were they both old lady Fielding's watchers? If so, they would have plenty to report back to their boss, many thanks to Rand's little exhibition with Alyse there on the lanai.

Damn Elaine Fielding!

"Rand?" Alyse took his hand.

"I'm sorry, Alyse. I . . ." He couldn't finish.

Rand didn't know how to begin to explain what was going on inside him at that moment. He wanted her, but he had a pretty good idea that Alyse already sensed that. What she probably didn't know was that a greater part of him *needed* her—and was absolutely petrified by that feeling.

Alyse reached up and touched his face. He gently took her hand away. With one last, longing look into the shimmering depths of her eyes, Rand forced himself to turn and walk away.

Some distance down the beach from the cottage, Rand broke into a slow trot along the water's edge. He needed to run off his mushrooming anxiety before it turned him into a paranoid basket case.

He needed, period. The word kept banging around inside his head like a loose ball bearing.

He hadn't intended to kiss Alyse.

No. That was not true. Rand had to admit that every last atom in his body had intended to kiss Alyse Marlowe. What he hadn't meant to do was add yet another complication to his long-running battle with Elaine Fielding over custody of Tommy. Embracing Alyse so passionately right out there on the open lanai had been absolutely stupid.

To be perfectly honest with himself — which was something Rand had been avoiding for some time now — he also might as well admit that Mrs. Fielding was only half of the problem. The rest of it involved a little-known fear that he had long managed to keep hidden even from himself: Rand wasn't sure he could cope with the kind of emotional risk that Alyse represented.

Rand was ready and willing to fight for Tommy in court, if it came to that. But what about Alyse? If she chose a different path, he couldn't fight for *her* in court. If she chose not to love him back — not to *need* him back — there wasn't a damned thing Rand could do about it.

A half mile along the curving beach, Rand stopped at a narrow, rocky point and peered out to sea. The red-and-orange catamaran still held its position three or four hundred yards beyond the surf line. He watched the bright sail tack back and forth parallel to the shore, as if it were taunting him.

If the boat pilot actually was working for Mrs. Fielding, he had probably gotten a dilly of a telephoto snapshot of Rand lusting after Alyse. Hell, for all Rand knew, the clown had videotaped the whole thing. Real nice courtroom material against a single man trying to adopt a six-year-old kid.

As if that weren't bad enough, Alyse could be undeservedly dragged through the whole sordid proceedings. Both Kiku and Tommy could be called to testify that Alyse had spent the night at the cottage. Then how was Rand to prove that he had slept on the couch? He had been up before Kiku this morning. So it would be his word against a shotgun blast of innuendo loosed by Elaine Fielding's lawyers.

Rand closed his eyes, recalling the warmth and taste of their kiss — reliving the feel of his soul unlocking and reaching out to Alyse. When he looked back out to sea, he had no illusions as to how much that momentary indiscretion alone might have cost him. And yet, to his amazement, he knew that if he had it to do all over again, he'd behave as he had. Alyse actually, suddenly, cosmically meant that much to him.

"And that, my friend, is grounds for a plea of insanity," Rand said aloud, reflecting on the fact that until two days ago, he hadn't even known Alyse existed.

He waded out into the surf to cool off.

Two days ago, he'd had his life under control — in a lifeless, battened-down sort of way. He had his career and Tommy. That was enough. But now, he suddenly couldn't think straight, with the taste of Alyse still on his lips. The feel of her soft body was still on his skin, the shock of her passion still played havoc with his own.

Alyse was more than just a beautiful woman. She was *decent*. A blind man could see it in the way she interacted with Tommy. Her insistence on wearing that hideously garish necklace the boy had given her was added proof.

Rand wanted to explore the wondrous universe of Alyse Marlowe so badly that his teeth ached. But he knew he couldn't afford to stick his neck out that far, even if he could muster that kind of nerve. No, he couldn't risk losing Tommy. He *couldn't*. He'd already lost too much in that nightmarish accident off Martha's Vineyard last year.

"Damnit, Chris," he whispered tightly. "I'd trade places with you if I could, Bro. I would!"

Later, wading slowly back through the surf toward the cottage, Rand dejectedly faced up to the reality that losing Alyse was unavoidable. Oh, she was decent all right, he told himself. And she was smart, and courageous, and so gloriously, maddeningly sensuous.

In addition to all that, however, the lady of his dreams was also bulldog-stubborn. When Alyse had to fly back to the mainland empty-handed, without the antique box for her boss, Rand figured that would just about tear it between them.

He kept telling himself that over and over. After a while, it almost stopped feeling like a lie.

Alyse sat at the glass-topped table on the lanai, her hands limp in her lap. She felt unplugged—as if Rand had kissed her very soul and then folded it up to take with him when he ran off down the beach.

What had she done wrong that had caused him to flee? Her fingertips moved to her lips. For that matter, what had she done right, to arouse him to such passion in the first place?

Alyse had never felt such physical and emotional attraction to a man in her life. It didn't make sense. She had slept in Rand's bed—in his pajama top, no less. She had consoled his orphaned nephew through a thunderstorm. And she had allowed Rand to kiss her practically into a catatonic state. But when it came down to bedrock reality, she barely knew the man.

"This is too rich for my blood," she muttered, taking a sip of cold coffee.

Between the sudden fortune resulting from her discovery of the dragonfly pendant, and the sudden passion that had erupted almost volcanically between her and Rand, Alyse felt as if she were losing touch with the world as she had known it.

At the same time, however, she experienced a heady, surprisingly exhilarating sense of power.

This feeling was rooted in the knowledge that whatever direction she took in the future would be by her own choice. For the first time since she was born, nobody else was in control of her life. Not Rob. Not Conrad Brace. Most certainly, she thought, gazing thoughtfully out to sea, not Rand Turnbull.

Alyse frowned. The red-and-orange catamaran was still out there, tacking back and forth at that slow, vaguely somnambulant pace at which most things moved around these islands. She was almost sure it was the same craft that had hung offshore yesterday afternoon.

She turned away from the sea, irritated. The whole idea that Tommy's grandmother had actually hired a detective to dog Rand seemed underhanded and shabby. No wonder he had suddenly cut and run. He had his hands full already. Why should he unbalance his load by adding another complication?

"So, now you're a *complication*," Alyse murmured, wondering if it was a bad sign that she had begun talking to herself.

A quick riff of piano notes came from inside the cottage. Alyse listened curiously as the random notes turned into a brief finger exercise before shifting to the opening movement of a Bach concerto. She followed the music for a moment, impressed by the skill of the pianist, then got up and crept to the door.

In the living room, she found Tommy perched on the piano bench with his back to her. Using extensions to work the foot pedals, he was off in a world of his own, playing only for himself. At once, she recognized that Rand hadn't exaggerated in the least—the child was indeed a prodigy. Alyse had taken piano lessons right up through high school, but had never come close to playing at Tommy's level.

However, according to Rand, the boy hadn't touched the instrument since returning from his stay with Mrs. Fielding. Alyse couldn't imagine what had caused him to resume playing, but she was delighted. She hoped it was a sign that Tommy was finally beginning to heal.

Kiku appeared in the kitchen doorway. Alyse quickly raised a cautioning finger to her lips. Kiku smiled and nodded. They both stood quietly, listening, neither willing to break the spell.

As the complex musical passages filled the air, Alyse let her gaze drift around the comfortable room. It settled on the tea box sitting on a low table near the piano. Packing materials lay in a neat pile on the floor. She stared longingly at the lacquered antique until Tommy finished.

Alyse and Kiku applauded softly. Tommy spun around, startled. Alyse quickly crossed the floor and slid onto the bench next to him, slipping an arm around his narrow shoulders.

"That was beautiful, Tommy!" she exclaimed. "You have such a wonderful gift."

A shy smile curled his lips, moving up to shine in his clear brown eyes. Too soon, the smile faded. He stared down at his fingers resting lightly on the ivory piano keys. Alyse was amazed that such small hands had enough reach and dexterity to execute the music that she had just heard.

"I don't want to play any more," he said.

Alyse squeezed his shoulder, recalling what Rand had told her about Mrs. Fielding exploiting the boy.

"Then, don't," she added lightly, sensing that he was testing her. "It's your gift, Tommy—yours alone. If you choose to share it with those you love—with those who love you—that's your decision."

Tommy looked up at her, his head cocked. The smile returned. She had passed his test.

"Maybe I could play just one more thing."

"That would make me very, very happy, Tommy," Alyse said, aware that his lisp and toddler grammar had completely disappeared.

He spread his small fingers over the keys, and then jerked them away. "Wait! I have something."

Tommy slid off the bench and raced out of the room. He returned a moment later clutching a small square of folded rice paper tied with gold string.

"For you." He held it out to Alyse.

The paper appeared old and brittle. Curious, Alyse gently slid the string off and carefully unfolded the paper just enough to see the Japanese characters drawn in black on its finely textured surface.

She had mastered a modest amount of conversational Japanese, but reading the language was a completely different ballgame. She hadn't even attempted to learn written Japanese. There was no alphabet, and she'd been told that some of the older characters had gone out of use over the centuries. From the looks of it, this particular item was quite old.

She glanced around to find Kiku still lingering in the doorway. Answering Alyse's questioning look, the diminutive housekeeper crossed the room to the piano.

"Ah—a haiku," she said, peering over Alyse's shoulder at the rice paper.

"Can you read it?" Alyse asked.

Kiku studied the characters for two or three minutes, then sighed wistfully.

"So lovely," she said.

How far today in chase I wonder has gone my hunter of the dragonfly.

Alyse gasped involuntarily. *Dragonfly!* She forced herself to smile at Tommy and Kiku, although a sudden chill had settled around her like hoarfrost. Kiku smiled back, patted Tommy on the head, and drifted off to the kitchen.

When they were alone, Alyse asked, "Where did you find this, Tommy?" She tried hard to keep her tone pleasant, afraid that her rising sense of dread might infect the boy.

"In that." To her astonishment, he pointed to the Tokugawa box on the nearby table. "It was with the necklace."

Her hand flew to the sand dollar that concealed the priceless dragonfly. Her knee-jerk reaction to the haiku must have been right on the money—the poem and the pendant apparently were companion pieces.

Alyse rose slowly and stepped around the piano to the low table. She knelt before the box, her trembling hands clammy as she touched the smoothly lacquered vermillion surface. She raised the heavy lid with its ornate dragon emblem and peeked inside.

The box was empty. She had to strain to get the next question out.

"Tommy, does your Uncle Rand know you took the haiku and necklace from this?"

Tommy shrugged noncommittally. "I found them in the secret place."

He slid down off the bench and joined Alyse at the table. With her help, he turned the teakwood tea box upside down. Pressing a hand against the age-darkened bottom panel, he pushed hard. The panel moved aside, revealing a shallow hidden compartment that was just large enough to have contained both the necklace and the haiku.

"Amazing," Alyse murmured, closing the panel and returning the antique to the table. The chill moved into her chest, then spread down into her stomach. Again, she had to force the question. "Does your Uncle Rand know about this secret place?"

"I found it, myself." Tommy shrugged again, and then looked troubled. "I guess I shouldn't have taken the things out. Maybe I should tell."

Alyse took him in her arms, suddenly afraid for

him. "Not yet, Tommy. Let's wait—this will be our secret. I'll tell Rand when the time is right. Okay?"

The boy thought it over. Finally, he nodded and hugged her back, obviously relieved that the matter was being taken out of his hands by a grown-up. "Do you think Uncle Rand will be mad at me?"

"Maybe not," she said.

Satisfied, Tommy wriggled free and climbed back onto the piano bench. As he resumed playing, Alyse sank into the cushioned hollow of a papasan chair, deaf to everything but the rising crescendo of suspicion and doubt that assailed her.

More than once, Rand had tried to talk her into letting him replace the garish necklace that Tommy had given her. Could it be that Rand knew it had come from the hidden compartment in the Toku-gawa box? That the sand dollar concealed the price-less stolen dragonfly pendant? Was his continued interest in replacing the tacky bauble with some-thing "nicer" just a ploy to cover the fact that he wanted it back?

Giving Rand the benefit of the doubt did little to still the clamor of suspicion. True, he might not know of the necklace or the haiku. But that didn't change the fact that he refused to part with the box. In fact, he hung onto it just as tenaciously as Alyse did the necklace.

She wanted to trust him—*yearned to*. But the devil's advocate in her warned that Rand could be totally unaware of what the antique had con-tained—and still be involved in the heist of these and other Japanese national treasures—perhaps

111

merely as a conduit in an intricate conspiracy of thieves.

The cynical devil's advocate flung yet another thought at Alyse, perhaps the most painful of all. If Rand was unaware that the dragonfly had been concealed inside a cheap plaster sand dollar, he might think the treasures were still hidden away in the Tokugawa box. That could explain why he refused to sell it to Conrad Brace at any price.

Gradually, the chill transformed itself into a sick feeling in the pit of her stomach. No matter how Alyse twisted and turned the jigsaw puzzle pieces, they created an ugly picture.

Her hands had grown icy in spite of the warm tropical breeze wafting through the open French door. Alyse knotted them in her lap, resisting the very real prospect that Rand was a part of the ugly picture. She didn't want to believe that her instincts could be that wrong. But neither was she willing to stand by and let history repeat itself. If she had anything to be thankful for after four miserable years with Rob, it was that he had permanently cured her of being a fool.

Even the shock of learning that the stolen pendant had come from a hidden compartment in the tea box hadn't succeeded in wiping the lingering sensation of Rand's kiss from her lips. Had that, too, been nothing more than a calculated deception?

Tears stung the backs of her eyes as an element of fear — for herself and Tommy — crept into the equation.

* * *

Rand returned grim-faced from his run along the beach to find Tommy and Alyse pounding out a frenetic, rapid-fire duet of "Chopsticks" on the piano. Alyse's mouth went dry when she saw him stride up onto the lanai, and then freeze in the doorway when he saw his nephew seated on the bench next to her.

She kept hammering away at the keys, pretending not to notice Rand until they finished with a flourish that left Tommy giggling with delight. Then Rand's expression shifted from disbelief to something between awe and joy, as if he were witnessing a miracle.

He rushed over and flung Tommy playfully into the air. With Tommy dangling like a wriggling bean bag under one arm, Rand turned to Alyse, his eyes bright with emotion.

"Thank you," he said softly. "I don't think I'll ever forget this moment."

He lightly brushed her cheek with the backs of his fingers. The touch and the look that accompanied it sent a river of warmth through her. The chill that had seized Alyse earlier thawed, floating a knot into her throat. Her doubts about Rand became less defined, as if they were evaporating before her eyes.

Alyse wasn't even close to solving the riddle of how the stolen dragonfly and its accompanying haiku had come to be concealed in the Tokugawa box. But that look on Rand's face—those words, whispered with such feeling—left their own indelible imprint.

They cast doubts on her doubts.

Rather than further confusing her, that suddenly infused Alyse with a tremendous sense of liberation. It was as if an unbearable weight had been lifted from her chest.

She had a sudden compulsion to spill everything she knew about the stolen treasures. But she had given her pledge of secrecy to the Japanese consulate official, yesterday, and she couldn't go back on that.

Alyse gazed into Rand's deep brown eyes, mentally replaying over and over again their impassioned kiss on the lanai that morning. The remembrance of their embrace was in Rand's expression, as well. But then, his eyes shifted, his attention drawn out the living room window wall toward the beach. Alyse knew he was searching for the red-and-orange catamaran. She could tell without looking that he found it there, still engaged in its endless, lazy tacking.

Rand's jaw knotted in steely resignation fraught with regret, and he took a step away from her.

"I'd better go change clothes," he said dully.

He put down Tommy and strode quickly from the room. Alyse stood awkwardly beside the piano, suddenly feeling like an intruder in paradise.

Chapter Seven

During the short mid-morning drive into Lahaina, the front seat of the car seemed as over-
crowded to Alyse as a New York subway at rush
hour. She sat pressed against the passenger door,
her face turned toward the endless expanse of sea to
her right. On the opposite end of the seat, Rand
gripped the steering wheel in both fists and stared
rigidly ahead. Tommy occupied the neutral zone
between them.

This time, Rand made no mention of his nephew's tendency to get carsick while riding in the middle. Alyse hoped the child could tolerate the brief
ride into town. For his part, Tommy seemed to
sense the unspoken tension separating his two adult
companions. He sat quietly twiddling his thumbs
between his knees, mutely looking first at Alyse,
then at Rand.

"Uncle Rand?" he said finally.

"Hmm?" Rand responded without taking his
gaze off the road.

"Are we mad?"

Alyse glanced across the top of Tommy's copper-blond head. Her eyes locked with Rand's for a long two seconds. The unexpected question forced him to acknowledge the intimacy that he had been working so hard to pretend hadn't taken place earlier that morning, and Rand's face reddened even as she felt the heat rise in her own. He smiled wryly at her and flicked his gaze toward the car's roof.

"No, my man, we most definitely are not mad," Rand answered with a pained laugh.

He took a hand from the steering wheel and gave Tommy a rough, man-to-man hug. Then he stretched his arm across the back of the seat so that his fingers lightly brushed Alyse's shoulder. Her skin prickled deliciously. She exchanged a rueful smile with Rand.

Some of the tension seemed to bleed out of the air. Rand strummed his fingers on the steering wheel. He suddenly appeared intent on recapturing the lighter mood that his last sighting of the red-and-orange catamaran had so thoroughly shattered.

"Lahaina was a whaling port back in the nineteenth century," he said, glancing down at his nephew as they neared the outskirts of town. "But that was a long time ago. These days, you can sometimes see whales swimming along the reefs between here and Lanai and Molokai."

He directed Tommy's attention out to sea, where the dark humps of two neighboring islands rose on the horizon. The boy craned his neck to peer

116

over the window sill. As Alyse squeezed tightly against the back of the seat so he could see past her, Tommy's gaze shifted to the clunky necklace that she wore, and he grinned up at her.

Alyse caught Rand, too, eyeing the necklace. He frowned and shook his head, markedly less pleased than Tommy that she insisted on wearing it everywhere.

"I've got to hand it to you, Alyse," he said. "You're a good sport about that."

She fingered the garish ornament, not wanting to say in front of Tommy that she didn't care how ugly it was—the thought behind it made the necklace beautiful. She smiled to herself. Alyse did not dare say in front of *anyone* that the treasure beneath the bauble made it equally beautiful, but in an entirely different way.

In town, Rand drove slowly past rows of tourist-clogged shops that occupied the restored nineteenth-century buildings along Front Street. Down by the waterfront, he found a parking space near the old Pioneer Inn—a broad, red-roofed Victorian structure surrounded by towering palm trees.

"Would you look at that veranda!" Alyse gazed up at the high porch running the length of the inn as they got out. "It looks as if it belongs on a plantation somewhere in the Deep South."

"Bite your tongue," Rand said, waiting for Tommy to slide out of the seat on his side before he locked the car. "Lahaina still fancies itself as a lusty whaling village. The whole town

117

is listed as a National Historic Landmark."

"I'm impressed," she responded.

"You'll also be impressed by the prices in the shops," he quipped.

Alyse dug into her straw bag and whipped out a credit card. "I came prepared. Would you guys care to join me?"

Rand rotated on a heel, fists on his hips, making a quick survey of the tourist population. "Tell you what, you go ahead and swashbuckle the shops. My matie and I are going to get a couple of soft drinks and go see if we can find some buried treasure under yon banyan tree."

He pointed to the sprawling, block-wide tree next door to the courthouse. Tommy's eyes lit up at the plan. He bounced at Rand's side like a tethered ball.

"Where will I find you when I'm finished?" Alyse asked.

"We'll have our feet propped on the brass rail at the bar inside, sipping ale and telling sea yarns," Rand teased, jabbing a thumb over his shoulder at the inn. He winked at her expression.

"Either that," he continued, "or we'll be holding a table for three on the lanai of the Old Whaler's Grog Shoppe. Just follow this walkway around to the other side. Twelve P.M. sharp."

"It's a date," Alyse said, smiling, and started to turn away.

"Oh — a thought," Rand added, holding up a finger and then pressing it to his chin pensively. "While you're running up your credit card debt, why not pick out a tog for Saturday's luau?"

Alyse stopped cold, startled. "I'm planning to fly back to Oahu today."

"I know." He placed a hand on Tommy's shoulder, his expression suddenly tense, expectant. "But we'd be more than pleased if you'd reconsider and stay on for the luau."

She glanced down at Tommy. He stared back at her, wide-eyed with hope, the fingers of both hands crossed tightly under his chin.

"If you need a special engraved invitation, I can arrange that," Rand volunteered. "How about a chauffeured limousine? Caviar with your roast pig? Your own personal ukelele player?"

"Stop!" Alyse threw up her hands and laughed. "Let me think about it. Okay?"

"Okay. You can think about it until lunchtime."

Alyse hurried off toward the heart of the shopping district, thinking that Rand's spur-of-the-moment invitation was foolhardy. How would it look to Mrs. Fielding's catamaran-sailing detective if she stayed at the cottage for two more days?

Alyse's hand went automatically to the necklace as she entered the first dress shop she came to. The reward for the dragonfly meant the world to her—an exciting, opulent world that she might never know otherwise. She found it astonishing that she was sorely tempted to delay stepping into that world, in order to spend two more days with Rand and Tommy Turnbull.

Temptation wouldn't get in the way of common sense, however. With great reluctance, she decided to forgo the luau. Two more days with Rand—and

Tommy—would only make her inevitable departure more painful. Worse, that blasted detective might have a field day.

She went through the dress racks like a whirlwind, trying on items that she could never have afforded until yesterday. The clerk, who evidently worked on commission, followed her like a happy puppy.

Alyse settled on a bright orange-and-white muumuu with matching sandals. But she didn't stop there. The pile of clothes next to the cash register rose higher and higher as she added screen-printed blouses, raw silk slacks, and linen culottes. She also found a variety of lacy, clinging undergarments that she wanted in a small alcove at the back of the shop. While the clerk eagerly totalled up the damage, Alyse kept tossing in little afterthoughts from the scarf bar next to the cash register.

Two shops later, she emerged from a beachwear side-alley arcade clad in a colorful tropical-weave jumpsuit and thongs. She was lugging two bulging hand-painted canvas shopping bags the size of suitcases. With fifteen minutes to spare before meeting Rand and Tommy, Alyse made a beeline toward the little post office across Front Street. She'd been told she would find a public telephone there.

She didn't notice Eddie Komake bearing down on her until he intercepted her in the middle of the street. He was decked out in a brilliant yellow-and-green pineapple luau shirt that contrasted sharply with his dark skin and black hair.

"Aloha, wahini u'i," he said with a courtly bow that drew stares from passersby.

Alyse pulled up short, trying not to show her annoyance. She was beginning to take it for granted that Komake would pop up at the most unexpected times. This time, however, his physical appearance startled her.

She couldn't help staring at the sling he wore on his right arm, recalling the car that had followed her and Rand back from the airport the previous night. The last she had seen of it was the wild whipping of its headlights as it spun off the wet road in the storm.

"It's nothing." Komake patted his arm. "I had a spectacularly clumsy fall on the stairway of the hotel where I'm staying up at Kaanapali. It'll be fine by Saturday."

"That's good," Alyse said politely.

She had forgotten that Rand had hired Eddie to entertain at the luau. The charismatic Hawaiian was a marvel of coincidences. Most of them seemed to involve turning up wherever Alyse happened to be. She wondered what would transpire when she turned down Rand's invitation to the party and flew back to New York. Would the singer crawl out of the woodwork of her Manhattan apartment on Saturday night, instead of performing for Rand's guests?

"I thought you were going to take the shuttle back to Oahu last evening," she added.

"So did I," he chuckled humorlessly, indicating his arm. "How about you?"

121

"Poor planning. I missed the flight."

"Will you be at the luau?" Komake asked casually.

"I haven't made up my mind," Alyse lied.

As usual, she sensed that he was on a fishing expedition. She began to wonder if he knew how to sail a catamaran, and hoped she wasn't being malicious.

"Well, then, I'll just have to hope our paths will keep crossing this way," he said.

"Yes." Alyse put on a smile that felt like warm plastic. "Meanwhile, Lahaina calls." She hefted the bulky shopping bags.

"So it seems." Komake laughed heartily and waved her on.

Alyse left him standing in the street and hurried on toward the post office. As she rushed through the open doorway into the cool shadows of the building, she stole one last look over her shoulder. Komake was gone. For some reason, his ability to vanish into thin air bothered her even more than his habit of suddenly materializing in front of her.

The small post office was jammed with tourists mailing postcards and packaged souvenirs. Alyse wormed her way through the crowd to the public telephone on the far wall. She placed the shopping bags against the wall beneath the phone and pressed her legs against them in the protective guard-dog stance that had become second nature to her in New York.

The call to the Japanese consulate in Honolulu was fruitless. Her contact had already left for lunch. Considering her vow of secrecy, Alyse wasn't willing to talk to just anybody at the office about her staying on Maui this extra day. She hung up, hoping for a chance to make contact later.

The missed connection with the consulate official made her think twice about the five-hour time difference between Hawaii and New York. She would have to hurry to get through to her bank.

She quickly placed the second call, using her long distance credit card. She did this after deciding it was worth the charge to find out if the dragonfly reward actually had been transferred to her bank account. She gave her personal access code to the clerk in bookkeeping, and tensely contemplated the two enormous shopping bags at her feet while she waited. When she shakily put the receiver back on the hook thirty seconds later, Alyse thought she had a pretty vivid idea how it felt to be one of those rare lucky stiffs who won a megabucks lottery.

According to the clock high on the post office wall, she still had five minutes before meeting Rand and Tommy. She had time for one last quick call. But her hand was still shaking so hard that she had to dial the number three times before she got it right.

Conrad Brace answered on the fourth ring.

"Alyse, darling!" Brace cried when he heard her voice. "Please, tell me you have good news."

"I wish I could," Alyse said truthfully. "I've followed Rand Turnbull all the way to Maui, but I'm afraid he refuses to give an inch on the Tokugawa Shogun box. The harder I try to talk him out of it, the more determined he becomes to present it to his Japanese clients this Saturday."

A heavy silence filled the line. Alyse could feel Brace's disappointment across the miles. She fingered her necklace distractedly, miserably aware of how badly she had let him down. She wished she could at least tell him about her discovery of the priceless jewel. As supportive as Conrad had been to her since Rob's death, he couldn't help being cheered by her good fortune—as well as intrigued by how she had come by it.

"Conrad, I've exhausted all angles," she said. "But there's still time for you to fly out here and try to negotiate something yourself."

"No—I can't do that," Brace said anxiously, as if rattled by her suggestion.

Alyse frowned. His reaction puzzled her. He sounded almost frantic—so unlike the gruff, sometimes officiously stuffy man for whom she had worked these past years. She wanted to ask him what was wrong, but this was the wrong time and place. The post office crowd pressed in closely around her, and she could hear his end of the conversation only by clamping a hand over her exposed ear.

"I can't possibly get away now," Brace said. "I'm counting on you, Alyse. Please—for God's sake, stay there on Maui and do whatever you must. *Just get me that box!*"

The line went dead. Alyse jiggled the switchhook, more out of frustration than out of hope that she could be reconnected with Brace. Perhaps that was for the best, she thought, again glancing at the clock. She had run out of time.

She stood there for a moment longer anyway, torn between two conflicting forces. She *couldn't* remain on Maui, knowing that her presence there might jeopardize Tommy's future with Rand. And yet, she still felt a powerful loyalty toward Conrad, and a strong desire to make up for her failure to bid on the tea box at the Bundys auction.

Conrad had told her he had promised the antique to a valued client. Alyse hadn't bothered to ask the identity of that person. But if the level of Conrad's anxiety were an accurate gauge, the client was among the select group of deep-pocket buyers who were capable of severely damaging the Brace Gallery's reputation. They could do so by simply spreading the news of their displeasure around the affluent art collecting community.

Grappling with her own anxiety now, Alyse picked up her bags and shouldered her way out of the congested post office. Except for its brightly colored attire and markedly less aggressive attitude, the crowd was not unlike what she contended with daily on New York streets. She even heard a snatch of Brooklyn accent as she emerged on the sidewalk outside.

The tide of pedestrian traffic seemed to be flowing against Alyse as she hurried back toward the Pioneer Inn. The heavy shopping bags dragged at her shoulders like two sea anchors, slowing her progress. She had just started to cross the last intersection when she thought she glimpsed a familiar yellow-and-green Hawaiian shirt moving away from her a dozen feet ahead.

Alyse tried to speed up. But the noonday crowd jostled her from all sides, causing her to lose sight of the shirt. She frowned and moved on across the intersection, wondering if she really had seen Eddie Komake once again.

She tried to shrug it off. After all, there must be a hundred such Hawaiian shirts in Lahaina that day. But the suspicion continued to gnaw at the pit of her stomach. The more she saw of the singer, the less she trusted him.

Something else ate at her as well. The Japanese consulate official had promised that she would be kept under constant surveillance as long as she had the dragonfly pendant in her possession. She was beginning to seriously doubt that gentleman's veracity.

Tommy sat across from Rand at a table near the entrance to the outdoor dining area of the Old Whaler's Grog Shoppe, where they couldn't miss Alyse. She was already over ten minutes late. Rand wouldn't have minded, if Tommy hadn't been already starved half out of his mind.

The boy hadn't said a word about being hungry. He just sat there patiently twiddling his thumbs, swinging his short legs. But Rand noticed that every time a waitress passed with a tray of food destined for a neighboring table, Tommy eyed it longingly and salivated like a bloodhound on a hot scent trail.

A ripple passed along the rapidly growing line of customers waiting to be seated. The line bulged, and Alyse popped through. She was wearing a crisp new jumpsuit that molded enticingly to her slender figure. But she looked slightly frazzled, almost as if she had just run some kind of gauntlet.

Rand got up and relieved her of two swollen canvas shopping bags that appeared to be in imminent danger of exploding. She sagged into a chair and breathed an exaggerated sigh of relief.

"Only twelve minutes late," she said, glancing guiltily at her watch.

Rand stowed the two bags on the floor between them, amazed that she had been able to move at all carrying that much ballast.

"What did you do, mug a bus load of tourists?" he asked. "You couldn't possibly have bought this much stuff in an hour and a half."

"I could and did," she insisted proudly. "Not only that, I tried on most of it."

"Wow!" Tommy said. "Uncle Rand, wouldn't it be fun to take Alyse to a Toys R Us store?"

Alyse burst out laughing. Rand smiled as she leaned across the table to plant a kiss on Tommy's forehead. The feel and taste of her soft, intoxicating lips came back to Rand in a rush. It was all he could do to keep from reaching out for her.

"Speaking of toys," Alyse said, bending to dig into one of the bags. In a moment, she came up with a small package wrapped in tissue paper. "I thought you might like this."

Tommy accepted the package reverently, his eyes

shining with expectation. He carefully unwrapped the tissue one layer at a time until he uncovered a hand-carved model of a killer whale mounted on a driftwood pedestal.

"It's *awesome!*" he exclaimed, stroking the elegant black-and-white markings. "Thank you a bunch."

Alyse dug into the bag again and produced a second bundle, which she handed to Rand. "For your gracious hospitality, kind sir."

Rand's eyebrows shot up in astonishment at the unexpected gift. Their gazes locked just long enough to send a white-hot spasm of pure pleasure through him. He unrolled the tissue, and whistled through his teeth as he revealed a brass-and-bone scrimshaw key ring.

"That isn't a real walrus tooth," Alyse explained quickly. "The shopkeeper says there is a craftsman down near Nuu Landing who carves these out of soup bones. First he makes soup, then he lets his dog chew off the scraps, then he makes these beautiful things."

"Remarkable," Rand said. The wedge of bone nestled comfortably in the palm of his hand. It had the feel of something he had owned for a long time. "But then, I've come to expect remarkable things of a certain remarkable woman."

Alyse flushed at his compliment. "You don't think soup bone scrimshaw is too . . . offbeat?"

"The walruses and I love it." To show his sincerity, Rand fished out his keys and snapped them onto the ring.

"It's nice to know our minds have been on the same track," he said, reaching into his pocket and pulling out a small purple velvet bag with a silk drawstring. "Now it's your turn, Alyse. Tommy and I didn't spend all our time under the banyan tree."

Alyse gasped as Rand upended the bag and a black coral necklace slithered out into her hands. He shook the bag, and a matching bracelet dropped out on top.

"I hope this shows in some small way how deeply I appreciate your plucking my little urchin out of the sea." He looked Alyse straight in the eyes while tilting his head toward Tommy. "If I were to truly match the reward with the deed, I'd have stolen the Hope Diamond for you. But I have a pretty good idea that you wouldn't accept anything that extravagant."

She suddenly paled at his crack about stealing the famous treasure. Rand did a mental stutter-step, thinking she couldn't possibly have taken him seriously. Then she blinked, shook her head almost imperceptibly as if to clear her mind, and smiled radiantly.

"Rand, it's gorgeous." Alyse slipped on the bracelet and then let the polished coral beads pour through her fingers. "But you didn't have to do this."

"After Tommy gifted you with such a classy piece of jewelry," Rand said, "I felt it was absolutely necessary that I do something to uphold my good name."

They both looked at Tommy, who eyed the sand dollar necklace and grinned importantly.

Rand helped Alyse find the clasp on the coral beads. Instead of taking off the garish monstrosity first, she simply looped the long strand of beads around her neck twice, choosing to wear both at the same time.

"They look incredible together, don't you think?" she asked, settling the coral beads in among the gaudy baubles.

"Extremely incredible," Rand said dryly.

"Extremely, *awesomely* incredible," Tommy put in. "You'll look real special at the luau."

Rand looked at Alyse, and she stopped fussing with the beads. He had made the invitation on the spur of the moment that morning, rashly casting aside every semblance of good judgment. Being around Alyse was doing that to him—turning him into an adolescent hormone factory with pudding for brains.

Without even seeming to try, she had worked her magic on his nephew, as well, saving the boy from more than just drowning. In a way, Rand felt that Alyse had somehow saved Tommy from himself. Tommy had stopped lisping and started playing the piano again. He had made one giant leap out of the dismal swamp of grief in which he had existed since his parents died—and since his stay with Elaine Fielding. Today, for the first time since that dark night when Rand had broken the news to Tommy that Chris and Pat wouldn't be coming home, the little trooper had expressed joy.

Besides, damnit, Rand just plain wanted Alyse with him at the luau. He'd had almost two hours in which to reconsider his invitation, and his desire to have her there by his side had done nothing but grow. He dreaded the thought of her flying back to Oahu—and quite possibly out of his life—later that day.

"Rand, you don't really want me there," she said quietly.

"We do!" Tommy piped excitedly.

Rand ignored the boy. Planting his elbow on the table, he rested his chin in his hand and concentrated on Alyse. Her worried expression held deeper meaning than her words. He knew what she was getting at. She was thinking of the Fielding Factor. But for once, he didn't give a damn.

"You don't want to stay," he said.

Her eyes flicked in Tommy's direction, signaling caution, and she bit her lower lip.

"Staying would cause complications," she said, choosing words cautiously.

Rand pursed his lips, and reluctantly nodded agreement. "That's a distinct possibility. But if you leave, you'll cause worse complications."

Alyse frowned, puzzled. "How so?"

"Separation anxiety," Rand explained. He glanced at Tommy, who was following their conversation closely, then back at Alyse. "You see, there are a couple of fellows here in Lahaina who are falling flat-out in love with you, Alyse."

He was looking straight into her blue-green eyes as he made the confession. Her irises dilated an instant before her jaw dropped open. She went white as a sheet, then a deep blush flowed up her neck and onto her cheeks. She was suddenly a delightful kaleidoscope of movement and color.

"Please, Rand," she chided softly. "Don't play games."

Rand turned his head to look at Tommy without lifting his chin from his palm. "Thomas, my boy," he said seriously, "are you in love with Alyse?"

Tommy looked startled by the concept. His grip tightened on the killer whale, and he glanced from his uncle to Alyse. Finally, he swallowed a hard lump of embarrassment and nodded.

"See?" Rand smiled at Alyse. "Smack out of the mouths of babes." He lowered his voice. "And I believe I've already shown you how I feel."

Her hand flew to the coral necklace, but her thoughts raced elsewhere. He could tell by the way she nervously licked her lips as if they had experienced anew the fiery pleasures of their kiss.

"This is ridiculous," Alyse said, totally without conviction.

"True."

"You know very well why I can't stay."

Rand sighed dramatically. "Well, Tommy, I guess our Alyse doesn't like us."

"Rand!" Alyse sputtered, as Tommy looked confused. "What are you trying to do?"

"Drum up a date for the luau," he replied innocently. "Tommy and I have our hearts set on you."

Tommy placed the whale on the table and folded his hands prayerfully under his chin, watching

Alyse with rapt attention. Rand leaned closer, waiting.

She closed her eyes to shut them both out, trying to hold onto the last vestiges of her common sense. The image of an orange-and-red catamaran drifted across her mind's eye, but it seemed pale and far away. After a moment, it disappeared altogether.

"If I stayed, I'd just keep badgering you about the Tokugawa box," she warned, making a last-ditch effort to throw a damper on Rand's invitation.

She wanted to stay so badly—but not for Conrad's sake. And that made her feel profoundly disloyal.

Rand smiled and shrugged. The prospect of being badgered by Alyse Marlowe didn't bother him one iota. In fact, he even looked forward to it.

"All right," she said finally, through gritted teeth. "I'll stay for the luau."

Tommy threw up his hands and let out a shriek that brought half the diners to their feet. Alyse glanced around at the staring faces and hunkered low in her chair. When she looked at Rand, he had his face buried in one hand, and was gripping his chest with the other. His shoulders shook with badly suppressed laughter.

"Oops," Tommy said in a small, repentant voice.

"It's okay, spud," Rand managed. "In fact, you expressed my sentiments exactly."

"What do we do now?" Alyse asked in an undertone as the other diners settled back into their chairs.

Rand plucked a menu from the stack the waitress

133

had left on the edge of the table and slid it over in front of Alyse. "I suggest the *opakapaka* with rice pilaf and papaya salad."

"What's *opakapaka?*" Tommy asked suspiciously.

"Snapper," Rand said. "It's a fish. What would you like to eat?"

"Pizza."

"That figures."

Rand glanced out over the dining area, and the smile died on his lips. Three tables away, almost hidden by the trunk of a palm tree, sat a man in a beige sport jacket, looking their way. As Rand watched, the man averted his gaze and eased farther out of sight behind the trunk.

Rand felt a chill in the warm breeze.

Chapter Eight

Low on the western horizon, the fading afterglow of sunset tinted a thin layer of clouds soft shades of deep coral and purple. As darkness settled in, Alyse turned and started slowly back along the sandy beach toward the cottage. Still deep in thought, she walked along the edge of the incoming surf, letting the waves foam over her bare feet.

She had been wandering up and down the sun-washed beach for what seemed like hours, since returning from the shopping excursion in Lahaina in late afternoon. After two days of almost continuous tension, she had needed to be alone for a while to clear her head and try to regain her sense of balance.

She hadn't gained much ground. Alyse still felt keyed up, as if some great cataclysm lay just around the corner out of her sight. She couldn't quite decide if it was fear, or dread, or just an itchy suspicion that she had waded in far over her head.

The evening breeze tugged at the pajama top that

Rand had loaned her to sleep in last night. The soft cotton felt almost sandpapery against her bikini-bared skin. The red-and-orange catamaran that seemed to have been patrolling the shoreline for the past two days had been nowhere in sight when she left the cottage, so she had taken the baggy top along to use as a cover-up. But her pale skin was unaccustomed to the intense tropical sun, and she could tell she had managed to get a slight sunburn anyway.

The solitude had not eased the deep misgivings that Alyse harbored about her decision to stay on for the luau Saturday. A wiser, saner part of herself said she should have taken the late flight back to Oahu and let Conrad Brace handle the hopeless quest to retrieve the tea box. But that voice was no match for the sticky spider web of emotion that already held her so inextricably.

She was loved.

After four miserable years with Rob Marlowe, Alyse had almost come to believe that love was an illusion. These past two days, however, she had learned that she had been only half right. Love was illusory only when it wasn't reciprocated.

Rand and Tommy love me, she thought, still shaken by the suddenness of that development. Even more astonishing was the very real fact that she had fallen just as quickly for them. Like an acute illness, sudden love had produced severe symptoms. She was suffering from transient aches and a kind of emotional vertigo that left her tottering on the brink of bewilderment.

She touched the sand dollar necklace against her breast. Love and riches. Was it too much to hope that she could hold onto both?

Alyse kicked at the water as she walked. Hope was cheap. She could afford all of it she wanted, even without the reward for the dragonfly pendant. But old habits die hard, as the saying went. Nothing in her history led her to believe that she should trust in her own good fortune. If she knew what was good for her, she warned herself, she would brace herself for a fall.

The welcoming lights of the cottage shone up ahead. Alyse picked up her pace, concerned that Kiku might be holding supper for her. Then she slowed again as she spotted a shadowy figure striding toward her along the wet sand. Her sunburn tingled as she recognized the familiar wedge of Rand's upper body silhouetted against the distant glow of the cottage. He was back in his comfortable old cutoffs, this time shirtless and shoeless.

They stopped a few feet apart. The surf that foamed around their ankles looked phosphorescent in the moonlight. The same breeze that gently stirred the folds of her makeshift cover-up brushed Rand's hair across his wide forehead.

"Alyse." He spoke her name softly, barely audible above the steady boom and whoosh of the waves. "You've been gone a long time."

"I hoped no one would notice."

"I notice everything about you."

Alyse tensed. Something in his tone had sounded wary. Or, was that her imagination — a trick of the

137

tropical darkness that had settled around them like a warm, caressing glove? If she weren't careful, Alyse warned herself, she would infect their love with the virus of her doubts.

Rand stepped closer. She quivered involuntarily as he reached out to her. But instead of touching her skin, he fingered the necklace.

"Don't you ever take that thing off?" he asked.

She saw his white teeth flash in a grin — or a grimace. She couldn't tell which in the darkness.

"It means a lot to me," Alyse said truthfully, feeling guilty that she wasn't wearing the black coral beads and bracelet Rand had given her at lunch. She had left them safely tucked inside their purple velvet bag back at the cottage.

"I suppose you plan to wear it to the luau," he muttered.

"Maybe," Alyse said, thinking *most definitely*.

Unless the Japanese consulate official showed up to relieve her of the camouflaged dragonfly pendant before she left Maui, she didn't intend to let the sand dollar necklace out of her sight.

Now was as good a time as any to ask Rand about the false bottom in the Tokugawa box, from which Tommy had innocently extracted both the jewelry and the haiku. But she couldn't bring herself to broach the subject while they were alone out there on the beach. Her reluctance confused Alyse for a moment. Then she realized that she was unfairly measuring Rand against the standards of deception and distrust established by her late husband.

Alyse was suddenly angry with herself for allowing Rob to control her actions even from his grave. She didn't have to settle for that kind of life any longer. Thanks to the reward for the pendant, she would never again have to *settle* for anything.

"Rand, I think we'd better get back."

Alyse started past him. Rand sidestepped and blocked her way. She looked up at him, alarmed in spite of herself.

He put his hands on her shoulders, cradling her jaw with the heels of his thumbs. While she stared uncertainly into the dark shadows of his face, he slowly bent and pressed his lips to hers.

She sucked in her breath as the fire of their kiss on the lanai that morning flared anew. Rand groaned softly, and Alyse flowed into his arms. His hands moved down, and then up under the pajama top, settling hotly into the bare hollow of her waist as he pulled her tightly against him.

The fragrance of plumeria blossoms drifted on the gentle night breeze. The slow, rhythmic pounding of the surf—coupled with the whoosh of foam that rushed across the sand to tease their feet— seemed to grow distant and otherworldly.

"Rand," she sighed as his lips moved into her hair, then down to the lobe of her ear and the curve of her neck where the pajama top had fallen away.

They stood there for a long time, locked in an exploratory embrace. Their kisses grew intense, demanding, until Rand suddenly drew back, tucking her head tightly against his shoulder. He held her like that for a moment and struggled to regain control of himself. Then he took a long, uneven breath.

"Do you want me to take you back to the cottage?" he asked hoarsely.

Alyse shook her head, not trusting her voice.

Rand held her hand and they walked together away from the surf onto dry sand still warm from the tropical sun. Alyse moved loose-limbed in a languid dreamworld, suspended in a seductive aura of heady fragrances and intoxicating desire. In a physical sense, she had never felt this way with a man before—so totally, unequivocally *right*. Love, and being loved, made all the difference.

Rand led her to the dappled, sheltering moon shadows of a leaning coconut palm. There he slipped the baggy top from her shoulders and placed it on the soft sand. He straightened, his hands spread wide without touching her, taking her in for an interminable, breathless moment.

Alyse felt suddenly exposed and unsure of herself under his probing gaze. Her body was fettered only by the meager fabric of her string bikini. She regretted the moonlight, wishing for the concealing cloak of total darkness. She closed her eyes, trembling, her hands fisted at her sides.

"You are so incredibly beautiful," he whispered.

Alyse opened her eyes, dizzy with relief. Her fists unclenched, and she traced her fingertips across his thick chest. His pectoral muscles twitched.

When she reached down to release the ribbon ties on her bikini, Rand gently but firmly stayed her hand. With slow movements that seemed neither clumsy nor practiced, he made a ritual of removing her skimpy attire—first the top, then the bottom.

140

He took his time. His tenderness touched her heart in places she had kept hidden even from herself.

When she stood before him clad only in moonlight and shadows—and the inevitable necklace—Rand leaned down and brushed his parted lips lightly across hers. His hands moved to his belt.

This time, Alyse was the one who took control. She pulled his hands away and raised them to her lips, kissing the strong, thick fingers. Then she finished with the belt buckle and slid Rand's cutoffs down over his athletic hips. She could hear the rasp of his breath—a catchy sound beneath the arhythmic pounding of the surf—as she rose before him as his equal.

They knelt together and a shiver of pleasure passed between them as they embraced again, bare flesh to bare flesh. When Rand finally eased her down onto the too-small patch of pajama top and pressed his lean, hard body alongside hers, tears of almost unbearable joy welled within Alyse.

I love you. She wasn't sure which of them said it, or if the words were even spoken aloud. It was there in every touch and in the silent eloquence of each kiss. It murmured in the fragrant night breeze, and in the strange singing vibration that raced through her body faster and faster.

A dove cooed high up in the crown of the palm. Alyse dug her fingers into the powerful, knotted muscles of Rand's back. He shuddered with her name on his lips, and something deep, deep, deep inside her took wing.

Later, neither of them seemed capable of words

141

as they lay in each other's arms and stared up through the gently waving palm fronds at the moon. Alyse shifted her head into the hollow of Rand's shoulder. She felt profoundly changed, as if a towering tsunami had swept over her and forever altered the very topography of her life.

A tsunami named Rand Turnbull.

"I think it's smirking," Rand said quietly.

"What?"

"The crescent moon. Look at it up there, tilted to one side. A smirk, if I've ever seen one."

"You're silly."

"Silly in love."

She placed a hand flat on the slight declivity of his sternum, feeling the strong, steady beat of his heart. The slow rise and fall of his chest with each breath reminded Alyse of a great ship forging through heavy seas — resolute and unsinkable. She felt safe. Then it occurred to her that, in the beginning, she had felt that way with Rob. A tiny frown line appeared between her eyes. The possibility that history might repeat itself was never far away.

Alyse tried to tell herself that Rand was different. Only a profoundly good man could be so generous and tender and caring in the heat of passion. Their lovemaking had been a totally shared experience. Rand wasn't just a gentleman. He was a gentle man.

Still, the invisible scars of her past remained. As much as she cherished this moment in Rand's arms, Alyse couldn't help drawing away slightly.

"Ow! That damned . . ." Rand squirmed in the

scratchy sand, resettling the sharp-edged beads of Alyse's necklace so they wouldn't dig into his bicep. "To show you just how silly I've become, I'll pay you a thousand dollars for that menace to lovemaking right now."

Alyse sat up abruptly. "A thousand dollars?"

A dull ache filled the pit of her stomach. She desperately hoped Rand had meant his offer as a joke. But how many times had he tried to persuade her to take off the clunky beads?

He rose onto one elbow, cupping the sand dollar ornament in one hand. Alyse bit her tongue, afraid that he would feel the chip that had broken off the back, revealing the dragonfly wing.

"You actually have that kind of money on you?" she asked in a strained voice.

"Do you see a wallet?" Rand released the bauble and spread his hands wide, chuckling. "What about it? I'll give you a verbal IOU if you'll hand over that piece of junk right now."

"No."

He stared at her for a long moment. Then, he reached out and gently pulled her to him again, rolling onto his back in the bed of sand.

"I value fidelity, Alyse, even if it isn't to me," he said as he tucked her head against his shoulder. "I admire your loyalty to Tommy."

Alyse lay against him and stared into the night as fresh doubts assailed her from all sides. Did he really mean that? Or, was Rand just telling her what she wanted to hear in order to cover one more failed attempt to talk her out of the necklace?

143

She couldn't be sure. Alyse closed her eyes, wanting to scream. She couldn't be sure of *anything* anymore.

Where did she get off, entrusting her love to a man she had known for only a few days? As a lover—as a man who professed to love her—Rand embodied her wildest fantasy. But it was a well-known fact that a woman's heart was a lousy judge of character. Hadn't she already proven that with Rob?

What she needed, Alyse thought, was some kind of test. She racked her brain, trying to come up with something that might reveal Rand's true colors once and for all, for better or worse. *Dear God, let it be for better.* But if it were for worse, she would rather know now, before she made a fool of herself a second time.

Then, it came to her—the haiku.

Lying there with her cheek pressed into Rand's thick shoulder, her breasts against his muscular chest, and her legs stretched alongside his, she was convinced that she would be able to sense his response as if it were her own.

Alyse took a shallow breath, trying to remember the words exactly as Kiku had translated them. "How far today in chase I wonder," she recited, "has gone my hunter of the dragonfly?"

Rand lay perfectly still for a full minute. She began to think he might have fallen asleep. Finally, he picked up a handful of sand and dribbled it onto her bare leg as if anointing her.

"You're not only beautiful," he said huskily,

"you're enchantingly poetic. Did you make that up?"

He shifted, moving his head down to kiss her shoulder. Alyse bit her lip and forced back the rush of pleasure brought on by the feathery brush of his lips on her naked flesh.

"It's an ancient Japanese haiku," she explained, and had to clear her throat to go on. "I thought you might have heard it before."

Rand shook his head. His lips inched along the hollow above her collarbone, then down toward her cleavage. Alyse struggled to keep her rationality from slipping away through his maddeningly probing fingers.

He could be faking ignorance of the haiku, she thought, clinging to the farthest extreme of doubt as a counterbalance against her reawakening desire. After all, he couldn't own up to knowing about the poem without also admitting knowledge of the dragonfly pendant. *And only the members of the theft ring know the dragonfly is in the sand dollar.*

Alyse shuddered, and Rand mistook it for a sign of pleasure. He was only half right. Out beyond the soft wallow they had made in the sand—beyond the reach of either passion or love-clouded logic—hung an icy noose of doubt. It settled around Alyse's neck, digging sharp frozen chips into her flesh. The sand dollar chilled her breast all the way through to her heart.

She sat up again. Rand tensed, startled. He watched her for a moment, then eased over and leaned back against the trunk of the palm tree.

"Did I do something wrong?"

Alyse was glad he hadn't reached for her again. Instead he had moved away a couple of feet, giving her space. She wrapped both arms around her knees and stared across the flat beach toward the sea.

"No," she replied honestly, knowing Rand was referring to the past three or four minutes.

A while later, he asked, "Would you like to go for a swim?"

She almost said yes. But she couldn't risk losing the necklace in the water, and she wouldn't take it off and leave it on the beach.

"It's getting late," Alyse said. "Let's just wade back up to the cottage."

She handed him his cutoffs. Rand slipped into them while Alyse dug her bikini out of the sand. He helped her tie the thin ribbons at her hips and back, then shook the sand from the pajama top and draped it over her bare shoulders. He held onto the collar, gently preventing Alyse from turning away.

"Before we go," he said softly, "is it all right if I just hold you for a moment?"

She thought it was a strange request, considering their passionate intimacy earlier in the evening. But when she slipped into his arms, Alyse understood. To be simply held was like being submerged in a soothing balm. In spite of her doubts, she let her heart go, and it flew straight to him.

Her mind stayed put.

When they finally started back toward the cottage, she felt as if her heart and mind were at war with each other.

"Something's bothering you," Rand said, one arm around her shoulder, matching his much longer stride to hers as they waded knee-deep in the surf. "I think I know what it is."

Alyse stiffened, her hand reflexively moving toward the necklace. She forced it back down to her side and kept walking. She held her breath, expecting his next comment to be about the haiku.

"Your husband—while he was alive—was one lucky bastard."

Alyse stopped. "What?"

"You loved him. It's only natural for you to feel guilty now about being in love with—*making* love with—another man." Rand shook his head. "I'm sorry, Alyse. I shouldn't have moved so fast. I should have given you more time."

She looked past him, back to the palm tree. He was so colossally wrong about everything. Her feelings for Rob had died long before he did, for want of nourishment. And if there was one thing in this world that Alyse didn't feel at this moment, it was guilt. Rand hadn't moved one bit faster than she had into their breakneck love affair.

The problem was, she couldn't tell Rand any of that. Not without then explaining what her real dilemma was. So, she turned back toward the cottage, reluctantly letting him go on believing in his error. And then, she *did* feel guilty—for Rand's unjustified sense of guilt. She wondered how complex

147

her life could get before it became downright ludicrous.

"You haven't changed your mind about going to the luau, have you?"

"I promised Tommy," Alyse said distractedly, trying to distance herself emotionally from Rand by bringing his nephew into the conversation. It didn't work. She realized with a jolt that she was coming to think of the two Turnbulls as a package deal.

Rand dropped his hand from her shoulder. "Funny," he said without humor, "I would have sworn I was the one who invited you."

Alyse stopped again. They were close enough to the light from the cottage now for her to see his face. The tight line of his mouth, coupled with the sharp cant of his jaw, was unmistakable. Rand was jealous!

"I thought I was going with both of you." She nudged him good-naturedly in the ribs.

His smile was as transparent as her playfulness. The old tension had returned, zinging back and forth between them like a shorting electrical wire.

This time, it was Rand who resumed their walk. He left the water's edge and struck out diagonally across the beach, charting the shortest possible course to the lanai. Alyse had to hurry to keep up.

By the time they crossed the lanai and entered the living room through the French door, she had progressed through surprise, then mild irritation, before settling on resignation. She was holding out on Rand, and he could sense that in spite of her best efforts to pretend otherwise. It wasn't fair to blame him for developing an attitude.

But don't completely lose your senses, Alyse thought. *This time around, let your head be the judge.*

What was the worst thing that could happen if Rand turned out to be another Rob Marlowe? She answered that swiftly: If she were lucky—if she didn't fall into a dangerous trap of some kind—she could simply walk away from Rand Turnbull and never look back. She could do that right now, she thought, and be over him in a month. Or, a year. Two, tops. Three, if she was already in deeper than she imagined, which was certainly bad enough.

Then, a mind-numbing thought came to her: What about Tommy? The child couldn't walk away. At his age, he couldn't even *run* away. If she did simply leave Rand—and there would be nothing *simple* about it—would she ever be able to scrape Tommy off her conscience?

The cottage was quiet. They stopped just inside the doorway, listening.

"I guess Tommy and Kiku have already gone to bed," Rand said with surprise, keeping his voice low.

"I guess." Alyse directed his attention to a tray of cheese and papaya slices on a table beside the couch. Next to the tray sat an open bottle of wine and two crystal wine glasses.

Rand stared at the arrangement, dubiously. "Looks downright romantic, doesn't it? I had no idea that Kiku had a devious side."

Alyse smiled, although it took some effort, and said, "She'll be disappointed if we don't graze."

"She'll keel-haul us and throw us to the sharks."

Rand looked at Alyse awkwardly, still more than a little confused. They had just shared something of extraordinary importance. At least, that was the way Rand felt about it. At the moment, however, he had an eerie feeling that they had somehow returned to square one.

I don't know how you managed it, Romeo, he thought, *but you've gone from lovers to former lovers in a span of about fifteen minutes, without a cross word between you.*

Rand had a bizarre feeling that he and Alyse were looking at each other through jailhouse bars. The crazy thing was, he couldn't for the life of him tell which of them was looking in and which was looking out. One thing was for sure, though—he didn't want the evening to end this way.

"You pour," he said. "I'll be right back."

Rand moved on across the room and disappeared down the bedroom hallway. Alyse had poured two glasses of Zinfandel and was nibbling on a cheese-papaya-and-cracker sandwich when he returned.

"Tommy's dead to the world."

"Or, going for an Oscar." Alyse handed him a glass. "Tommy is a very bright little boy. Plenty smart enough to enter into a conspiracy with Kiku to leave us alone for the evening—and see what happens."

Rand peered down into the wine glass, his jaw muscles knotting. "What did happen, Alyse?"

She looked up at him quizzically. "Are you trying to say you've already forgotten?"

"I'm not likely to forget the most . . ." he clenched his lips, searching for the words, "earth-shattering hour of my life. But I don't want to believe that all we had was just an . . . *interlude* out there on the beach." He waited for her to respond. When she didn't, he demanded, "Was it?"

Alyse stared up at him, her heart racing as if she had just run a wind-sprint. She tried to swallow, but her mouth was too dry. What was real, and what wasn't? Did Rand really mean what he was saying? Or, was he manipulating her, attempting to push her over the edge into an emotional commitment that would leave her easy to control?

The necklace and its priceless secret felt like a lead weight around her neck.

"I'm in love with you, Alyse," Rand continued. "I know this sounds crazy, but I wish it hadn't happened so fast. It would have been nice to ease into this, instead of feeling like a bull elephant crashing around in a tea room."

He reached out and touched her face, feathering his thumb down the delicate line of her jaw. "Tell me I'm not in this alone," he said softly.

Alyse bit her lips, desperately hanging onto her will. Rand's touch was addictive. If he took her hand again—led her down the beach to the coconut palm again—she wasn't sure she could resist. But he didn't. He just stood there sipping his wine, challenging her with the probing seduction of his gaze.

Gradually, common sense born of hard experi-

ence gained the upper hand. Especially after she reminded herself that Tommy was at stake here, as
well. Even if she had lost her heart, she had to hang
on to her rationality at all costs.

"I can't," she managed finally, and watched the
fierce light go out of his expression as if she had
snuffed a candle.

With a dull ache in her chest, Alyse looked past
him at the Tokugawa box on its low table near the
piano. The dragonfly pendant was her secret — she
had to know, once and for all, that the hidden compartment in the tea box wasn't Rand's.

Alyse placed her wine glass on the snack table
and went over to the antique. Rand hesitated, then
followed. She lifted the heavy box and turned it
over, careful to not mar its lacquered vermillion surface. Clenching her teeth, she commanded herself
not to turn back as she looked straight into Rand's
eyes and slid aside the bottom panel, revealing the
concealed compartment.

The change came quickly. Rand's face turned to
granite, his dark eyes narrowing into a steely scowl.
He stared down at the false bottom in the box until
Alyse began to wonder if he were in a trance. When
his gaze drifted up from the box to fasten on Alyse,
it was all she could do to keep from touching the
sand dollar as if it were some kind of protective tal-
isman.

"How did you know about that?" Rand inquired
evenly.

Alyse slid the panel back into place and righted
the antique. She couldn't quite decide how to de-

scribe his reaction. Anger seemed close. Cold, contained anger. And something else—something she couldn't put her finger on.

"What difference does it make?" she asked, suddenly anxious to keep Tommy out of this.

Rand grabbed her arm, his fingers biting into her flesh. As if realizing that he might be hurting her, he yanked his hand away and took a half step back.

"I want to know, Alyse!"

His sudden intensity frightened her, but Alyse didn't let her fear show. She lifted her chin defiantly. Again, she detected that separate element beneath his apparent hostility. Strangely, it took away her fear—but not her uncertainty.

She realized with a sinking sensation that she couldn't tell if Rand had known about the false bottom before she showed it to him. But if he hadn't known, wouldn't he be intrigued instead of angered by the discovery? Alyse couldn't overlook the possibility that her unresolved suspicion that Rand might be somehow involved in the theft of the pendant was clouding her view of everything—including his innocence.

Alyse stepped back, distancing herself from him. Her arm burned where he had gripped her. She rubbed it slowly, absently. Everything in her cried out for reassurance that she hadn't committed her love to another disaster. But she knew there was nothing Rand could say at that moment that would take away the sting of her doubts.

Chapter Nine

At eight A.M. sharp Friday morning, Conrad Brace unlocked the steel rear door to the gallery, complimenting himself on his punctuality. He switched on the overhead fluorescent lights and quickly punched in the proper code numbers on the control panel next to the door to deactivate the building's elaborate silent security alarm system.

He checked to make sure the tiny light on the panel had gone from red to green.

"What the . . . ?"

Both of the indicator lights were out. Brace bent down and tapped the cover plate on the panel. The plate rattled, then fell off into his hand.

Frowning, he set aside the plate and pulled his reading glasses from his inside coat pocket. He placed them fastidiously on his knobby nose, leaned close to the control panel, and examined the wiring. A fine bead of sweat broke out on his forehead as it became apparent even to his untrained eye that the wiring had been tampered with.

Brace took off his glasses and reached for the extension wall phone nearby. He quickly and nervously punched in the number for the security company. When the person on duty answered, Brace gave her his private code word and requested a routine check of his security system.

He shifted from one foot to the other, sweat trickling down into his shirt collar as he waited. Finally, the woman came back on the line and informed him that their monitors indicated that the gallery's system was engaged and functioning properly.

Brace hung up, wondering as he did so why he hadn't told her that the security alarm might be activated on her end, but it sure as hell wasn't on his. Instead, he left the rear entry area and moved cautiously down the broad, carpeted service corridor toward the front showroom, dreading what he would find.

A quick inspection of the walls and lighted display cases, however, revealed that nothing in the showroom had been disturbed. He stood in the middle of the room for three or four minutes, puzzled. From the looks of the alarm system control panel, the gallery had been broken into by a professional. But nothing seemed to be missing. Not a thing.

He wandered back down the corridor to his walnut-paneled office. Everything there, from the elegant tufted leather chairs to the ornate cherry-wood desk, was just as he had left it last night. Still bewildered, Brace circled the desk and sat down.

That's when he noticed the scars gouged into the wood around the lock to the lap drawer. His eyes widened as the air suddenly rushed from his lungs. Brace yanked open the drawer. The contents were a jumbled mess.

He worked his way down the three drawers on each side of the desk. The same. Bolting from the chair, he moved rapidly around the office, checking the oak filing cabinets, and even the dozen or so cardboard boxes in which he stored old records. Absolutely everything showed signs of having been pulled out, examined, and then hastily wadded back into place.

Panting with alarm, Brace swung aside a gilt-framed oil painting on the wall behind his desk, uncovering his safe. He worked the combination lock with shaking fingers, and pulled open the thick steel door. Clawing out the contents, he searched frantically for the one thing that he most feared that he would find missing.

"Please—no!" he gasped, sorting through the papers again and again.

The cryptic message from his "client" instructing Brace to purchase the Tokugawa box was gone. With a guttural curse, he flung a handful of documents across the room and collapsed into his desk chair.

He had to pull himself together. After all, he should have expected this. Just days ago, he had allowed the antique to slip through his fingers — and then he had compounded the problem by entrusting its recovery to Alyse Marlowe. Almost a week had gone by since the Bundys auction, and Brace still had nothing to show for it. Could he blame his "client" for growing impatient — perhaps even suspicious?

He got up and paced the carpeted office, mopping his perspiring face with a crisp linen handkerchief. Besides Brace, only one living person — his "client" — knew the total story behind the tea box. The man was rich and powerful. If he got it into his head that Brace was double-crossing him, that misconception could be fatal to the gallery owner.

He moaned out loud. The rifled files and missing instructions were a clear indication that his "client" had already come to that misguided conclusion, and had taken measures to cover his own tracks. Brace was seized by a jarring stab of panic.

He had asked too much of Alyse. Instead of sending her blindly after the box, Brace knew now that he should have gone himself. Unlike Alyse, he had known the dangers — what he could lose, and what there was to gain.

Perhaps it still wasn't too late, he thought, grabbing for his desk phone to book the next flight west. He had to get to Maui and retrieve the thing, even if he had to steal it. That was the only way his "client" could ever be convinced that Brace wasn't trying to cut him out.

Damn Rand Turnbull!

Dawn thrust narrow fingers of pale light between the closed louvers of the plantation shutters covering the bedroom window. Alyse eased the door open and peeked out into the hallway, holding her breath as she listened.

The house was silent. As she had hoped, she was the first one up.

She slipped out into the hallway and quietly closed the door behind her. With catlike steps, she crept down the corridor toward the living room. After a sleepless night, she desperately needed fresh air to chase the cobwebs from her mind. And she didn't want to have to talk to anyone—least of all, Rand.

The room was surprisingly empty. Alyse had expected to have to tiptoe past Rand. But he wasn't on the couch, and the fluffed cushions showed no indication that he had slept there during the night. She glanced toward the Tokugawa box on its low table near the piano and felt a dull twinge somewhere in the vicinity of her heart.

Alyse hurried on across the room and let herself out onto the lanai through the French door. The flagstone paving felt cool and damp beneath her bare feet. She relaxed, relieved that she had made it out of the cottage undetected, and headed down the path to the deserted beach.

A trawler rode the gentle swells in the distance, hauling a drag net in its wake. She could just make out an unruly mob of sea gulls wheeling and dipping above it in the cloudless blue sky. Unfortunately, Alyse was in no mood to appreciate the picture-postcard day unfolding before her.

She had gone to bed in despair, and gotten up depressed. In a way, she had nobody to blame but herself. In just three short days, her life had somehow caught a ride on the granddaddy of all roller coasters—and she wasn't at all sure she had the strength or will to ride it out.

A swim might have helped, but she was still wearing the blasted necklace. If the thing got wet, the plaster would probably fall apart, and there she would stand with the stolen pendant exposed to the whole world.

No, she corrected herself, not the whole world. Just in front of Kiku and Tommy—and Rand.

Alyse walked down to the edge of the surf, sorely tempted to wade on in, soak off the costume jewelry, and then march back to the cottage and parade the dragonfly right under Rand's nose. Get it over with. Find out once and for all how the man she loved balanced out on the great scales of life. Was he a romantic? Or, a rogue?

She was tempted, but not out of her mind. If she broke her vow of secrecy to the Japanese consulate official, she could kiss the official recognition of her cooperation good-by. And there was no way she was going to let that happen. The reward would buy her new gallery—the recognition would insure its early success. She would keep her mouth shut.

Alyse took off jogging along the shore, intent on whipping her mood into shape. She was through with the emotional Ping-Pong game she had been playing ever since she met Rand Turnbull. From now on, she would make use of some sage advice that her father had given her when she was just a child.

"Trust everyone," he had said, "but always cut the cards."

From here on in, Alyse decided, she would give Rand the benefit of the doubt. But she wouldn't show him the dragonfly.

She kicked up sand as she ran, occasionally dodging sea urchins and ocean debris that had washed up onto the beach during the night. A few hundred yards down the shoreline, Alyse realized she was coming up on the coconut palm. *Their* coconut palm. She would not permit herself to wish she had gone in the opposite direction.

"This is a test," she muttered through her teeth. "Breeze your fanny right on past."

Alyse started to break into a sprint, when she spotted movement in the shadows near the trunk of the palm. She stumbled to a halt. *Rand?*

"Aloha, wahini u'i."

Eddie Komake stepped out of the shadows.

160

Clad in colorful shorts, his dark skin shone like burnished copper in the sunlight. He flashed a smile, but didn't even try to make an excuse for yet another chance meeting.

This time, there was no doubt at all in her mind that Eddie was following her. Alyse eyed the stocky, muscular singer warily. Then she glanced past him at the palm tree and felt a different kind of unease. Had he been tracking her last night? When Rand made love to her in the moonlight beneath that palm, was Komake lurking nearby, spying on them? The thought left her feeling sullied.

"I see your arm is better," Alyse said, noting that his sling was gone.

Komake grinned and rotated his shoulder. "Good as new." He crossed the short stretch of beach separating them, his stride fluid and graceful, as if he were strolling out onto a stage.

"Why are you following me, Eddie?" she asked bluntly. No more beating around the bush, Alyse thought. She was steering her own bus now, and she would make the stops whenever and wherever she chose.

He chuckled softly, digging his toes into the loose sand. Eddie Komake was an attractive man, but Alyse didn't find him so at the moment. From where she stood, he seemed more threatening than alluring—all the more so because of his disarmingly exotic appeal.

"I was just standing there enjoying the view," he said. "Then along you came and improved it."

"You didn't answer my question."

His dark eyebrows rose languidly. "Oh? I thought I did."

"All right," Alyse said, containing her annoyance and trying another tack. "What are you doing out on this particular patch of deserted beach at this hour?"

"I was born on Maui. When I'm not working, I practically live on the beaches around here—and in the water. But you, *wahini u'i*—what brings you running along with fire in your eyes, talking to yourself?"

His description of her startled Alyse. She wished she had kept right on jogging when she spotted Komake. She didn't like the way he kept dodging her questions, bobbing and weaving like a shadow boxer.

"I was sent here by my employer to buy a Japanese antique," she replied. "I'm just a little frustrated over not being able to obtain it from the current owner."

Komake glanced back toward Rand's cottage. "What kind of antique?" he asked.

"A rare one," Alyse answered, thinking it was none of his business. "Why do you ask?"

"Just making polite conversation, *wahini u'i*," he said, smiling engagingly. "People tell me I'm a very curious *kanaka*."

"I'll bet they do." Alyse smiled back stiffly. "Are there any other curious itches you'd like scratched before I continue my jog?"

"Not at all." The singer grinned, then made a grand, sweeping gesture with one arm, motioning her on down the beach. "By all means, go on. And may the rest of your stay with Mr. Turnbull be most pleasant."

Alyse ran a few steps, and then halted abruptly. She turned back and looked at Eddie. "How did you know I was staying at the Turnbull cottage?" she asked.

His ever-present smile became guarded. Alyse waited, sensing that she had scored a hit—Komake was stumped. She let the silence drag on, her steady gaze driving home the point. He stared back, apparently unable to come up with a plausible substitute for the truth, which he was clearly unwilling to divulge.

Finally, Komake's smile curled bemusedly and he bowed to her. Alyse nodded back. She had no idea what the singer was up to, but she was satisfied that he now realized she wasn't fooled by his on-going charade. That was to her advantage. The next time they just happened to run into each other, he wouldn't be able to pretend it was purely by accident.

Alyse turned back up the beach, again breaking into a slow jog for which she had lost her enthusiasm. But she didn't want to leave Komake with the impression that their verbal skirmish had disturbed her sufficiently to send her fleeing back to the cottage.

* * *

When Alyse retraced her path twenty minutes later, she was relieved to find Eddie had gone. In spite of their encounter, the lope along the shoreline had lifted her spirits. Her stomach spasmed hungrily, and she found herself fantasizing about cinnamon bagels, peanut butter, and fresh pineapple rings.

She spotted Tommy crawling on the beach in front of the cottage before he heard her coming. His back was to her, and he was using an old metal pie plate to scoop great quantities of wet sand into a pile.

Alyse slowed to a walk to catch her breath, the sound of her approach silenced by the soft sand and the continuous rush of incoming waves. She stopped a few feet away, forgetting her hunger as she watched Tommy toil over the wet mound. A slightly lopsided box emerged, gradually taking the shape of a slant-roofed house. With a twig, Tommy carefully dug out a door and half a dozen windows.

When he sat back on his haunches to survey his creation, Alyse started to compliment the boy on his handiwork. Her jaw snapped shut when he spoke first.

"This room will belong to Mommy and Daddy." He pointed to an upstairs window. "Uncle Rand can have that one. I will have the one in between. And Kiku can have this one down here next to the kitchen, where she can bake us all lots of cookies and stuff."

164

Alyse realized with a jolt that Tommy wasn't talking to her—that he probably hadn't detected her presence behind him. She wondered if Rand knew that his orphaned nephew talked to himself.

At first, she couldn't decide whether to barge in on his private conversation with himself, or make a wide circle around to the front of the cottage and leave Tommy undisturbed. But she couldn't just go off and leave him alone on the beach.

"Wow," she said softly. "That's a pretty house. Did you design it yourself?"

Tommy's back stiffened at the sound of her voice. He nodded without looking up, and busied himself laying out a driveway as Alyse dropped down beside him. She watched him quietly for a while, trying to figure out how to broach the subject.

"I'll bet you miss your mom and dad and the friends where you used to live," she began, opting for a head-on approach.

He chewed on his lower lip for a moment. "Well, it's not so bad, living with my Uncle Rand." Tommy glanced at Alyse from the corner of his eye.

"I played by myself a lot when I was your age," she said, pitching in to help him bulldoze a street in front of his house.

"You did?"

"Yup. I was an only child, too. One year, I was sick for a long time, and my friends weren't allowed to visit me much. Sometimes, I got real lonesome." Alyse didn't mention that, unlike Tommy, she had rolled through her bumpy childhood under the guidance of two loving, *living* parents.

Tommy looked at her then. "What kind of games did you play?"

"Oh, I had dolls and coloring books and comic books and stuff. But mostly, I liked to pretend I was a penguin."

"Huh?"

"Penguins are real cute birds that live in big flocks down at the South Pole. I used to think that if I was a penguin, I'd be surrounded by hundreds and billions and jillions of friends."

Tommy slapped a hand across his mouth and giggled. Alyse winked at him, and drew a neat sidewalk across the front yard with the flat of her index finger.

"Alyse, when I grow up, will you marry me?" he asked seriously.

She leaned over and gave him a peck on the forehead. "Sweetheart, if I'm not hitched by then, I'll certainly keep you in mind."

"Great! You can come visit us in our new house," he said, patting a gob of extra sand onto the roof. This was presumably intended as a chimney.

"How nice of you to invite me. Where's the guest room?"

Tommy pursed his lips in thought. "We don't

have one, but that's okay. You can share Uncle Rand's room. If he doesn't mind."

"Oh, he won't mind," Rand said.

Alyse whirled to find Rand slouched on a large rock at the foot of the path leading up to the lanai, his long legs sprawled in front of him. He cradled a big coffee mug in both hands. She couldn't tell how long he had been sitting there eavesdropping.

Tommy looked up at him and grinned. "Uncle Rand, you snored last night."

"And you hogged the covers," Rand shot back. He took a long swig from the mug.

So, that's why the couch didn't look as if it had been slept on this morning, Alyse thought. Rand had bunked with his nephew.

He looked past Tommy at Alyse, his speculative gaze warming her skin even more than the tropical sun. What was on his mind couldn't have been clearer to her if it had been written on his forehead. Rand was thinking about last evening. He was remembering their lovemaking, as well as the tense confrontation over the Tokugawa box that had followed and wondering where all that left them this morning. He stared at her until they both became aware that Tommy was watching them.

"Hey, spud," Rand said, holding out the mug to the boy. "Kiku said to tell you she's fixing blueberry waffles for breakfast."

Tommy whooped with delight and bolted for

the cottage. He snatched Rand's mug from his hand as he passed. When they were alone, Rand propped his elbows on his knees and folded his hands under his chin, his gaze riveted on the abandoned sand house.

"Damn it all," he said wearily. "I'll never be able to replace what he's lost."

"Of course not. Just being someone who loves him is enough—if it's permanent. He's already been through so many changes. He doesn't need any more tough breaks."

"I'd die before I let anything happen to Tommy," he said fiercely.

Alyse nodded. "I think Tommy already knows that, deep down. When he learns to trust what he knows, he'll start feeling like part of a family again."

Her voice trailed off as it occurred to Alyse that she could just as well be talking about herself. If she learned to let herself trust Rand, perhaps she could at last overcome her own doubts.

Rand frowned in thought for a long moment, then smiled hopefully at Alyse. "I think you're wrong about one thing."

Alyse gave him a quizzical look.

"You wouldn't have liked being a penguin," he added. "You're too special to ever be just one in a jillion."

She laughed. "You didn't know me as a six-year-old. I was a freckled butterball in desperate need of braces. I'd have been thrilled to fade into the masses."

"From caterpillar to butterfly," Rand said admiringly.

Alyse felt her skin flush. The way he looked at her made her feel so desirable. He must have had that same look in his eyes last night under the coconut palm. But it had been dark then, and she couldn't see the tender longing. Only now did she realize what she had missed.

"How about you?" she said, nervously wrenching her mind away from plumeria-scented moonlight. "Didn't you ever have an imaginary friend?"

Rand winced and turned his face away, a bleak look replacing the warmth in his eyes. Alyse bit her upper lip, mentally kicking herself for being so stupid. She got up and moved to the rock. There wasn't much room on the flat surface, so she sat very close to Rand. When he didn't get up, she slipped her hand into his.

"That was pretty insensitive of me. Of course, you didn't need a pretend friend. You had your brother."

He clasped her hand tightly between both of his and pressed her fingers to his tight lips, staring out to sea. His grip was hurting her, but Alyse remained still, sensing the silent struggle going on inside him. When Rand finally spoke, the words came haltingly and with difficulty. It was as if he were dragging them into the blinding sunlight from a locked and windowless room.

169

"Chris was the best," he said. "The funny thing was, he was four inches shorter than I, but I always felt I was looking up at him. I don't think I'll ever get over losing him."

"At least he left you Tommy. You still have a little part of him in your life."

Rand kept his gaze fastened on the far horizon. "I'd like to think I could look forward to having you in my life, too," he said in a hoarse near whisper.

Alyse took a deep breath and let it out slowly. If he hadn't been holding her hand so tightly, she felt as if she might have floated off into the stratosphere. She couldn't find the right words, so she simply leaned over and kissed him lightly on the lips.

Rand rose and pulled her into his arms. He kissed her again, deeply, one hand tangled in her windblown hair. When their lips finally parted, he clutched her, swaying unsteadily, her head pressed against his shoulder.

"Precious Alyse," he whispered. "I feel as if I've been searching for you all my life."

Alyse pressed her mouth to the ridge of his collarbone and sighed. "I'm a very lucky woman."

"No, I'm the lucky one." Rand held her out at arm's length to look at her face, smiling. "But if I don't take my hands off you, we might get ourselves arrested for a wanton display of affection right out here on the beach."

"That didn't seem to bother you last night," Alyse pointed out impishly.

"Not my fault," he said, tweaking her nose with a knuckle. "I was moonstruck. And I seem to be suffering from a relapse. Would you care to join me for a curative swim?"

Her hand went to the necklace. "I think I'll pass. I've already been for a jog this morning, and I've worked up a positively savage appetite."

"So have I." Rand traced a thumb down the side of her neck, sending a shiver through Alyse. "That's why I need a swim."

Alyse peeled herself out of his clutches, smiling apologetically. She started up the beach path toward the lanai, then turned back.

"By the way, I ran into Eddie Komake this morning," she said.

Rand stared at her, then spun around and scanned the sea, his body tense. Alyse followed his eyes all the way to the horizon. A couple of fishing trawlers still worked their drag nets. Farther in the distance, a destroyer plowed northwest toward the Kaiwi Channel. It was heading to its berthing at the big naval base in Pearl Harbor, over on the southern coast of Oahu. But there was no sign of an orange-and-red catamaran.

"Did you talk with him?" Rand asked, facing her.

"Yes." Alyse contemplated Rand's stony expression with growing disbelief. Gone was the warmly amorous gaze of only a moment ago. In its place was a look of chilling, almost predatory watchfulness.

"What about?"

"About what I was doing here," she said. "He was full of questions, as always."

"What do you mean, 'as always?' "

"Komake pops up everywhere I turn. I know it sounds silly, but I've about decided he's following me."

Rand wiped a hand across his mouth and again scanned the sea.

"What is it, Rand?" she asked worriedly.

"Nothing. Probably nothing."

When he turned back to face Alyse, his gaze fell briefly to the clunky beads. He blinked, and looked off to one side, but not before the bottom fell out of her stomach.

"I was just wondering if Elaine Fielding might have recruited Komake to keep tabs on me," Rand said. "That would explain why he would be interested in you."

Rand was rattled by the news of her encounter with Eddie, Alyse thought. Worse, she had a sickening feeling that Rand was lying to her. She didn't think he believed the singer's suspicious behavior had anything to do with Tommy's grandmother.

She had seen the way he had eyed her necklace—as if it were far more than a piece of worthless junk jewelry. Had Rand just given himself away? The question catapulted her forward to wondering if he and Eddie Komake could be in cahoots over the pendant theft.

Alyse turned and fled the thought, racing up the path to the lanai. She wouldn't let herself believe that the man who had stolen her heart could be a low-life thief of material treasures.

Rand watched her sprint up the beach path like a frightened gazelle. He cursed under his breath, wanting to chase after her. He turned toward the sea instead, raging inside.

Komake had lied to him!

Chapter Ten

Early that evening, Alyse leaned toward the small mirror over the dresser in Rand's bedroom, hurriedly putting the finishing touches on her makeup. Rand had rushed home less than half an hour ago and pretty much steamrolled her into going out to dinner with him.

Sunburned, windblown, and coated with salty sand, Alyse had declared dibs on being first in the shower. She had been racing around at a frenetic pace ever since. She hadn't had time to think, and that made her edgy. Every instinct she owned told her that she was swimming in deep, treacherous seas—and that only by using her brain could she keep her head above water.

She leaned closer to the mirror with the mascara wand, clad in a filmy silk slip over lace-trimmed bikini undies. Behind her, a low-cut mauve cocktail dress that she had picked up in Lahaina during yesterday's shopping spree lay ready on the end of the bed. She planned to wear it with a pair of matching silk pumps. When she splurged on the outfit, she'd had no idea she would have an opportunity to don it so soon.

She could faintly hear the shower running in the bathroom that separated Rand's bedroom from Kiku's at the end of the hallway. The thought of Rand lathering his lean, muscular body just a few feet away made her hand quiver. Alyse had to take a deep, calming breath before adding one last dab of mascara.

Rand had been gone nearly all day, supposedly looking after details for tomorrow night's luau for his new Japanese and American clients. His absence had left Alyse with a discomforting sense of emptiness and relief. She had missed him dreadfully—and yet, these past few days had left her emotionally frayed. She had needed those precious hours of slack time to mend her nerves and regain her balance.

Alyse had remained at the cottage to bask in the sun and help Tommy construct an entire Medieval village of turreted sand castles. Afterwards, following a leisurely picnic lunch on the beach, they had taken origami lessons from Kiku.

Alyse put away her makeup kit and picked up the intricate little folded paper crane that Tommy had made for her, under Kiku's patient guidance. She considered wearing it in her hair this evening, but reluctantly decided against it.

All the priceless things in her life lay spread before her on the dresser. The paper crane. The black coral beads and bracelet that Rand had given her. The necklace containing the dragonfly pendant. She felt profoundly guilty about her choice, but there was never any doubt in her mind which she would wear that evening — and which would have to be left behind.

The sound of the shower shut off abruptly. Alyse quickly returned the origami bird to the top of the dresser, suddenly in a mad rush again. She grabbed the cocktail dress from the bed as the shower door banged shut. She shimmied into the soft, clinging garment, stepping into the matching pumps as she zipped the form-fitting bodice.

Dashing back to the dresser, she snatched up the sand dollar necklace and draped it around her neck. Alyse had time for only one quick peek in the mirror, which was enough to give her pause.

The neckline of her dress dipped far lower than she had remembered from when she tried it on in the shop. It revealed a startling amount of cleavage. Combined with the snug fit of the bodice, the garment left little to the imagination.

Alyse gave a moan of dismay. But she didn't have time to change into something else — if, indeed, she had anything else suitable for a night on the town. Rand needed the bedroom now so he could get dressed.

She pulled open the top dresser drawer that Rand had graciously loaned her, and grabbed her beaded evening bag. A slip of brown paper beneath the bag caught her eye. Alyse picked up the square of folded rice paper containing the dragonfly haiku, and hesitated.

Should she take it with her? Unfortunately, the

poem wouldn't fit into the small evening bag without additional folding, which she was afraid might damage the fragile old paper fibers. Alyse reluctantly slipped it back into the drawer under a package of stockings. As an afterthought, she placed Tommy's crane on top before closing the drawer.

The velvet drawstring bag containing the black coral beads and bracelet lay on top of the dresser. She paused, then snatched it up, loosened the drawstring, and dug out the bracelet. She slipped the glossy black band over her wrist and tucked the pouch containing the beads into her evening bag.

After quickly checking to make sure she hadn't left any of her things lying around in Rand's way, she rushed from the room and down the hall.

Ten minutes later, Alyse was standing on the lanai watching the pastel splendor of the tropical sunset when Rand opened the French door behind her and stepped outside. She spun around as though startled from a reverie. He stopped short, one hand on the brass door handle, and stared at her, enthralled.

A tremor of electrified heat passed through Alyse as she took in the tall, dark-blond figure before her. Rand could have been a male model, in his white linen dinner jacket and dark slacks. He wore a fresh plumeria blossom in his lapel. Even in the fading half-light of dusk, she could see the glow of desire in his warm brown eyes.

"Ravishing!" he said, stringing out the word appreciatively.

"Handsome!" Alyse said at the same time.

They both laughed nervously, revealing a thread of underlying tension that neither was prepared to openly acknowledge. His gaze snagged on the gaudy necklace. Alyse was about to apologize for not wearing the coral beads, when he glanced down at the bracelet she was wearing and smiled, apparently satisfied with her compromise.

Rand took his hand off the door handle and she gasped at the splendid lei of pale violet orchids looped over his wrist. He ambled across the lanai and stood looking longingly at her as he draped the lei over her shoulders. The cool, fragrant blossoms nestled delicately against her neck. They framed her face enticingly.

"I've never seen anything so gorgeous," Alyse said, inhaling the lei's exotic perfume as she traced the curled edge of a petal with her fingertips.

"I have," Rand said huskily.

He looked deeply into her upraised eyes — so deeply that her toes curled. Alyse held her breath, lips parted, waiting for the kiss that lurked behind his hungry, longing expression.

With brute force, Rand tore his gaze from Alyse and glanced out past the lanai toward the water. A catamaran skimmed across the gentle swells a hundred yards offshore. He couldn't make out the colors of the striped sail in the rapidly waning light, but he wasn't about to take any chances.

"We'd better go," he said. "I made reservations."

Alyse felt vaguely disappointed as Rand escorted her along the stone path that skirted the cottage. His hand hovered near her back, ushering her over the slightly irregular stones without once touching her. In the driveway, he held the door of his car open as she slid into the passenger seat.

She watched him stride around to the driver's side, his fingers snapping out a quick cadence. He climbed in behind the steering wheel without so much as glancing at her. In fact, he suddenly seemed to be making a point of not looking at her. When he started to twist the key in the ignition, she reached over and touched his arm.

"Rand, are you all right?"

He looked at her then, blinking. "I'm fine. Why do you ask?"

"You seem kind of . . . antsy, all of a sudden."

His shoulders drooped and he sagged back in the seat, grimacing. "It shows, huh?"

"What?"

Rand laughed dryly and cast a supplicating look at the ceiling of the car. "You're going to think I'm losing my mind, Alyse. Especially after what happened out on the beach last night. But one look at you against that sunset a while ago, and my knees almost buckled. I don't think you have any idea how devastatingly beautiful you are."

Alyse sat speechless for a moment. Nobody had

179

ever told her she was devastatingly *anything,* before.

"Rand, that's just about the nicest thing anyone has ever said to me."

"Then, consider this. It was a gross understatement of how I feel about you." He gave her a crooked smile. "That dress ought to be registered as a dangerous weapon."

She flushed, a little embarrassed, but mostly glad that she hadn't had time to change into something else. Neither of them spoke as Rand pulled onto the highway and headed toward Lahaina.

"I feel badly about not letting Tommy come along," she said finally. "He was so disappointed."

Rand shook his head emphatically. "Tommy had you all day. I told him it was my turn. He's bright. He understands the principle of sharing."

Alyse looked at him askance. "Why do I suddenly feel like something that two little boys are toting around in an old cigar box?"

He grinned and gave her a look that wasn't even remotely little boyish. Then his gaze drifted down to the necklace peeking from beneath the orchid lei, and his smile became brittle, then vanished altogether. Alyse watched his profile as he returned his attention to the road, her hand moving protectively to the garish beads.

She couldn't blame Rand if he were offended that she hadn't worn the black coral necklace he had given her, even though she had compromised and worn the bracelet. Oddly enough, however,

Alyse didn't think that was the problem. A louder, clearer, and far more disturbing inner voice told her that something else entirely was bothering him. Something that had absolutely nothing to do with black coral.

Their table in a secluded corner of the Lahaina Palms overlooked a lighted sailboat dock at the edge of the town's small harbor. Beyond lay the broad Au'au Channel, separating Maui from neighboring Lanai. The floating strains of traditional island music drifted to them from the far end of the dining room, where a slightly rotund singer crooned plaintively into a hand-held microphone.

"Eddie Komake, he isn't," Rand commented under his breath as he studied the oversized menu.

"Thank heaven for small favors," Alyse murmured distractedly. Every item on the list was written in Hawaiian. She felt like a foreigner.

Rand glanced over the top of his menu at her. "You don't like Komake, do you?"

"I don't like the way he pops up everywhere I turn." She would have added *like the red-and-orange catamaran that bugs you out of your mind,* but there was no point in casting a pall over their evening.

"Oh, come on." Rand smiled. "He isn't here now, is he?"

Alyse smiled back at him, pretending that he

had a point. In truth, however, she was afraid to look. She wouldn't have been surprised to find Eddie smirking languidly at her from the next table.

"Besides," Rand went on, "if you stop and think about it, Komake just might be wondering how come *you* show up everywhere *he* goes."

"Then I won't stop and think about it," she said, at the same time shoving aside the impression that Rand was going out of his way to defend the ubiquitous singer.

The Lahaina Palms was extremely proud of its food, Alyse noticed, scanning the righthand column of the menu. Less than a week ago, the prices would have intimidated her. She would have selected the cheapest thing she could find, regardless of who was picking up the tab. But lucking onto the dragonfly pendant had radically changed her perspective on such matters. Ignoring the price column, she chose something easy to pronounce.

"I'll have the *puhi,*" she said, putting down the menu.

"Eel, huh?" he remarked, still scanning the list, trying to make up his mind.

Her eyes widened. Alyse snatched up her menu again and reconsidered. "Or, maybe *mahimahi.*"

"Ah. Dolphin."

She winced at a vision of Flipper staring up at her from her plate. "What are you having?"

"*Hapuupuu.* Black sea bass."

"Sounds too good to pass up."

The waiter came and went, taking the huge menus with him. Rand folded his arms on the edge of the table and drank in his unobstructed view of Alyse. She held his gaze for a long moment, mesmerized by the flickering reflection of the amber glass-domed candle centerpiece in his dark brown eyes.

Last night came back to her in a rapid sequence of dreamlike but strangely vivid images, which crowded out all thought in a dizzying rush of recalled emotion and sensation. The soft cooing of brown doves. The boom-whoosh of the surf. Rand's touch. Her touching. Whispered words carried on the gentle night breeze.

He raised his wine glass in a silent toast that needed no words. Rand's dilated pupils told Alyse in no uncertain terms that, if they hadn't been in a public place at that moment, he would have kissed her.

She raised her own glass by its delicate stem, feeling something deep within herself come into perfect, vibrating harmony with Rand. It was as if they were parts of the same tuning fork. They drank without blinking. Then Alyse tilted her glass toward Rand, the pale liquid catching the candlelight.

"To you, Rand," she said softly, her voice carrying no farther than to his ears. "You've given me something to take with me all my life."

Rand flinched as if her words had physically struck him and shattered the idyllic mirage that had settled over the table. His free hand shot out and grabbed her hand before Alyse could raise the glass to her lips.

"What . . . ?" he rasped.

Alyse froze, her hand vised in his. The slightest additional pressure, she feared, and the stem of the wine glass would snap. Rand stared at her imploringly for ten long seconds. Twenty.

"Rand . . . please, let go."

Her words didn't seem to register on him at first. When they did, he glanced down at their hands, then snatched his away. Rand sat staring at the white tablecloth, his jaw muscles knotted, until Alyse reached out and touched the back of his fist.

"I'm sorry, Alyse," he said tightly. "I didn't mean to come unglued. I'm not in the habit of overreacting that way. It's just that you made it sound as if we wouldn't be seeing each other any more."

"I will be returning to New York after the luau tomorrow. You knew that."

Rand nodded. "Yes. But I won't be. I intend to keep Tommy as far away from Elaine Fielding as possible until the adoption proceedings are finalized. That could take months, many months. We'll be staying here on Maui, and at a small condo I keep for business purposes in San Francisco."

Alyse felt a prickle of excitement. She came precariously close to telling Rand that she planned to make arrangements to move to the West Coast and open her own art gallery as soon as she got back to Manhattan. But she feared that spilling those beans was bound to arouse his curiosity as to how she intended to finance such an ambitious undertaking.

Yet again, she anguished over the war within herself. Her heart wanted to trust Rand with everything she knew about the dragonfly pendant. She wished she could give him a chance to deny that he was aware that the stolen treasure had been concealed in the false bottom of the Tokugawa box when he purchased it. But her mind kept repeating her father's advice—*trust everyone, but always cut the cards*.

In the end, Alyse played it safe and kept her mouth shut concerning the jewel hidden inside the tawdry necklace. Even as she hung onto her secret, however, her greatest fear was that it wasn't a secret at all. As much as she loved Rand, she couldn't bring herself to trust him without question.

That doubt ate away at her like battery acid. Had her ability to trust any man been damaged beyond repair by Rob's endless lies and deceptions?

"Rand, these past few days have been pretty wild and mixed up," she said, trying desperately to chart a course through the chaos. "You're running scared half the time, worried sick over Mrs. Fielding's low-life detective digging up something—who knows, maybe even *manufacturing* something—that could destroy your chances of adopting Tommy."

"That's a real threat, Alyse."

"I'm sure it is. And if I were in your place—with Tommy at stake—I'd have my wagons circled, too." Alyse took a sip of wine and closed her eyes briefly, waiting for its calming puddle of warmth to spread in her stomach.

"What I'm getting at," she continued, "is that these are crazy times for both of us. Maybe what we're feeling for each other isn't real. Maybe love is just a lie we're telling ourselves, so we won't have to face up to those fears. Maybe nothing that's happening to us is what it seems to be."

"No!" Rand reached a hand across the table, palm up. Alyse hesitated, then placed her hand in his. This time, his grip was firm but gentle. He stared straight into her eyes and repeated, "No."

His gaze had become steely, determined. "Alyse, listen to me," he said evenly. *"Believe* me. What's happening to us isn't some kind of imaginary, combat zone relationship. It's more real than anything you could ever imagine."

Alyse swallowed hard. His words seemed to have a double meaning that she couldn't quite grasp. What did he mean, more real than she could imagine? Was Rand trying to tell her something without actually saying it? Perhaps, something that he wasn't certain she would want to hear?

Mentally reeling from confusion, Alyse withdrew her hand from his. She felt oddly as though she were releasing a life preserver. Rand's fingers curled into a tight fist on the tablecloth. He ducked his chin, baring his teeth in a grimace of frustration. And suddenly, Alyse knew he was hiding something.

She *knew!*

She sat waiting for him to open up, every fiber in her body aflame with dread. Part of her was terrified of what he might say—the rest of her needed to hear it at all costs.

Rand said nothing. Instead, he turned and looked morosely out the window at the gaily lighted dock.

A small boat left its slip, moving smoothly down the quiet channel toward open water. Alyse watched it until she lost its running lights in the darkness and felt lost herself.

"These past few days," she said after a long while, "I think we've both sometimes lost sight of what I'm doing here." When Rand looked at her, she added slowly, carefully enunciating each word, "I came to retrieve the Tokugawa tea box."

"Believe me, Alyse," Rand said, his voice suddenly weary, "if it were up to me, I'd *give* you the damned thing. Unfortunately, it's out of my hands now. The box will be presented to my clients tomorrow night, whether we like it or not."

His words only deepened her bewilderment. Why did Rand think it was out of his hands? The question was on the tip of her tongue when the waiter appeared with their dinner.

Alyse stared down at the exquisitely prepared meal. Everything was so perfect—soft candlelight, romantic music, a picturesque view. The orchid lei enveloped her with its heady perfume, and she only had to raise her eyes to see the handsome cat burglar who had stolen her heart in spite of all the locked doors Rob had left behind.

Scratch the perfect surface, however, and another world shone through like the black roots on a bad hair dye job. Beneath the fragrant lei hung the sand dollar. Within the gaudy ornament lay the dragonfly pendant. Layer upon layer. Behind the dragonfly lurked — what? Alyse wasn't sure she wanted to know.

Rand refilled her wine glass from the crystal carafe the waiter had left. She couldn't bring herself to look him in the eye. Alyse took a small bite of succulent green kiwi fruit, and found that it tasted like sawdust to her.

The short, silent drive back to the cottage seemed to take much longer than the drive into Lahaina. When Rand reached over and took her hand, Alyse didn't try to pull away. But the physical contact was no more a comfort to Rand, she suspected, than it was to her. They were both miserably aware that the evening was turning out all wrong, and yet neither seemed capable of changing that.

"What the devil!" Rand said as they turned into the driveway.

Lights shone from every window in the house, and all the exterior landscaping floodlights had been turned on. Alyse could tell from the way

Rand accelerated down the driveway and skidded to a halt near the front door that he was alarmed.

He leaped out of the car, shouting for Alyse to stay put. She slid across the seat and scrambled out after him. By the time she caught up, Rand had the front door unlocked.

They ran inside. As they reached the living room, Rand suddenly halted in his tracks and threw up both hands. Alyse smashed into his back, knocking him forward another step. She regained her balance and peered around him — then gasped.

Kiku stood in her bathrobe next to the piano, a razor-sharp kitchen cleaver raised overhead. The tiny housekeeper glared at them fearlessly for one breathless second, then lowered the cleaver with a quavering sigh. As the weapon fell to the floor, Tommy darted from behind her and raced toward his uncle.

"What the hell's going on?" Rand demanded as he swept Tommy into his arms.

"A bad guy broke in," Tommy cried, throwing his arms around Rand's neck. "Kiku scared him away."

"He ran out the lanai door toward the beach, Mr. Turnbull," Kiku said, sinking down on the piano bench, clearly shaken now that help had arrived.

"When?" he asked curtly.

"Just a few minutes ago."

Rand tore Tommy's grip away from his neck and tossed the child into Alyse's arms. In an instant, he had barged across the room and out the door. He sprinted out of sight into the darkness beyond the halo of landscaping lights.

Alyse took Tommy over to the piano bench and sat down next to Kiku. They clung to each other, staring at the open French door through which Rand had vanished. After what seemed like a very long time, he returned, his face glazed with sweat and his shoes caked with sand.

He stopped in the doorway and looked back out into the night, his fists slowly opening and closing at his sides. Then he came on in and took Tommy back from Alyse. His expression was tense and anxious. He held the boy in an iron embrace for a moment, still breathing hard, then knelt down in front of Kiku.

"Tell me what happened," he said quietly.

Alyse squeezed Kiku's shoulders reassuringly. The housekeeper took Alyse's free hand in both of hers and held it tightly.

"I had just put Tommy to bed and turned out the lights. Then I heard a noise in your bedroom, Mr. Turnbull. I crept into the kitchen to call the police, but the telephone wasn't working."

Rand bounced to his feet and rushed to the kitchen. Seconds later, he was back.

"We passed a phone company truck, coming out from town," he said. "They must be working on the lines. Did you get a look at the intruder?"

Kiku shook her head. "Just a shadow. I was standing in the kitchen doorway trying to decide what to do, when he came down the hallway into the living room. He must have seen me, because he suddenly ran for the lanai door."

"He was alone?" asked Alyse.

"Yes. As soon as he was gone, I switched on the outside lights and ran through the house turning on everything. Then I heard a car drive up and thought he must be coming back, because I never expected you to return this early."

Alyse glanced at Rand. Just a short while ago, she never would have dreamed she would be glad that their evening together had gone so sour that they had cut it short. From the look on his face, she guessed that Rand shared her feeling.

"Do you have a gun, Uncle Rand?" Tommy asked.

"No, no," Rand replied, patting his nephew's back. "I don't think we need anything like that. If Kiku scared off the intruder that easily, he must not have intended any harm."

"Then you think he was just a random burglar?" Alyse asked.

"What else? He probably expected to catch everyone sleeping. Kiku must have scared the bujeezus out of him."

Alyse hoped he was right and that Rand wasn't just telling her what they all wanted to hear. Her attention strayed toward the tea box on the low table against the wall. She shivered, and Kiku looked up at her sharply. Alyse forced a smile that only made Kiku's frown deepen.

"Trooper, it's time you hit the sack again,"

Rand said, giving Tommy an affectionate pat on the backside.

The boy looked at him with wide, apprehensive eyes. "Will you sleep in my room again tonight, Uncle Rand?"

"Of course. You'll be safe and snug as a bug. Trust me."

Rand turned back toward the housekeeper. "Kiku, check around to make sure nothing's missing. As soon as I get Tommy tucked in, I'll lock up the place."

"I can take care of the locks," Alyse volunteered. "Rand, don't you think you should go somewhere and call the police?"

He seemed to consider that for a moment. "Whoever broke in is long gone now," he said finally. "Let's check around. If he didn't have a chance to take anything, there's no point in making a big deal of this tonight. I can notify the authorities when the phone lines are back in operation."

"That's a remarkably casual attitude toward crime, coming from a lawyer."

"Well, I'm an extremely tired lawyer. And I'm not thrilled by the prospect of generating a bunch of extra paperwork for some bored cop, when there isn't a chance in a hail storm of catching the creep."

"We're in Hawaii," she said. "But you sound an awful lot like New York."

"What can I say? It's in my blood." He turned and shambled off toward the hallway and Tom-

192

my's bedroom.

Alyse stared after him for a moment and frowned. Then she started with the French door leading out onto the lanai. She made sure the bolts were securely in place at the top and bottom. From there, she worked her way methodically through the house, checking windows and doors. By the time she made it to Rand's bedroom, most of the adrenaline rush brought on by the scare had worn off. In its place, she felt post-traumatic anger at the sleaze who had dared to break in.

The first thing she noticed as she entered Rand's bedroom was the plantation shutters. She had left them closed that evening. They stood slightly askew now, the wide louvers tilted partly open. Alyse moved around the bed to inspect the window. The glass was raised all the way, and the screen had been removed. She had no doubt that she had just found the burglar's point of entry.

After making sure the window was securely locked, Alyse closed and latched the shutters. She was heading back toward the door when she spotted the small origami crane that Tommy had made for her that afternoon. It was lying on the floor in front of the dresser.

She glanced around the bedroom, as if expecting the long-gone intruder to leap at her from the shadows. Then she reached down and picked up the paper crane. Alyse distinctly remembered having left it atop a package of stockings inside the dresser drawer. She cradled the bird in one hand as she eased open the drawer and peeked inside.

Her lingerie looked as if it had been stirred with a stick. She dug down through it carefully, her heart tripping wildly. The package of stockings lay on the bottom where she had left it. Alyse raised it by one corner, and bit her lip to keep from crying out.

The haiku was gone!

She plucked out every article in the drawer, just to make sure. The slip of antique rice paper most definitely was missing.

Alyse dumped everything back into the drawer, the words of the haiku spinning through her mind.

How far today in chase I wonder has gone my hunter of the dragonfly.

The intruder had obviously come in search of the stolen pendant, she realized, her hand flying to her neck. He had found the poem. He knew he was close, and would surely return. How many more hunters of the dragonfly lurked out there, Alyse wondered, feeling chased.

She closed the drawer and stepped out into the quiet hallway, moving toward the living room like a sleepwalker. The door to Kiku's room was closed. The housekeeper had apparently gone off to bed. Tommy's bedroom door stood slightly ajar, the night light burning. She leaned inside just long enough to reassure herself that he was sleeping peacefully in spite of the night's excitement.

A light was still on in the living room. Alyse crept on down the hallway, fatigue finally catching up with her. She paused to kick out of her silk pumps and carried them in one hand as she stepped into the living room.

She stopped just inside the doorway, surprised to find Rand kneeling on the floor near the piano. A rectangular section of the woven rice straw floor mat had been folded back and a wooden panel removed to reveal a floor safe, the heavy door of which stood open. While Alyse watched, Rand lifted the Tokugawa box from its table, carefully placed it in a cardboard carton, and lowered it into the safe.

He was reaching back for the door to the vault when Alyse dropped a shoe. It hit the floor with a soft thump.

Rand looked up, clearly alarmed at finding her standing there, but quickly regained his composure. His expression became guarded, as if a mask had fallen over his face. They stared at each other for a wordless moment, Alyse barely able to breathe around an icy lump in her chest. Then Rand eased the safe door shut and spun the combination lock.

He carefully fitted the wooden floor panel into the opening. As he settled the rice straw mat back into place, patting down the edges to conceal the seam, the paralysis that had held Alyse in the doorway suddenly released her. She snatched up her shoe, retreated quickly to Rand's bedroom, and locked herself in. Locked Rand out.

With her back to the door, she closed her eyes and held her breath for as long as she could before letting it out slowly through her lips. When she opened her eyes again, she was able to concentrate with some semblance of clarity.

There was nothing strange about Rand locking away the tea box following the break-in. After all, he had paid a bundle for the thing. If she'd had any idea that Rand had a safe in the cottage, Alyse would have strongly advised him to keep the antique there from the beginning.

What bothered her was Rand's reaction when he realized she was watching. He had behaved as if he hadn't meant for her to see the safe—as if he had something to hide.

Alyse moved over to the end of the bed and sat down. Rand had been hiding the safe, just as she was concealing the dragonfly pendant. Her head began to throb as she conceded that Rand's deception had been no greater than her own.

She squinted through the dull ache at the top dresser drawer. She also had been hiding the haiku. But the burglar had taken that off her hands.

Or, had he?

Alyse stiffened. After she left the poem in the drawer that evening—but before the intruder had broken in hours later—Rand had spent ten minutes alone in this bedroom while dressing for dinner.

"Stop it!" she whispered aloud, hammering a

fist into her lap.

A light knock sounded on the bedroom door. Her head snapped around to stare at the door knob. Again, the feathery tapping—a soft rattle of fingertips on the door panel.

"Alyse . . . ?" Rand's barely audible voice.

She sat unmoving, her gaze riveted on the door knob. It never moved. He never tested the lock. After a while, the sound of his footsteps receded.

Her relief that Rand had gone away was matched by an overwhelming sense of loneliness. Alyse wanted to run to the door and call him back, but she couldn't. Instead, she clutched the sand dollar necklace in both hands, shaking her head in mute dismay.

The dragonfly had made her rich. But so far, that hadn't bought her freedom from the prison of distrust that Rob had built around her. Now, she feared that it never would—at least, not in time to keep her doubts from tearing her life apart. Alyse doubled over and held her stomach as hot tears trickled down her bunched cheeks.

Chapter Eleven

After the previous night's excitement, Saturday morning didn't exactly arrive with a bang at the Turnbull cottage. Alyse had been lying in bed for nearly an hour watching tiny sunbeams filter through the chinks in the window shutters before she detected muted sounds in the hallway outside her door.

Within minutes, the smell of coffee reached her. That meant Kiku was up, she thought, then corrected herself. Putting together a pot of coffee was just the sort of puttery thing that she could envision Rand doing on a laid-back weekend morning.

A frown line deepened between her eyes. Where had she gotten the idea that there was anything laid-back about this particular day? Wishful thinking? After last night's break-in, and with the luau on tap for this evening, it felt more like the eye of a hurricane.

Alyse yawned, fuzzy-headed from the sleepless

night. She heard Tommy giggle in the hallway as though he had been playfully tweaked, then the bathroom door clicked shut. More giggling.

She listened carefully, wondering if the boy was sharing the cottage's only bathroom with his uncle. The question was answered by the buzz of an electric razor. When the door clicked again, indicating that the Turnbulls had finished with their morning ablutions, Alyse crawled out of bed.

She stood in front of the dresser mirror for two or three minutes and studied the wreckage. Her hair was a tangled mess and she had dark circles under her eyes. Incredible, she thought dully — just a dozen hours ago, Rand had told her she was ravishing.

Alyse dug out her toothbrush, finding little consolation in knowing that the night apparently hadn't treated Rand much better. She had heard him roaming around at three in the morning.

At one point, she had almost gotten out of bed and gone out to talk to him. But in the cold light of day, Alyse was intensely thankful that she had remained in bed and kept her mouth shut. Considering the state of mind she had been in last night, she probably would have come right out and asked Rand if he had taken her out to dinner in order to give Eddie Komake a chance to break in and steal the valuable haiku. And when he looked hurt and said no — as she knew he would whether he was telling the truth or a lie — Alyse would be no closer to knowing the truth than she was now.

Of course, Rand had at least one opportunity

to take the haiku on his own, but not without casting suspicion on himself.

Back and forth, back and forth. Was she betraying Rand by doubting him? Or, making a fool of herself for trusting him? Alyse was sick of the unending debate raging within her.

"Trust everyone, but always cut the cards," Alyse murmured mockingly, as she looked her mirrored image squarely in the eye. "Well, you aren't just cutting them, you fool. You're hacking them up into confetti."

The sum total of her sleepless night was that she had managed to cast a wildly popular Hawaiian club singer as a thief of Japanese national treasures, with a prominent attorney as his accomplice. At the rate she was going, Alyse thought dismally, by nightfall she would probably have Tommy pegged as a sinister midget posing as a child.

Only that wasn't going to happen. This farce had gone on long enough. Too long, in fact. Twenty-four hours from now she would be on her way back to New York, with or without the Tokugawa box—but definitely *with* the reward for the pendant.

Tomorrow was the critical day in her life, she told herself, not today. Today—well, she would get through it the best way she could.

Alyse was late for breakfast. Kiku followed her out onto the lanai with a fresh carafe of coffee. From the looks of the table, Rand and Tommy had already grazed on cinnamon bagels and Kiku's home-baked muffins. Alyse settled into a chair and shaded her eyes against the brilliant morning sunlight, squinting toward the beach.

"What in the world are they up to?" she asked.

Tommy and Rand lay on their backs at the edge of the water, their extended arms making rhythmic butterfly sweeps in the foaming surf.

"Swimming lessons," Kiku answered before disappearing back inside.

While Alyse watched with interest, picking absently at a wedge of fresh papaya, Rand got up and waded in knee-deep. He held out his hand to Tommy, who shook his head vigorously.

"Dream on, counselor," Alyse said aloud. After Tommy's recent near-drowning experience—not to mention what had happened to his parents—getting the boy back into the ocean was going to require time, along with some high-powered persuasion.

Still holding out his hand, smiling, Rand spoke quietly to Tommy. The words were unintelligible to Alyse at that distance. A moment later, she arched one eyebrow as Tommy took a small, tentative step into deeper water—then another.

Rand stretched out prone and ducked his head under the water, obviously demonstrating breath control. The tense, unenthusiastic student at his side repeatedly shot anxious glances back toward dry land.

"He'd rather eat broccoli," Alyse commented to herself, expecting all-out revolt at any moment.

Within ten minutes, however, Tommy was facedown in the water of his own free will. Before Alyse had finished her first cup of coffee, Rand

201

had the boy stretched out in the rolling surf, propped up on both hands, paddling his short legs for all they were worth.

"Amazing," she said under her breath.

Apparently deciding to quit while he was ahead, Rand suddenly scooped Tommy out of the water. He hoisted the youngster onto his shoulders and came galloping ashore, racing toward the beach path in a wild zigzagging pattern that produced shrieks of delight from his passenger. Not until they reached the lanai and Rand swung Tommy into a somersaulting dismount did Alyse realize that she was laughing along with them.

"Did you see me in the ocean?" the boy shouted, charging toward Alyse.

"Yes. And I was so proud of you!" She caught him in her arms, startled by the strength of his hug. She squeezed him back hard, a lump swelling in her chest, not caring at all that Tommy was soaking her polka dot shorts and blouse.

Just as suddenly, he was off again, leaving a trail of wet tracks as he pounded on into the house calling for Kiku. As Alyse watched Tommy go, it struck her that her trip to Hawaii was turning out to be worse than useless. She had first lost the tea box—and then her heart.

Rand stood smiling at her as he slowly dried his chest with a thick towel. Water dripped from his hair onto his broad, sun-bronzed shoulders. She took in his lean, muscular body and, for the life of her, couldn't recall how he looked in a business suit.

"I was impressed," she said, as she nodded toward the beach. "If that was an example of your powers of persuasion, counselor, I'd love to watch you strut your stuff in a courtroom. What magic incantation did you use on Tommy?"

He laughed and flipped the towel around his neck. "I tried explaining to him that the human body was about four-fifths water, so he had a lot in common with the ocean. But that didn't work."

"I can imagine how it might not."

"Then I tried assuring him that I was big and invincible, and wouldn't let anything happen to him. That didn't work either."

Alyse nodded. She could tell Rand had already figured out where he had gone wrong with that tack. At one time, Tommy had undoubtedly viewed his father as invincible, too.

"So, what finally worked?" she asked.

Rand grinned ruefully. "Easy. I told him you were watching."

He chuckled at her expression and settled into a chair at the table. "Male ego," he said. "A fellow's never too young."

"That must make life difficult for you guys," Alyse teased. She was still rocked by the news that Tommy had been willing to confront what must be his greatest terror, just because he knew she was sitting in the bleachers.

"Sometimes." Rand nodded, suddenly serious. He leaned toward her and lowered his voice, weighting their light conversation with a heavy charge of intimacy. "Especially when a man wakes up one day and discovers that it's become extraordinarily important to him to impress one special woman."

His gaze locked onto hers. Alyse sat utterly still and stared deeper and deeper into his riveting brown eyes, feeling eerily as if she were being hypnotized against her will. And then she realized that it wasn't against her will at all. She wanted to simply let go, and fall farther and longer and with more perfect abandon than she had ever dared before.

She had done that once with him, under the coconut palm tree two nights ago. But once was not enough.

He reached out and covered her hand with his. Rand's touch jolted her consciousness back into gear. Alyse blinked rapidly and looked away. But she couldn't bring herself to withdraw her hand. She told herself that she didn't want to bruise his fragile male ego. As she madly scraped her thoughts back together, she told herself a lot of things, most of which didn't make much sense.

"Speaking of waking up," Alyse said, blindly seizing the first inane subject that came to mind. "I heard you roaming around the house in the middle of the night. One of us must have had a highly contagious case of insomnia."

Rand stared at her blankly. "Not me. I turned in about a half hour after you, and slept like a log — Tommy's nocturnal thrashings notwithstanding."

"But I heard you creeping around in the hallway," Alyse protested. After a pause, she added, "Unless it was Kiku."

He shook his head, frowning. "Nothing can part Kiku from her pillow once she's packed it in for the night. While visiting relatives in Tokyo last year, she slept through an earthquake that measured 5.8 on the Richter scale."

Alyse bit her lower lip pensively. "Rand, I'm not dreaming this up. I heard someone outside my . . ."

"Mr. Turnbull!"

They both turned toward the French door, where Kiku stood wringing her apron. One look at the disturbed expression on her normally placid face brought Rand to his feet, his chair raking harshly over the paving stones.

"Mr. Turnbull, I think you better come see," Kiku said, vanishing back into the cottage.

Rand shot a quizzical look at Alyse and hurried after the anxious housekeeper. Alyse caught up with him before he reached the door.

They found Kiku waiting near the piano in the living room, holding Tommy's hand. The boy was still clad in wet swim trunks, but now he looked frightened. *No!* Alyse corrected herself. *He looks guilty.*

"I didn't mean to bother your stuff, Uncle Rand," Tommy blurted, tears welling in his eyes. "I just saw a lump in the mat and lifted it up. I didn't touch anything. I promise!"

"Whoa, there, trooper," Rand said in a calming tone. He went down onto one knee and placed a hand gently on the back of Tommy's neck. "Settle down and tell me what's happened."

Tommy opened his mouth. Nothing came out.

His breath hitched in his narrow chest, apparently rendering him incapable of speech.

"The safe, Mr. Turnbull," Kiku said softly as she stroked Tommy's damp head.

Rand's attention snapped down to their feet. Alyse noticed a slight bulge in the section of woven rice straw mat—the same section, she realized, that covered the floor safe. He clawed up the edge of the mat and flung the entire section back, uncovering a wooden panel that no longer lay quite flush with the rest of the floor. Alyse knelt next to him, one arm around Tommy's waist, as Rand lifted away the portion of false flooring to reveal the vault.

"Maybe you didn't get the panel fitted down properly when you finished with the safe last night," Alyse said.

"Not a chance." He ran his hand along the underside of the board. "It dropped right in. I always double-check the corners."

A sliver of ice wormed its way up Alyse's spine as she recalled the muted sound of footsteps she had heard in the hallway last night.

"Maybe you'd better open the safe and make sure the Tokugawa box is okay," she suggested.

"It's fine," Rand replied curtly.

Alyse looked at him sharply. His jaw muscles bunched. She couldn't be sure, but he seemed to have paled slightly.

"Rand," she said evenly, her voice changing tone, becoming less uncertain, more uncompromising. "I think you'd better open it."

His lips tightened. Rand stared down at the

combination lock, as if debating with himself. Finally, he leaned down and worked the mechanism with angry, nimble jerks to the left and right, then hauled open the heavy fireproof door.

Alyse gasped. The safe was empty!

"I didn't take anything!" Tommy choked.

"Of course, you didn't, sweetie," Alyse said, pulling him to her.

Rand reached out automatically and patted Tommy's bare leg reassuringly without looking at him. The four of them remained in a frozen tableau for a moment, gazing down into the empty steel safe. Finally, without a word, Rand slammed the door shut, spun the combination lock, and fitted the floor panel and woven mat carefully back into place.

"I locked every door and window in this house last night," Alyse said flatly.

"The telephone is working this morning. I will go call the police," Kiku volunteered.

"*No.*" Rand sliced a hand through the air for emphasis, making it clear that he would brook no objections from anyone.

He rose slowly and scowled. Then, as if only now realizing that he was the focal point of their collective stare, Rand pawed a hand through his hair and stalked out of the living room to the lanai.

"Is Uncle Rand mad at me?" Tommy whispered.

Alyse glanced up at Kiku, who was frowning confusedly at the French door through which Rand had just exited.

"Absolutely not, Tommy," Alyse answered. "He's just upset. In fact, we're all very happy that you noticed the lump in the floor mat."

The boy looked from Alyse to Kiku to the French door. "You don't *look* happy," he said doubtfully.

Alyse planted an emphatic kiss on his furrowed forehead. "Well, appearances can be deceiving, sweetheart," she said, thinking *how right you are*. "Why don't you go change into dry clothes while I have a little talk with Rand?"

She glanced up at Kiku. Still frowning, the diminutive housekeeper nodded agreement with Alyse and gently herded Tommy toward the bedroom hallway. When they were gone, Alyse got slowly to her feet. Her movements had become sluggish, as if she were struggling up out of cold, clinging quicksand.

Rand paced the far edge of the lanai, feeling like a caged animal. The house had been locked up tighter than a drum last night. He had made doubly sure of that after Alyse went to bed. So, whoever she had heard skulking around in the hallway at 3 A.M. — undoubtedly the same person who had tried to tamper with the safe — had to have been a professional. Someone who could get inside without awakening the whole house.

Damnation! He had known since yesterday that he was dealing with much more than just Mrs. Fielding's sleazy detective. But he had been left with the impression that the situation was under control. Nothing had prepared him for anything like this.

He cursed again under his breath and rubbed his forehead hard with the fingers of both hands, trying to think. The location of his floor safe was no secret. Over the years, any number of visitors might have seen him access it. He used the vault mostly as fireproof, waterproof protection for important papers when he was working at the cottage. For security against theft, he relied on bank safety deposit boxes.

That was probably why he'd had second and third thoughts about locking the Tokugawa box in the safe overnight. After Alyse turned in, he had done more than just recheck the windows and doors. He had gone back to the safe, hauled out the box, and found another hidey-hole for the thing. But if he'd had any idea the cottage would be broken into a second time in the same night, he would have slept with the blasted antique.

A chair scraped on the paving stones behind him. Rand tensed, but gave himself plenty of time to get his mind focused on the here-and-now before turning.

He found Alyse seated at the table watching him. She looked pale and drawn. That was perfectly understandable under the circumstances. What hurt was knowing that, for the time being, there wasn't a damned thing he could do about it.

"I guess it's over, isn't it, Rand?" she asked.

"What's over?"

"My reason for staying. Now that the tea box

is gone, I might as well head back to New York."

He resisted a powerful urge to rush toward Alyse. He sensed that if he crowded her—if he pushed too hard in a desperate attempt to hang on—she would slip away like an evaporating dream. Instead, Rand instinctively fell back onto what he knew best, and that was his contract negotiating skills.

Whether in a boardroom or a courtroom, he had one proven rule of thumb: never employ a frontal attack on the other party's position when a flanking action is available.

"You'll break Tommy's heart if you don't stay for the luau tonight," he said.

Alyse lowered her face into her hands. Rand relaxed slightly. He could almost hear her defensive ramparts crashing down.

"Okay," she sighed wearily, the word muffled by her hands.

The quick capitulation surprised him. He hadn't expected it to be that easy. Part of him hadn't *wanted* it to be—the part that feared Alyse would have reacted quite differently had she known it was Rand's own heart that was in danger of being broken. He would have felt guilty about using Tommy as a tactical weapon if he hadn't been so concerned for Alyse's safety.

"Hey, there," he murmured tenderly.

Alyse looked up, aware of the sudden change in Rand's tone. He had moved closer, his back to the sun. For a moment, he seemed to be the sun— brilliant angles of light and shadow.

She felt cornered. She needed to distance herself from Rand, to escape his glare so she could see him for what he was—for *whatever* he was. New York might be far enough. If not, then the dragonfly pendant had brought her the means to keep right on going to London or Paris or Outer Mongolia, if that's what it would take to get both feet back on solid ground. But Tommy made all of that out of the question.

Alyse remembered how she had felt when she came across the little boy playing all alone on the beach. She hadn't been able to leave him there until she knew for sure just what was going on in his badly bruised heart and mind.

She clenched her fists in her lap, knowing that she couldn't leave Tommy now—not until she found out once and for all what kind of man Rand was.

"Come on, Alyse," Rand said quietly. "Go change into that terrific little scrap you call a bathing suit and we'll take a quick swim before the day gets out of hand."

"The day is already out of hand. And I'm in way over my head."

He sucked his lips in between his teeth and looked down at his feet. "It means nothing that I love you?" he asked so softly that she could barely hear.

"It means everything," Alyse said with feeling. "But it doesn't fix anything."

"Fix?" Rand spread his hands. "What's broken?"

"Call it faith."

"This conversation is turning into a riddle,

Alyse. Can't you just tell me straight out what has you bugged?"

"Let's see," she said, unable to keep the edge out of her voice. "Where shall I begin? How about if *you* tell *me* why you seem so willing to let a thief get away with stealing the Tokugawa box, when you wouldn't even consider selling it to me for *any* price?"

When Rand didn't answer right away, Alyse rose. Fear and frustration had formed an amalgam of anger that threatened to spiral out of control.

"Why haven't you run to the nearest phone to call the police?" she demanded, wanting to pound her fists into his chest. "Why?"

"I don't want to have a police cruiser parked in the front yard," Rand said finally. "That would make too nice a picture for Elaine Fielding's detective to send off to her. It wouldn't make any difference why the cops were here. She'd manage to twist it around into the image she's trying to paint of me as an unfit guardian for Tommy."

Alyse took a step back from him, her breath coming out in a rush. "Is that the best closing argument you can come up with, counselor?" she retorted coldly.

"What do you mean?"

"You don't want a police car to show up here, supposedly because of how it would look to Mrs. Fielding's detective," she said. "But you're suddenly quite comfortable with the idea of my slipping into that 'terrific little scrap that I call a bathing suit' so we can go for a swim right under the jerk's nose!"

She pointed out past the beach, to the orange-and-red catamaran that had sailed into view just as she came out onto the lanai. Alyse studied Rand's face as he eyed the familiar boat. She found no sign of the guarded expression that she had come to associate with the appearance of the colorful craft.

Instead, Rand shifted his gaze to the middle distance, his lips hardening. An overwhelming ache rose in Alyse's chest as she waited for him to say something—anything—that would help dispel the suffocating blanket of suspicion that his silence had cast over her.

She wanted to trust Rand. She didn't want to believe that he was lying to her. But he was giving her no choice.

"I'll go to the luau this evening, Rand," she said in a strained voice. "But I'll be staying in Lahaina tonight, I don't care if I have to sleep on a park bench. And I'm leaving for home first thing in the morning."

As Alyse turned and walked back into the house, a terrible pain shot through her. She had an even more cruel thought—that wicked old Elaine Fielding just might be right about Rand.

A tense, sickroom hush settled over the cottage for the remainder of the morning. Alyse tried to call Conrad Brace to report that her quest for the tea box had ended in disaster. But all she got was his answering machine at the gallery.

Depressed, she retreated to Rand's room, where

she lay on the bed for over an hour simply marking time. She listened to Kiku teaching Tommy how to play some convoluted Japanese stick game in the shaded side yard outside the shuttered window. Just before noon, she got up and padded silently back down the hallway toward the kitchen in her bare feet. She was determined to take one more shot at reaching Conrad.

She had just reached the kitchen door when she heard a soft thump. Alyse halted, suddenly alert. Then it occurred to her that she hadn't stumbled onto yet another burglar. Kiku and Tommy were outside, but Rand undoubtedly was not.

She marched on into the kitchen, and found Rand bent over a large metal produce bin in the adjoining pantry, his back to her. Her mouth was already forming his name, when she suddenly clamped her jaw shut.

He clearly hadn't noticed her silent approach from behind. Something about the quiet, stealthy way he removed the lid from the bin and set it aside made her want to keep it that way, just for the moment. She quickly backtracked two paces and ducked behind the door frame to watch.

Rand lifted out two five-pound mesh bags of citrus fruits, then bent almost double to reach down to the bottom of the metal container. His back muscles knotted as he straightened with effort, cradling a heavy object wrapped in a large toucan-print beach towel. He carefully lowered the object to the floor.

While hefting the citrus fruits back into the bin, he snagged one of the mesh bags on the towel, partially uncovering the top of the object beneath. Alyse stared wide-eyed at a golden dragon's tail emblazoned on bright vermillion.

The Tokugawa tea box!

Stunned, Alyse backed silently away from the door, her eyes frozen in shock. No wonder Rand had refused to call the police about last night's break-ins. The antique hadn't been stolen from the safe. But why hadn't he told her? Dear God, what was Rand up to?

She turned and ran cat-footed back to the bedroom, her heart pounding. She stood there in the middle of the floor, clenching and unclenching her fists. Alyse was convinced that she should be taking some drastic and immediate action. But why? Toward what end?

After all, Rand hadn't actually done anything— at least, nothing illegal. He had simply taken a box that he already owned and stashed it at the bottom of a pantry bin.

"Simply, my foot!" Alyse whispered. There had been nothing simple about Rand Turnbull since the day she had met him.

Tommy suddenly squealed outside the shuttered window. He uttered a high, shrill note of excitement that continued around the house and in through the lanai door, intensifying in volume as it approached down the hallway. He came barrelling through her door out of breath.

"Look what Kiku gave me!" he cried and held out a chunk of white coral.

Managing a smile, Alyse sat down on the end of the bed to give his prize a dutiful inspection.

Kiku had obviously put in a lot of effort to re-build Tommy's frame of mind following the incident over the safe, earlier. Alyse didn't want to undermine that.

"Why, look," she said appreciatively as she fingered the coral's tall, startlingly white peaks, "it looks like a sailing ship."

"Wow—yeah!" Tommy gave her a suddenly shy look. "We could share. Would you like to keep it until you go home tomorrow?"

Alyse cleared her throat, touched by the child's generosity. She didn't know how to tell him that she wouldn't be coming back to the cottage after the luau that evening.

"I'll tell you what," she said finally, "let's put it right over here on this wicker table by the window."

When the coral was properly centered on the table, she returned to the bed and patted the coverlet. "Come sit here for a little while, and we'll look at our clipper ship together."

Tommy grinned and plopped onto the mattress next to her. He settled into the crook of her arm with a contented sigh.

"Shouldn't you take a nap after lunch, so you'll be rested for the luau?" asked Alyse. She was amazed at how easily her mothering instincts surfaced when she was around Tommy.

He sighed again and nodded. "I'm kinda tired. Uncle Rand snored again last night."

"He kept you awake, huh?" Alyse patted his cheek sympathetically.

"Well, he quits snoring if you sorta poke him a

little. Except if you punch him too hard, he wakes up and tickles you."

She raised an eyebrow. "I see. That's what happened last night?"

"After."

"After what?"

"After Uncle Rand quit talking to that man and came to bed."

Alyse looked down at the top of Tommy's head. "What man, sweetheart?"

"I didn't see him. But my window was open. I could hear them whispering outside." Tommy squirmed around sideways, still looking at the chunk of white coral on the table, and laid his head on Alyse's lap. "I heard Uncle Rand call him Eddie."

Eddie! Alyse clamped her eyes shut. She tried to shut out a sudden flurry of images, all hammering at her with the same question. How could she have done it all over again? How could she have allowed herself to twice fall in love with the wrong man?

Tommy yawned, and she automatically reached down to stroke his fine fair hair, her mind racing like a runaway flywheel.

"Sweetheart," she said in a tight voice, "do you know what time you heard them?"

Tommy yawned again. "Uh-huh. I looked at the clock. The big hand and the little hand were all bunched up at the top."

Alyse frowned. Rand had held a whispered meeting with Eddie—Eddie Komake?—at midnight. But that still didn't account for the foot-

217

steps in the hallway that she had heard some three hours later.

She had more questions, but the gentle inquisition was foiled by a six-year-old's physical limitations. With a faint sigh, Tommy fell asleep. Alyse sat stroking his head, envying his escape — and fearing for his innocent vulnerability. How could she possibly leave this boy in the hands of a frightening unknown?

Alyse detected movement in the doorway from the corner of her eye and turned her head. Kiku stood in the hallway, a finger pressed to her smiling lips. After a moment, she silently crept away.

Later, when Tommy was too soundly asleep to be disturbed, Alyse slipped a pillow under his head and covered him with a corner of the bedspread. With a parting kiss on his smooth cheek, she stole quietly out of the room.

She could hear Kiku rattling around in the kitchen preparing a late lunch. The very thought of food made Alyse's stomach shudder. She hurried out onto the lanai, needing to be alone for a while. Fearing that Rand would appear, and that she was in no condition to carry on a conversation with him as though nothing were amiss, she kept on going down the beach path. She headed toward a grove of palm trees and banana plants.

A brisk sea breeze rustled through the palm fronds. Alyse climbed a small knoll into the cool shade. Lush banana leaves shielded her from the view of the cottage. She sat with her arms wrapped around her knees and forced herself to think days, weeks, even months ahead.

She would locate her gallery in San Diego, or perhaps Phoenix—definitely not San Francisco. She would specialize in European or Eastern Mediterranean antiquities—steering clear of things Oriental. If nothing else, falling in love with Rand Turnbull had defined her taboos.

Alyse straightened her back, her grip loosening on her knees as she squinted into the brilliant afternoon reflections off the water. The red-and-orange catamaran was back, moving parallel to the beach from left to right, skimming nimbly across the surface of the waves. Just as it passed her, the cat suddenly veered toward shore and beached itself on the wet sand.

The pilot was hidden for a moment behind the flapping sail. When he stepped off the canvas deck platform onto the near float, Alyse sucked in her breath. Eddie Komake bounded onto the sand, his coppery skin aglow in the bright tropical sunlight.

He stood on the beach, looking back toward the Turnbull cottage, as if waiting. Within five minutes, Rand came trudging along. He was carrying a large rectangular object swathed in a familiar toucan-pattern towel.

Alyse sat perfectly still and watched as he handed the tea box over to Komake. Then, she slowly lowered her forehead to her knees, her fists white-knuckled, shivering with pent-up fury.

What was going on? Having been thwarted in his conspiracy to steal the dragonfly pendant, had Komake now roped Rand into some kind of insurance scam involving the Tokugawa box?

219

That sort of thing went on all the time. Owners collected theft insurance on a supposedly stolen object, then turned around and sold it on the black market to an unscrupulous art collector. But why in this case?

Rand was successful and wealthy in his own right. Why would he risk sacrificing his reputation, his beloved brother's child, and the woman he supposedly loved — all for money that he couldn't possibly need? *Why?*

Chapter Twelve

Alyse awoke to a delicate, insistent tapping sensation on her arm. She opened one eye and peered straight into Kiku's round, smiling face.

"I guess I dozed off," Alyse said apologetically. She sat up and looked around, her senses still fuzzy with sleep.

"Yes," Kiku agreed. "You dozed off three hours ago. Mr. Turnbull says you will sleep right through the luau if someone doesn't go wake you. Then he looked at me very hard."

The tiny housekeeper laughed musically and headed for the door. "It's time for all of us to put on our party clothes and get happy," she said.

"You're going, too?"

"Yes. Mr. Turnbull says nobody stays home tonight." Kiku left, closing the door behind her.

Alyse crawled off the side of the bed and padded to the closet. Her heart wasn't in it, but she had already made up her mind. She would go to the blasted luau *and* wear the necklace containing the jeweled dragonfly, come hell or high water.

By this time tomorrow, she would be well on her way back to New York, having fulfilled her duties to the Japanese hunters of the dragonfly. Concentrating on that objective to the exclusion of all else was the only way she could keep her emotional distance from Rand and make it through the coming ordeal of the luau.

She dressed in her new orange-and-white muumuu. The gaudy sand dollar looked more at home with the bright, flowing Hawaiian dress than it had with the outfit Alyse had worn to dinner last evening. She found a fresh orchid on top of the dresser, apparently left there for her by Kiku. Brushing her tawny hair up over one ear, Alyse pinned it back with the orchid, and then whirled before the mirror.

Not bad. From the looks of her, Alyse judged, forcing a smile, nobody would ever know she was slowly bleeding to death from a broken heart.

The contingent from the Turnbull cottage made quite a festive picture as they drove up the coast to the luau site. Rand had distributed enormous leis as they left the house. Alyse noticed that hers matched the orchid in her hair.

She also noticed that the lei completely hid the tawdry sand dollar. She couldn't help wondering if, in her case, that wasn't the reasoning behind Rand's floral largess.

With what struck Alyse as strained high spirits, Rand claimed he was the tamest member of the colorful flock, in his tropical white shirt and royal blue slacks. In the back seat, Tommy sported a gaudy Hawaiian shirt over hot-pink shorts. Next to him, Kiku sat primly in a crisp blue-and-green kimono tied with a broad green silk obi.

A glorious flaming sunset splashed the western

horizon as Rand pulled off the highway into a parking lot. A dozen or so cars and a big catering van were already parked at the far end of the lot. He turned in next to a new black Land Rover and killed the motor.

Alyse caught Kiku eyeing the flower in her hair as they started to get out, and leaned over the back of the seat to thank her for leaving it on the dresser.

"Oh, but it wasn't me," Kiku whispered in a conspiratorial manner. "Mr. Turnbull picked it specially for you."

Alyse glanced around at Rand, but he was already standing outside the car. She sank back in the seat, fingering the orchid. He might have wanted to camouflage the tawdry necklace with the lei, but that hardly explained the single blossom. She got out, nonplussed.

"We're a little early," Rand said. "I see that my new clients haven't arrived yet."

"How can you tell?" Alyse asked.

Rand waved a hand, taking in the entire parking lot. "No limousines."

"Where's the party?" Tommy inquired, bouncing around the car.

"Follow the torches—and your nose." Rand pointed toward a double row of torches burning on either side of a path leading away from the parking lot through a stand of towering coconut palms. The tantalizing aromas of a roasting pit drifted to them on the shifting evening breeze.

Tommy went skipping off down the path with Kiku in hot pursuit. Her wooden soled sandals clacked rapidly on the carefully raked ground.

Alyse started to hurry after them, seeking safety in numbers, but Rand grabbed her arm and held her back.

Her skin burned where he touched her bare flesh. She walked along stiffly at his side, not daring to look at him. Her hand pressed the gaudy necklace firmly against her chest beneath the lei as a stern reminder of her pledge to herself.

The band had come early, as well. Alyse could hear them tuning their instruments at the luau site up ahead. As Rand guided her along the winding path, the band drifted into one of the corny, albeit seductively haunting island melodies to which Alyse was becoming addicted.

They climbed a low rise through the palms and looked down a slope of greensward into a large, torch-lit clearing shaped like a natural amphitheater. Near the center, the coals of a roasting pit glowed beneath layers of cut palm fronds. Two long tables bracketed the pit, laden with a staggering array of elaborately arranged island fruits and delicacies. These were tended by a small army of waiters decked out in floral leis and ornate Hawaiian headbands and loincloths.

A small wooden stage had been set up on the far side, with spotlights discreetly suspended from the surrounding palms, which were strung with colorful Japanese lanterns. Through a broad cleft in the hillside, Alyse could make out the nearby Pacific Ocean. It shimmered like molten lava beneath the last rays of the sunset.

"Incredible," Alyse murmured, barely aware that she had spoken.

"That's what I thought the first time I set eyes on you," Rand said.

His fingers traced a feathery stroke down the inside of her upper arm, sending a burst of heat in the opposite direction. Alyse quivered, stunned by her own response. With it came the searing recognition that Rand already owned a part of her that she could never get back. Tearing herself away, she started to run down the path toward the clearing.

Rand caught up with her before she had gone three paces, and pulled her up short. "I have to talk to you."

"I'd rather not."

Alyse strained against his iron grasp. He tightened his grip still more and bent so his face was close to hers.

"Look, love of my life," he said in a low, firm voice. "These clients mean a lot to me. This entire evening does. But I happen to know it means a hell of a lot more to you. So would you give me just ten minutes of your time, *please?*"

He emphasized the last word with a quick jerk of her arm, and then released her.

Alyse stared up at him, suddenly bewildered. Her fight-or-flight instincts seemed to have locked up completely. She didn't know what to do. When Rand indicated that he wanted her to follow a narrower side path leading along the wooded rim of the clearing, she paused, then hesitantly followed his directions.

They moved deep into the shadows of a palm grove, beyond the lights from the cup-shaped clearing below. The band's tempo had changed. It had taken on the more frenzied rhythm of Tahitian drums, as if trying to match the pace of her triphammering heart. Alyse stopped, her back to a tree trunk, unwilling to go farther.

"What is it, Rand?"

He propped a foot on a large flat rock five feet away, as if sensing that she needed space. Rand toyed pensively with his car keys, twirling the soup bone scrimshaw fob Alyse had given him.

"There are some things you have a right to know," he said, then shook his head in apparent irritation at himself. "Things you *need* to know."

"Oh?"

Rand pocketed the key ring and rubbed his hands together. "I don't quite know where to begin."

"Let me help you out then." Alyse dug her fingernails into the tree trunk behind her as if she were about to slip off the face of the earth. "What kind of fancy footwork are you and Eddie Komake planning for the Tokugawa box?"

His foot came down off the rock. Rand stared at her in surprise.

"I saw you give it to him this afternoon, after you dug it out of the bin in the pantry."

Rand walked away a few paces, then turned and faced her. Alyse could see the shock on his face even in the rapidly fading twilight. As angry and hurt as she was, it still gave her no satisfaction.

"Damn! I thought I was being more careful than that," he said.

"You're a first class lawyer, Rand. But when it comes to cloak-and-dagger work, you're a washout."

"I guess so." He raked a hand through his hair. Then, to her astonishment, he laughed. "Come to think of it, Eddie said practically the same thing."

"I'm sorry, Rand. I don't see the humor in that."

"Frankly, neither do I." He moved closer, leaning a hand against a neighboring tree. "Okay, let me begin by telling you something you *don't* know."

"You have a lot of material to choose from."

"Komake is a hell of a singer — for a U.S. Customs Service undercover agent." Rand nodded when her jaw dropped open. "It seems he's a specialist in Far Eastern history and art. He's been undercover here on the islands for over two years now, tracking a theft ring that's been hitting museums and private Oriental artifact collections from Tokyo to Singapore."

He rubbed a hand down his face. "Here I've had my eye out for Mrs. Fielding's detective skulking around in his ratty beige sport coat — and Komake comes along and does his spying right out in the open."

"I don't believe it!" Alyse hung onto the tree trunk for dear life, her mind reeling.

"Neither did I until he showed up at the back door of the cottage, Thursday night, and shoved some pretty convincing identification in my face."

"Thursday night?"

"Right. Eddie is annoyingly partial to midnight meetings of the clandestine sort."

"You've known about him since Thursday, and you didn't say anything?" Alyse let go of the tree.

Rand held up both hands defensively. "There are

227

two reasons I didn't mention it. First, when he initially contacted me, Eddie laid down a pretty convincing snow job. He claimed he was doing routine undercover work, spot-checking to make sure U.S. import/export licensing rules weren't being violated. He inspected the tea box—including that false bottom gizmo—and then said there was nothing amiss, so there would be no further investigation."

He shook his head. "God only knows why I believed him. I guess I was too busy trying to reconcile myself to the fact that he was an undercover agent. That seemed so out of character."

"I know the feeling." Alyse thought back on all the times she had suspected Komake of villainy, and a part of her felt like a complete idiot. The other part still hadn't quite worked itself around to believing it was wrong.

"I finally dug myself out of the snow yesterday, and threatened Eddie with dismemberment if he didn't come clean," Rand went on. "He did—reluctantly. But I had to give my word that I would keep a lid on it."

He stepped closer and reached under her lei to cup the sand dollar in his hand. "The same way you gave your word to the Japanese consulate, Wednesday morning, when you reported finding the stolen dragonfly pendant."

Alyse suddenly felt weak. "You knew?"

"Just since yesterday. According to Eddie, the Customs Service has been cooperating with a team of Japanese investigators trying to crack the case. They had unconfirmed information that the pendant would be smuggled into the United States inside the Tokugawa box."

"I think I need to sit down," she said, astounded that the consulate official had kept her in the dark about the pendant's connection with the box. She'd had to find that out on her own.

Rand helped her over to the rock. There wasn't room for both of them to sit. So he knelt in front of Alyse and held her hand while he explained the rest.

"The box was closely followed from the moment it entered the country," Rand said. "Once its existence became known, Conrad Brace's extraordinary efforts to obtain the antique earned him a red flag in Eddie's case file."

"Conrad?"

"Kind of makes you stop and think, doesn't it?" Rand smiled ruefully. "Then, in steps one Randall Walton Turnbull, attorney at law, who proceeds to throw a large wrench into the works."

"You bought the tea box."

"Right out of left field." He nodded. "When you came scrambling after me, offering any price I cared to name for the thing, Eddie just naturally figured you were part of the conspiracy and gave you a red flag, too."

"What conspiracy?" Alyse demanded. "Surely, no one actually believes Conrad Brace has anything to do with an international theft ring!"

Rand just looked at her, and Alyse suddenly fell silent. She turned her face away, a crushing sense of guilt bringing hot tears to her eyes.

"What a stupid thing to say," she whispered,

choking on the words. "I believed worse about you."

He pressed the heel of his hand against her jaw, turning Alyse toward him. She closed her eyes, unable to look at him.

"I'm so sorry," she said.

Rand's lips covered hers tenderly, drawing a muffled sob from her throat. The kiss deepened and warmed dizzyingly. Then he drew back, still cradling her head in his hands, his face so close that Alyse could feel his breath on her tear-dampened cheeks.

"Don't you *ever* tell me you're sorry again," he said hoarsely.

"But I should have trusted you!"

"Stop it! Trust isn't a given, except among naive Pollyannas. Trust has to be earned—and God knows, you've had plenty of reason to wonder about me, these past few days. Especially after last night."

He took out a handkerchief and helped Alyse dry her eyes. She felt lightheaded with relief, sitting there amid the rubble of her exploded misconceptions.

"I still don't understand," she said. "I was told by the Japanese consulate official that I would be under surveillance the entire time I had the dragonfly. But I haven't seen anybody watching me."

Rand rubbed a knuckle lightly against the tip of her nose. "It's been there, right under your nose. Eddie Komake."

"No." Alyse stared at him. Then she laughed. "But of course! He was tagging around after me, waiting to nab my accomplice."

"Well, the authorities had it figured two ways. Either you were planning to hand it off to someone else, or you really were going to follow through and collect the humongous reward. It wasn't until last night's break-ins that they finally started getting the news that you weren't trying to pull a fast one when you called the Japanese consulate." .

"Then Eddie Komake wasn't the person who broke into the cottage while we were gone?" she asked, struggling to rearrange the players in her mind.

"No." Rand smiled tightly. "He said after you caught him skulking around in your hotel room on Oahu, he would throw in the towel and go to work sacking groceries for a living before he'd try breaking in on you again."

Alyse was too overwhelmed to feel surprise any longer. Instead, she asked, "What was he after?"

"Evidence. You see, at that point, he didn't know the dragonfly was inside that — thing," he said, tapping the sand dollar. "Eddie was just hoping to stumble onto some proof that you were tied into the theft."

Alyse rubbed her temples. "I have to say, I'm having a little trouble swallowing all this at once."

"So did I, until I called a former client in Washington, D.C. and had him do some checking," Rand said. "Sure enough, Eddie's for real."

"I'm glad you didn't just take his word for it."

"By the way, when I finally persuaded Komake to give me the big picture, he read me a haiku and asked if I'd ever heard of it." Rand worked his finger into Alyse's hair, pressed his lips to her fore-head, and whispered, "It was the same haiku you recited to me after we made love."

"You told him that?" Alyse asked, grateful that darkness had fallen so Rand couldn't see the blush that she felt surging up into her face.

"No way!" He nuzzled her neck. "Not about the lovemaking, anyway. That was hardly any of his business. But I did mention that you had quoted the poem. Eddie came unglued. He knew Tommy had given you the pendant, and figured he must have forked over the haiku as well."

"He had."

"Eddie said my 'damned good-hearted nephew' was giving away the imperial treasures *and* his case, one piece at a time."

"Well, I'm afraid I have some seriously bad news for Eddie."

Alyse told Rand about how she had left the poem at the bottom of the dresser drawer last night, only to find that it was missing when they re-turned from dinner in Lahaina.

Rand whisper-whistled through his teeth. "Ed-die's going to love that bit of news."

"Whoever broke in the first time," she said, thinking out loud, "must have been the same per-son who returned later and tried to tamper with your safe."

"Not knowing that I'd already moved the Toku-gawa box elsewhere," Rand added. "When I called Eddie this morning and told him about that second break-in, he suggested that I give him the box for safekeeping until tonight's luau. It's part of his case now. He said if he allowed the box to slip through his hands, he'd have to go to his Japanese counterpart and take instructions on how to commit *hara kiri*."

"He's going to wish he had taken possession of the haiku earlier, too." Alyse took Rand's hand. "By the way, Tommy's having second thoughts about whether he should have played finders-keepers with the things he took from the hidden compartment in the box. I told him I'd talk to you about it."

Rand squeezed her fingers. "His conscience is coming back. That's encouraging. I owe *you* that — among many other things."

He kissed her again, and Alyse slid her arms around his neck. Down in the clearing, the band changed rhythm again, drifting into the languid melody of a traditional Hawaiian song of welcome.

Rand groaned. "I think my guests are arriving."

"That sounds like a complaint."

"It is." He glanced up toward the crown of the palm tree under which they were sitting. "Some people get amorous under mistletoe. For me, I guess it's coconuts."

Alyse smiled, kissed his earlobe, and rose. She smoothed her muumuu, and he helped her repin the orchid in her hair. They reluctantly started back toward the main path, their arms around each other.

"There's one last thing you ought to know, Alyse." Rand lowered his voice as they approached a group of colorfully attired revellers making their way toward the clearing from the parking lot.

"Conrad Brace is on the islands."

"What?"

The clearing was filling rapidly with guests. Rand spotted his new clients — three elderly Japanese gentlemen and their American partner, Lyle Eason — receiving lavish orchid leis from the luau's official greeting party of grass-skirted dancers.

He took Alyse's hand and headed around the glowing pit, where a roast pig turned slowly on an iron spit. The Japanese closed ranks and smiled when they saw Rand coming. He couldn't help a sense of undeserved pride when their almost ceremonially polite expressions crumbled into broad grins as their collective gaze shifted to Alyse.

"Alyse, my sweet, I'm glad you didn't wear that extraordinary little dress you had on last night," Rand said under his breath, drawing her hand into the crook of his arm. "I'd have to beat those distinguished old men off you with a stick."

Alyse looked up at Rand, startled from her anxious preoccupation with the news that her employer was on the islands. He winked, trying to conceal his own concern, which had only slightly diminished now that the luau was underway. He didn't put much faith in the schooling instinct when it came to security measures.

When they reached the foursome, Rand quickly shook hands all around. He ended with stout, square-jawed Lyle Eason, stoically subjecting himself to the older man's two-fisted, knuckle-popping grip. As he introduced Alyse to the real estate investment group, Rand noticed with amusement that she received the deeper bow from the three Japanese. The latter managed to appear serenely dignified in their gaudy print shirts, floral leis, and sandals.

"*Konbanwa*," said the youngest of Rand's Tokyo clients, a rail-thin seventy-year-old with brush-cut white hair.

"*Dozo yoroshiku*," Alyse replied softly, continuing in a brief flurry of Japanese that expressed her delight in meeting such eminent guests. Rand was more than a little impressed.

The elderly businessmen uttered a grunt of pleasant surprise. "How remarkable, Miss Marlowe," said their septuagenarian spokesman. "You have a perfect Nipponese accent."

"All credit goes to my tutor," Alyse smiled.

"Lyle, you should hire Miss Marlowe's instructor," said the old man, revealing an astonishingly pronounced Boston accent of his own. "After all these years, you still speak Japanese like a New York cabby."

The other two Japanese laughed heartily. So did Rand until Eason deftly nudged him and neatly separated Alyse from his arm.

"You say you're with the Brace Gallery in New York?" Eason asked, wiping a hand back over his thinning hair.

"Yes, so was my husband. In fact, Rob was on a buying trip to Japan for the gallery when he died six months ago."

"I'm sorry to hear that. So sad," Eason murmured, his steel-blue eyes boldly roaming over

Alyse. "I'm sure he must have been a fine young man."

Alyse ducked her head, accepting Eason's vision of her husband without comment. But Rand was beginning to read volumes into her silences. She wasn't exactly charmed by the brassy Texan, and Rand didn't blame her. In sharp contrast with his Japanese partners, Eason sometimes had the social grace of a falling rock.

"I believe you're being paged, Alyse." Rand pointed toward the roasting pit, eager to provide her with an easy out.

Tommy stood on the far side of the pit, jumping up and down and semaphoring his arms at them. When Alyse saw him, she waved back, then shot a grateful look at Rand before excusing herself from his clients.

"What an exquisite young woman," said the youngest Japanese, folding his hands behind him as they watched Alyse hurry off through the crowd.

"Hai," Rand agreed quietly, nodding.

When he turned back to his guests, Rand realized Lyle Eason had wandered off without so much as a go-to-hell to anyone. The trio of wizened Japanese investors stood avidly eyeing the wildly gyrating hips of a troupe of Tahitian dancers. They looked like three bespectacled entomologists who had stumbled onto a flock of exotic and heretofore undiscovered butterflies.

Rand signaled a nearby waiter, who made a pass with a tray of drinks served in coconut shells. When the Tahitians moved on, soon to be replaced by the more sedately sensual movements of five

Hawaiian dancers, Rand offered a measured bow to the youngest Japanese investor, drawing his attention.

"There has been some small difficulty with the Tokugawa box," Rand said. "If you wish, I could provide security for it after the presentation ceremony this evening."

The old man looked up at Rand, his lidless eyes blank. "Forgive my ignorance, Mr. Turnbull." He shrugged, clearly confused.

"Lyle didn't tell you?" Rand frowned, a little confused himself by now. "I've acquired the box that you requested . . ."

"Requested?" the old man interrupted sharply.

"Yes. Lyle Eason was very specific about the gift you desired."

The old man drew himself up straighter. "I dare say, Mr. Turnbull, we would hardly be so arrogant as to request a specific gift—or *any* gift, for that matter."

Rand looked dumbfounded. "My apologies."

"Quite unnecessary." The old man raised a hand, smiling agreeably, cutting him off. "I'm sure it was a simple misunderstanding."

"I'm sure," Rand murmured with a puzzled frown.

As soon as he could extricate himself from his guests for a few minutes, Rand went off in search of Eddie Komake, wondering what in heaven's name was going on.

Making her way toward the roasting pit, Alyse

warned herself that her imagination was getting the best of her — she couldn't really feel Lyle Eason's roving eyes still undressing her from behind. That was stupid. Just because Eason had known Rob was no reason to label him as a jerk. She wasn't being any fairer to Eason than she had been to Eddie Komake.

Tommy ran around the glowing pit to meet her. His wide-eyed excitement provided a welcome distraction.

"Kiku says she knows a real spooky place we can walk to," he said, grabbing one of her hands. "Will you go with us?"

"Sounds too good to pass up." Alyse let him lead her through the crowd to where Kiku waited on the far side of the clearing. "Where are we off to, Kiku? A haunted house?"

The diminutive housekeeper laughed softly and shook her head. "I know of a *heiau* nearby — one of many on the islands."

"It's an ancient burial ground!" Tommy said.

"An old Hawaiian temple," Kiku corrected, producing a small flashlight. She turned and led the way up a steep, narrow path.

The wide beam of the flashlight illuminated a tangle of lush vegetation on either side of the path as they passed through a fern dell. Enormous fronds of shoulder-high ferns intermingled with split banana leaves and flowering tropical shrubs.

They were halfway to the top of the rim surrounding the clearing, when they heard the sound of hurried footsteps approaching from above. Kiku raised the beam of her flashlight.

Seconds later, Eddie Komake came into view. He seemed as surprised to see them as they were to come across him. He did a stutter-step, then grinned and continued toward them.

"I'll be singing in about an hour," he said, easing past them on the narrow path. "You'd better make your escape while you can."

Alyse watched Komake go bounding on down the slope toward the clearing. If Rand hadn't told her that the Hawaiian was an undercover agent for the U.S. Customs Service, she would have been alarmed at yet another supposedly chance encounter with Komake. As it was, she felt only a vague uneasiness.

When she turned back around, Alyse discovered that Kiku and Tommy had continued along the path. She had to run to catch up.

At the top of the rim, the path turned sharply to the left before opening onto a flat shelf on which a crumbling stone temple rose inside a low rock wall. Kiku's flashlight beam played over the primitive structure, sending eerie shadows leaping and cavorting like ghostly dancers.

"You must not pick up so much as a piece of stone," Kiku warned. "The legends say that to disturb the spirits of a *heiau* brings bad luck."

"And you believe that?" Alyse stepped through a low breach in the wall.

"I only repeat the legend." Kiku remained where she was. She used the flashlight beam to show Alyse the rough stone walkway leading to the altar. "It is said that visitors who took stones from the *heiau* have later mailed them back and asked that

239

they be thrown into the sea off the island."

Alyse ran a hand across the stone altar. Her skin prickled as if brushed by a chilled breeze. *Or a ghostly breath.* She took her hand away.

"I'm ready to go back now," Tommy said in a quavering voice, his eyes darting continually at the surrounding darkness.

Alyse stepped back from the altar. "There isn't much to see at night, is there?" *Oh, but there's so much to feel creeping around in your mind,* she thought, suddenly matching the six-year-old's anxiousness to be away from there.

Her toe stuck on a loose stone. Alyse stumbled, caught herself, and hurried on to the low wall.

The trek back down the path went faster than the climb. They had just emerged into the brightly lighted clearing below, when Tommy jerked on Alyse's hand.

"Your necklace!" he said, his eyes round.

Alyse's hand flew to her breast, where the lei had shifted to one side. The sand dollar was gone! She gasped, rocked by an icy wave of panic. The clasp must have broken. *The dragonfly!*

"Kiku!" she cried, grabbing for the housekeeper's flashlight. "I'll be right back."

Alyse whirled and raced back up toward the *heiau*. The searching flashlight beam jitterbugged up the steep path two or three feet in front of her. Her anxiety grew by leaps and bounds with each step. She had to find the necklace, she thought, with mounting hysteria. *She had to!*

By the time she reached the top of the rim and turned left, her breath was coming in short, sharp

240

rasps. At the *heiau,* Alyse clambered over the breach in the old rock wall, near tears as she swept the stone walkway with the flashlight beam. She spotted the loosened stone that had tripped her earlier, and checked the surrounding area carefully.

She was about to give up, when the beam swept over the altar itself. Her heart leaped painfully in her chest and, for a moment, she thought her knees would buckle. The necklace lay broken on the altar stone.

With a choked cry of relief, Alyse lunged for the prize. The sand dollar was shattered. The pendant protruded from the irregular clump of ragged plaster, apparently undamaged. Several of the large, garish beads had broken, revealing a heavy gold chain. As she had suspected, the clasp securing the necklace had snapped, apparently when she stumbled.

Alyse clutched the treasure to her breast for a moment. She felt strangely as if the not-always-benevolent spirits of the *heiau* had played a part in helping her find the priceless key to her dreams. The necklace could just as easily have slipped over the back of the altar, in which case she might never have found it in the dense, junglelike undergrowth.

She gathered up the scattered, broken beads and made her way back to the path leading down toward the clearing. Now that Alyse had found the necklace, she was suddenly conscious of how alone she felt.

Her pace grew cautious. She played the flashlight beam along the sides of the path rather than down the center, trying to penetrate the black shadows beyond the cool, damp foliage of the fern dell.

A night bird cooed off to her right. Alyse turned her head toward it, her scalp tingling. Suddenly her shoe caught on something solid on the path, sending her sprawling. The flashlight went spinning out of her hand.

She didn't drop the necklace. She doubted if a fall down the face of a hundred-foot cliff could make her lose her grip on the precious dragonfly.

The flashlight had landed a few feet away, the beam shining straight back into her face. Alyse got up, brushed off the front of her muumuu, and picked up the light. When she pointed the beam back up the path to check out whatever she had tripped over, she almost dropped it again.

A silent scream strained at her throat as Alyse stared, horrified, at Conrad Brace's blank, lifeless eyes. He lay prone across the path, one hand clawed into the soft, loamy soil, the other reaching around toward a bloody stain on the back of his tweed jacket.

She backed away slowly, her knees wobbling loosely with each step. Her brain kept screaming, over and over, the barely audible sound whistling from her lungs like air escaping a tiny pinprick in a balloon.

Alyse turned, every fiber of her body tensed to run—and the flashlight beam snagged on something lying on the loamy ground. It jutted from the dense undergrowth a few feet farther down the path.

The sleeve of a beige sport coat, from which a bloody hand protruded.

Chapter Thirteen

Alyse ran.

Her mouth gaped in terror. Her constricted throat still produced only that strange, whistling sound, but it was louder now, more like a distant, runaway tea kettle.

She stumbled twice, catching herself both times, hardly pausing in her headlong plunge through the tunnel of wildly bouncing light toward the clearing.

Conrad Brace—dead. Mrs. Fielding's detective—dead.

Alyse recalled having encountered Eddie Komake on that same path less than half an hour ago, and, at last, a voicelike sound escape her tortured throat. She groaned and her grip tightened on the dragonfly pendant.

Could it be that Komake had only hoodwinked Rand into believing he was a U.S. Customs Service agent? The smooth, exotically attractive Hawaiian apparently had the wherewithal to engineer a phenomenally popular career for himself as a club singer, simply as a cover. That cover could just as easily hide a thief—and a cold-blooded killer.

Alyse forced herself to slow as she reached the

foot of the path within sight of the clearing. It wouldn't do to go charging down into the luau in a state of hysteria. That would be like shouting Fire! in a crowded theater. No telling what the killer might do in the resulting pandemonium.

Kiku and Tommy were not at the bottom of the path where she had left them. Alyse stopped there anyway, taking advantage of the slightly elevated ground to scan the crowd.

Waiters had hauled the cooked pig off its spit. They were carving it at a large table near the roasting pit, where a double line of guests was forming. To her great relief, Alyse spotted Tommy standing at the tail end of the nearer line. He was chattering animatedly to Kiku. Alyse waved at them, trying to attract their attention, but neither glanced her way.

On second thought, Alyse decided, perhaps the food line was the safest place for the boy. Especially with Kiku there to watch after him. She stood on tiptoe, straining to see beyond them, and searched for Rand's familiar dark-blond head.

She found him diagonally across the clearing, at the edge of a palm grove elaborately festooned with Japanese lanterns. He stood behind a low table draped with a pale blue cloth. A large package rested on the table. His Japanese clients stood nearby, and he seemed to be making a speech. She realized that Rand was formally presenting the Tokugawa box to his guests of honor.

Alyse began forcing herself toward him through the luau crowd, drawing startled looks from all sides. She didn't care. Her only thought was to

244

reach Rand and to tell him that the hunters of the dragonfly had turned deadly.

After bowing respectfully to the eldest and most senior of his clients, Rand backed away from the table. The rotund old man stepped forward and returned the bow, his face a polite mask of formality. After a brief acceptance speech delivered in rapid bursts of guttural Japanese, he turned toward the elaborately wrapped package waiting on the table.

Rand glanced at Lyle Eason, who had finally shown up after the presentation ceremony had already begun. The stout Texan's jowls were flushed and he was sweating heavily. This led Rand to suspect that Eason had already filched too many drinks from the trays that were continually circulated by roving waiters.

Money had a way of bringing together strange bedfellows, Rand thought, as he mentally compared the gracious Japanese real estate investors with their loud-mouthed, hard-drinking partner from Texas.

In spite of their denial, he still wasn't totally convinced that the Japanese hadn't at least dropped a few hints to Eason concerning their desire to own the antique. But Rand was willing to give them the benefit of the doubt.

On the other hand, he wasn't inclined to cut Eason much slack at all. With little effort at all, the Texan could be flat-out obnoxious.

Rand returned his attention to the old man, who

245

examined the package in minute detail before ever laying a hand on it. Many Americans had finally caught onto the fact that gift-giving was an important element of Japanese business culture. But where many Americans still missed the boat in a big way was in not understanding that the wrapping was as important as the gift. The American habit of hastily ripping off the ribbons and paper and tossing them away was considered downright insulting.

The old man carefully unfastened the origami ornaments atop the package and respectfully set them aside along with the wide satin ribbon. He next began delicately, fastidiously removing the elaborately folded, untaped wrapping paper. He performed this little rite without adding so much as a crimp to the original folds and creases.

Rand's gaze wandered off into the crowd. A small group of guests had gathered to watch the presentation. However, most of the crowd was either queued at the lavishly appointed food tables, or still dancing to the haunting strains of a steel guitar.

A sudden ripple moved through the crowd about two-thirds of the way across the clearing, as if a small stone had been forcefully thrown into a large pond. Rand watched the crowd intently, trying to figure out where the ripple had originated. A moment later, it came again, several yards closer than the first time.

Alyse! He glimpsed her barging through the double lines near the roasting pit. The lines split, heads turning in confusion.

What the hell?

Rand started toward her, then remembered the ceremony under way and backtracked. With the ritualized care of a high priest, the old man was lifting away the intact husk of loosened wrapping paper. Rand fidgeted, one eye on the startled groove Alyse was cutting through the gathering, the other on the table.

The tea box suddenly lay revealed, brilliant vermillion against the pale blue cloth. The rampant gilded dragon on its lid glimmered beneath the overhead lanterns. The Japanese clients sucked in their breaths, uttering sharp exclamations of pleasure.

"Hell of a nice cigar box," Eason commented in an undertone, slapping Rand on the shoulder. "I'll bet that baby set you back a yen or two."

Rand was relieved to see that the three Japanese businessmen apparently hadn't overheard Eason. For the sake of expediency, Rand ignored the embarrassing Texas dinosaur and quickly directed his Tokyo clients to a low table surrounded by woven rice straw seating mats. The seats were alongside the stage where Eddie Komake soon would be performing.

As his clients moved off in that direction, Rand craned his neck, searching for Alyse. He found her barely a dozen yards away. She was still fighting her way toward him through the vibrant luau crowd, close enough now for him to see her deathly pallor—and the look in her eyes.

Rand plowed into the crowd, dodging waiters and guests, throwing out distracted apologies to faces he barely registered. As he closed the distance between himself and Alyse, something caught his attention.

Tommy! The boy seemed to be floating above the crowd. Rand hesitated, focusing on the familiar copper-blond head moving away toward the wide path that led up over the rim of the clearing to the parking lot. A fraction of a second later, he realized that Tommy was being carried on someone's shoulders.

Eddie Komake's shoulders.

"What the . . . ?" Rand stopped cold and watched Komake disappear up the steep path with his nephew. Something about that picture disturbed him — *frightened* him — but he couldn't quite put his finger on it.

The maddeningly festive crowd ebbed and flowed like thick, clinging molasses. Alyse halted every few steps, closed her eyes, and took a deep breath. That was the only way she could keep from going stark raving hysterical.

Twice, she lost sight of Rand. But she kept her bearings, using the cluster of Japanese lanterns over the presentation table as a landmark. She moved toward them like a storm-tossed skiff struggling toward a beacon marking the entrance to safe harbor.

The crowd suddenly parted and Alyse had a clear

view of the presentation table beneath the lanterns. She stood still, trembling, as her mind took a giant lunge toward panic. Rand was gone!

Someone grabbed her from the side and almost jerked her off her feet. Alyse started to strike out in self-defense. But Rand's voice washed over her, and she threw her arms around him instead, hanging on with the desperation of a shipwreck victim.

"What happened?" His strong arms closed around her protectively.

"Dead," she choked. "They're both dead."

"What? Wait, let's . . ."

With a supportive arm around her waist, Rand led Alyse out of the crowd. They went past the presentation table where a pair of burly Hawaiians stood guard over the Tokugawa box, their traditional garb making them look more ceremonial than they were.

He found a relatively secluded location near a twisted palm tree growing horizontal to the ground, only to glance back and discover Lyle Eason tagging along. The oiled Texan held a coconut shell containing a frothy drink in one hand while eyeing Alyse.

"Now, who's dead?" Rand asked in an undertone. He had to force Alyse down onto the contorted tree trunk. She was so stiff with fear that her knees didn't want to bend.

"Conrad." Alyse took a deep breath and held it until she thought her lungs would burst. When she finally let it out, some of her overwhelming tension went with it. Her voice still didn't sound like hers, but at least she could talk coherently.

"I found Conrad's body lying on the trail to the *heiau*," she said, pointing across the clearing. "And close by, the body of a man in a beige sport jacket. I think it might have been the detective who worked for Mrs. Fielding."

Alyse swallowed hard, and had to squeeze out the next words. "There was blood. I think they'd been knifed."

Eason had been leaning close to listen. He straightened suddenly, sloshing the milky contents of his coconut shell onto the front of his shirt. "You mean there's a goldanged *murderer* on the loose?"

"Keep your voice down!" Rand snapped at Eason. He knelt in front of Alyse, cupping her trembling hands in his and peering searchingly into her eyes. "You're sure about all this, sugar?"

She nodded, her hunched shoulders quivering in a violent shudder. "I fell over Conrad. He was just lying there across the path in his tweed jacket. Can you imagine wearing a tweed jacket in Hawaii?" Alyse clamped her jaws shut, aware that she was babbling.

Rand looked down at the ground for a moment, his eyes narrowed. "I have to find Komake," he said.

"No!" Alyse shot to her feet. Her mind was in a turmoil. Nothing was clear to her except the fear wedged in her stomach like a razor-edged icicle. "I saw Eddie on that same path just a little earlier."

She watched Rand turn ashen as the blood

drained from his face. He rose slowly and stood gaping at Alyse as if trapped in a state of suspended animation.

"Oh, my God," he whispered finally. He spun around, staring wildly across the clearing toward the path leading to the parking lot. "Komake has Tommy."

Tommy! Alyse felt dizzy, almost disoriented. Too much was happening too fast. She was overloading. She needed to put everything on hold long enough to sort out the madness, but there was no time. She had a sick feeling that, for Tommy, time might be dangerously close to running out altogether.

Kiku came bustling out of the crowd, her kimono billowing around her. A look of worried indignation had replaced her usual serene expression.

"Mr. Turnbull!" she called, heading straight for Rand. "Did you tell that Eddie Komake fellow it was okay for Tommy to go with him?"

Rand seemed to stop breathing. For a moment, he looked as if he had taken a staggering blow. He took a step in the direction where he had last seen Komake with Tommy, but Alyse pulled him back, trying frantically to attract his attention.

"I have to go after them!" Rand said, prying at her fingers knotted in the front of his shirt.

"They already have a head start," Alyse insisted. "We need to notify the police, Rand. The only way Komake can get Tommy off the island is with a boat or a plane."

"Would somebody kindly tell me what the hell's

251

going on?" Eason demanded, flinging aside the coconut shell. His face retained its usual flush, but his steel-blue eyes had taken on a predatory sharpness.

"Komake's a U.S. Customs Service agent," Rand explained, distractedly clawing a hand through his hair. "He's been tracking some Japanese national treasures that were smuggled into this country inside the Tokugawa Shogun box."

Eason wheeled on one heel to look at the tea box on the blue-clothed table, whistling softly through his front teeth. "Well, I'll be damned," he said. "And now, you think Komake's one of the smugglers?"

"I don't know what I think," Rand replied, wondering if he could have been that badly duped. What kind of renegade government worker were they dealing with here?

"Eddie could be working for Mrs. Fielding," Alyse suggested. "Maybe she hired him to steal Tommy again."

Rand dragged a shaky hand down his face. It didn't make sense. What could Elaine Fielding offer Komake that would make it worthwhile for him to throw away a successful career?

Still, Rand had been played for a sucker somehow. That was enough of a shock to cause his stomach to turn over even at such a highly unlikely scenario involving Elaine Fielding. With a hissed curse, he rushed toward one of the costumed Hawaiian security personnel standing watch over the Tokugawa box.

"Who's this Conrad guy who got himself killed?" Eason asked.

Alyse blinked at Eason in surprise. The Texan had dropped his brash wheeler-dealer's bluster, his voice taking on a low, authoritative tone. She realized she was getting her first look at another side of Lyle Eason—the pragmatic international businessman.

He's a chameleon, she thought. *He's a redneck jerk only when he wants to be.*

"Conrad Brace is . . . was owner of the Brace Gallery in New York," she said. "I worked for him. In fact, that's why I'm here. Conrad sent me to try to buy the tea box from Rand."

Eason nodded slowly, frowning, then shook his head. "Incredible. First, you lose your husband to a heart attack. And now, this."

Alyse flinched at the unexpected reference to Rob. At first, she half suspected that Eason was suggesting she was a jinx. But she discarded that notion when he reached out and patted her arm sympathetically.

One of the burly Hawaiians with whom Rand had been talking suddenly dropped his ceremonial staff and sprinted off around the perimeter of the clearing. By the time Rand turned and strode back toward the twisted palm, the fleet-footed guard was already racing up the torch-lit path to the parking lot.

"I sent one of the security guards up to radio for the police and seal off the parking lot so nobody else can leave," Rand said, taking Alyse's hand and

253

slipping an arm around Kiku's shoulders.

"Good thinking," Eason remarked, eyeing the crowd. "When word starts circulating that there's been a double homicide, most of these people will try to hightail it out of here so fast it'll make your head spin."

"I don't blame them. But what about Tommy? Where would Komake take him?" Alyse asked.

"God knows," Rand replied, his tone equal parts terror and rage. "But if he hurts that boy . . ."

"Miss Marlowe was right, earlier," Eason said. "The only way Komake can get off the island is by boat or plane. You need to light a bonfire under the authorities. Make sure they put a tight clamp on all docks and airstrips."

Rand nodded. "As soon as the cops get here."

"You can't wait!" Eason said in exasperation. "The first squad car that's going to show up out here will likely be some two-bit patrolman who wouldn't have the moxie or the authority to put out an all-points bulletin if a Force Five tidal wave was headed his way.

"He'll have to call in his supervisor, and that'll take time, Rand, which you don't have. What you need to do is burn rubber all the way to Lahaina, where you can climb the head honcho's frame in person."

"*Hai!*" Kiku agreed, reverting to Japanese in this time of stress.

"You have a strong argument," Rand conceded. "But I'm not leaving here."

Eason looked at Rand as if he had lost his mind.

254

"Why the hell not?"

Rand closed his eyes, his grip on Alyse's hand tightening until her knuckles popped painfully.

"Tommy's my only brother's only son," he said slowly through bared teeth. "If Komake knows that — and I think maybe he does — he might not be trying to get the boy off the islands. Komake might intend to use Tommy for leverage against me."

"To what end?" Eason asked, clearly not buying Rand's argument.

"To get to that." Rand pointed to the Tokugawa box.

"But he had it once," Alyse said.

"The box, yes," he replied. "But not what was originally in it."

Rand looked down at her. A chill reverberated through his body when he realized for the first time that she wasn't wearing the tawdry necklace. Then he noticed the strand of garish beads — some broken — looped around her other hand.

Alyse saw him staring at her clenched fist and felt suddenly numb.

"What's that got to do with your staying here?" Eason asked, scowling.

"It could be that this is where Komake expects me to be, where he expects to negotiate."

"You don't know that's the case," Eason shot back.

"I don't know that it isn't, either," Rand pointed out. "And until I do, I'm not taking any chances. Not with Tommy hanging in the balance."

"Then we'll cover both bases," Alyse said,

equally torn between the two arguments. She didn't want to leave Rand, but she couldn't do anything for Tommy by staying. "I'll go to Lahaina."

"No way." Rand shook his head emphatically. "I'm not letting you out of my sight."

"She'll be all right," Eason said. "I'll drive her to Lahaina. As soon as we're through with the police and the mayor and whoever else we can get moving on this, I'll bring her straight back here."

Rand looked at Alyse. She nodded, not letting him see how much she disliked the idea of going with Eason. This wasn't the time or place to get bogged down in personalities. Until they got Tommy back safe and sound, they were all on the same team.

"I don't like it," Rand said, "but then, there isn't anything about this situation that I do like."

Eason set off in a lumbering gait toward the path leading to the parking lot. Rand released her hand so Alyse could follow, but she didn't move. Instead, she gazed up into his tormented eyes and held out her other hand—the one holding the dragonfly.

"Trade it to Komake for Tommy," she ordered, surprised by the forcefulness in her own voice.

Rand stared at the delicate jade and mother-of-pearl pendant amid crumbling remnants of the sand dollar. The magnitude of her offering staggered him.

"The Japanese authorities would blow a fuse. You could lose the reward," he cautioned.

"You could lose Tommy."

Her hand remained steady, unlike the pandemonium taking place in her heart and mind. The reward and what it would bring meant everything to Alyse. To another, deeper part of her, so did Rand and Tommy. Losing the reward would break her heart. But she had a sure feeling that placing riches above this small boy's life would do even greater damage to her very soul.

Rand took her hand in his and gently curled her fingers back over the pendant. His eyes ached. He looked at her through a haze of tears.

"You hang onto it for now," he managed, deeply moved. "We can cross that bridge when we come to it. Who knows? I might be totally wrong about what Komake's after."

Alyse blinked back tears of her own. "I'll hurry back with it," she promised.

He bent and kissed her quickly. Alyse turned and ran after Lyle Eason, her mind still in a turmoil. Beneath the fear and anguish, however, was a nagging, itchy feeling that she had overlooked something important — perhaps, something deadly.

Chapter Fourteen

The gentle night breeze had picked up. It fitfully
tossed the crowns of palm trees alongside the highway and raised the luminescent surf in ever-higher
breakers that boomed hollowly onto the moonlit
beach. Alyse hoped it was just another storm blowing in off the Pacific. But in the back of her
mind—and in the pit of her stomach—it felt more
like an ill wind threatening to sweep them all over
the edge of a sheer precipice.

The mad scramble up the path from the clearing
had only heightened her sense of being caught in a
disaster. She was filled with the angry terror of a
young lioness whose cub is threatened. It didn't
seem to matter that Tommy wasn't hers. She would
do *anything* to get him safely back to Rand.

The moment Lyle Eason accelerated his dark
rental sedan out of the parking lot onto the highway, Alyse had leaned heavily against the passenger
door and closed her eyes. She tried desperately to
find her center of calm. She would need to have her
wits about her when they reached Lahaina.

The high wail of a siren sounded in the distance, approaching rapidly. Alyse opened her eyes in time to see a brilliant flash of rooftop strobe lights as a police cruiser shot past toward the luau site. Then another. And a third.

"The cavalry charges to the rescue," Eason said in an oddly dull tone.

She looked at him sharply, then out the side window. Something seemed eerily out of focus. No—*askew*. Alyse sat up straighter and glanced around at the car's interior as if seeing it for the first time.

"You didn't ride to the party in the limousine with your Japanese partners." She stated the obvious.

Eason didn't look at her. After a while, the corner of his mouth curled into what struck her as an almost cruel smile.

"As a matter fact, I did," he replied.

Alyse remained perfectly still for a moment. Then slowly, she turned her head to peer over the back of the seat. A black leather carry-on valise lay on the rear seat. The pale backwash of the dashboard lights reflected off two one-inch polished brass initials bradded to the wide luggage strap that extended under the padded handle.

C.B.

Conrad Brace!

She snapped her head back around to find Eason watching her. The total lack of expression in his wintery blue eyes froze the breath in her lungs. Her mouth went chalk-dry.

"Your late employer is no longer in need of his

259

wheels," Eason said, returning his gaze to the dark road. He patted the steering wheel. "This seemed the logical car to appropriate on the spur of the moment."

"Where did you get Conrad's keys—on the spur of the moment?"

Alyse regretted the question almost as soon as she had asked it. There was only one place he could have gotten the keys. From Conrad's pocket.

The disturbing half smile returned to the corner of Eason's hard mouth. She shivered under a sudden wave of icy-hot panic at the realization that she might be in the company of a killer.

"Your husband once told me his wife was too smart for her own good. I'm beginning to see what he meant."

Alyse licked her dry lips. Eason made it sound as if he had known Rob far better than he had earlier implied.

Another thought wormed its way insidiously into her consciousness. Back at the luau, Eason had expressed surprise when she informed him that Rob had died six months ago. But later, although she was certain she hadn't mentioned the cause of death, Eason had made specific reference to Rob's heart attack.

A sharp pain suddenly stabbed her hand. Alyse realized she was clenching her fists together in her lap, and that an exposed wing of the pendant was cutting into her left palm. Incredibly, she had forgotten all about the precious stolen treasure.

Her mind made another belated connection.

Rand had bought the Tokugawa box for his new Japanese clients at Lyle Eason's suggestion. The dragonfly had been smuggled into the country inside the box. It seemed logical now that the stolen treasure's intended destination must have been Eason. The big, brash Texan was one of the dark hunters of the dragonfly!

Careful not to attract Eason's attention with a sudden movement, Alyse slowly eased her left hand out of sight under the voluminous folds of her muumuu. Raw animal instinct told her that her life depended on his not knowing that she possessed the pendant.

The road curved. Alyse braced herself as Eason steered into the sharp bend without slowing, tires squealing on the smooth pavement. She peered out past him at the moonlit beach beyond the opposite shoulder of the highway.

The wrong side.

She realized too late what she had probably sensed all along—that the sea was on the wrong side of the road. They were not speeding toward Lahaina.

The colorful luau festivities had taken on surreal undertones that were detectable only by Rand and a very select handful of others. He paced at the periphery of the crowd, which continued to eat, drink, and make merry in blissful ignorance of the fearsome drama being enacted all around it.

Resisting his own urgent desire to go off like a

Roman candle, Rand had intentionally refrained from sounding a general alarm that would undoubtedly turn the party into a mob scene. The luau site wasn't exactly remote, but neither was the location within the reassuring environs of town. He had to keep a cap on things until the police arrived.

Besides the security guard whom he had sent out to the parking lot, Rand had posted a waiter at the foot of the path leading to the *heiau*. His presence would deter wandering guests from stumbling onto Conrad Brace and Elaine Fielding's detective.

It occurred to Rand that he might be saving his guests from more than just an unpleasant shock. The person—*Eddie Komake!* Rand wanted to scream—who had already disposed of the two men on the *heiau* path could very well have an accomplice. Perhaps more than one. Until that was known for certain, it was safer to keep everyone bunched together.

"When I get my hands on you, Komake," he muttered tightly under his breath, "you'll wish you'd never set eyes on Tommy!"

If he lived to be a very old man, Rand would never forget the sight of his nephew riding off up the path to the parking lot on Komake's shoulders. With a low growl, Rand suddenly turned and pounded a fist into the trunk of a palm tree.

"Pardon us . . ."

He spun around at the quiet voice. His three Japanese clients stood shoulder to shoulder. They bowed to him as one. Rand was too stunned by events to return the courtesy. He absently rubbed his bruised hand, staring dumbly at the elderly men.

"We could not help noticing that you seem to be experiencing some distress," said their spokesman, the rail-thin seventy-year-old. "We took the liberty of inquiring of your housekeeper, Miss Hiakawa, who tells us your nephew is missing."

Rand noticed that he didn't mention anything about what Alyse had stumbled across on the *heiau* path. He decided to let sleeping dogs—and Conrad Brace—lie for the time being.

He glanced over his clients' heads at the crowd. Keeping his voice low, he said, "It appears that Tommy might have been kidnapped by the singer who was to perform tonight."

The gaunt old man looked surprised. "You are speaking of Eddie Komake?"

"Hai," Rand nodded.

The old man turned to his wizened associates. The trio conversed briefly in Japanese that was far too rapid and guttural for Rand to follow. The senior partner uttered a sharp exclamation and jabbed a fist angrily into the air.

"What is it?" Rand interjected in Japanese.

"Perhaps nothing," replied the youngest partner, scratching his snowy brush-cut hair. "Perhaps a great deal."

Rand waited impatiently through another flurry of incomprehensibly colloquial Japanese. Finally, the rail-thin spokesman turned to him with a puzzled sigh.

"Forgive our confusion, Mr. Turnbull," he said,

rubbing his narrow chin. "You see, we were approached by your Eddie Komake late this afternoon at our hotel."

"You don't say. What did he want?"

"At first, he asked to speak with us about our American attorney."

"Me?" Rand wondered what in hell Komake had been up to.

"Yes, Mr. Turnbull. But then, he seemed more interested in the gift you intended for us." The old man nodded respectfully toward the tea box on the blue-clothed table a dozen yards away. "He gave us specific instructions on what we were to do with the gift at the end of the evening."

He glanced at his partners, frowning. "We thought it exceedingly strange, Mr. Turnbull, that you would send a cabaret singer to handle such a security matter. Of course, we had no idea what sort of gift you had in mind. But even now, his call on us seems rather . . . inappropriate, shall we say?"

"Yes, let's say that." Rand thought *suspicious* was a better word, and had an idea that his courteous clients might agree. But this wasn't the time to split hairs. "Exactly what were Komake's instructions?"

"That we take the gift directly to our hotel following the luau, and turn it over to a security detail that will look after it for the duration of our stay in Hawaii."

I'll bet, Rand thought. But the news only compounded his own confusion. Why would Komake

264

bother to set up a net to haul in the Tokugawa box, when he'd had the thing in his hands that very day? How could the Hawaiian singer possibly use the box to suck in the priceless pendant?

Rand felt like a laboratory rat trapped inside a maze. The harder his mind raced around searching for a solution to the puzzle, the more dead-end walls he ran up against.

He realized he was unconsciously grinding his bruised fist into the opposite palm. Rand looked up and saw that his clients had noticed as well.

The eldest of them bowed slightly. In Japanese, speaking slowly and distinctly so that Rand would be sure to understand, he said, "There is an old samurai saying, Mr. Turnbull. 'He who stands still moves backward.' "

Rand stared at him. The longer they stood there looking at each other, the more convinced he became that he had already stood still far too long. But where could he turn? Where should he go? He had no idea where Komake had taken Tommy.

"Your hotel?" he asked finally.

The three old men stared back at him, unblinking. The decision was his to make—and Rand made it with a sudden decisiveness.

The hotel.

The police would be converging on the luau at any moment. Whether Komake was a renegade undercover U.S. Customs agent, or a dyed-in-the-wool world-class felon, he wouldn't hang around there one second longer than necessary. Why had Rand ever thought otherwise? Komake was long gone — with Tommy. Rand would have to find him somehow.

Alyse and Lyle Eason were already halfway to Lahaina by now. And Alyse had the dragonfly pendant, the bargaining chip.

Everything had shifted to Lahaina.

Rand went down the row and quickly pumped his three clients' hands. Each of them uttered guttural words of encouragement. Then he sprinted up the torchlit path toward the parking lot, praying that he could make up wasted time.

An aching dread filled him. Komake had Tommy. Now Alyse, too, was racing into harm's way. Rand had thought she would be safe, going to Lahaina with Eason, at least for the time being. But if Komake spotted her in town before Rand got there, he might take her as a hostage, as well. Or he might do something worse if he found out she was carrying the pendant.

Rand was partway across the parking lot to where he had left his car parked when three police cars whipped off the highway in rapid succession. Their roof lights flashed and their sirens died in a somber moan. Rand barely broke stride to glance back at them before continuing on to his car.

"Keep moving," he said to himself, his voice a harsh rasp of urgency. "Forward, forward. *Move*." He couldn't afford to waste another second.

The scrimshaw key ring that Alyse had given him was in his hand before he realized he had reached for it. He dived into his car and jammed the key into the ignition, slammed the gears into reverse, and bore down on the accelerator. The car shot backward, tires spinning wildly. Rand braked to a skidding halt just inches short of broadsiding the stretch limousine that he'd hired to bring his new clients out from Lahaina.

Rand jerked the steering wheel around to the left. At the same time he slapped the gear stick with the heel of his hand and again stomped on the accelerator pedal. The tires kicked up a rooster-tail of dirt as the car raced to catch up with the roaring, whining engine. The rear end tried to creep around for just a few seconds, but he counter-steered, and the car went thundering down the ragged aisle separating two rows of parked vehicles.

The police cruisers had stopped roughly abreast near the parking lot entrance. Before the officers could so much as throw open their doors, Rand aimed for the opening between two of the vehicles and locked both elbows, bracing himself, hoping he had enough room.

He heard the slightest "chink" sound as his side mirror clipped the mirror on the cruiser to his left. And then he was through the gap, charging on out of the parking lot onto the highway. He made a skidding left turn; the bottom slid out of his stomach until the tires gained traction on the pavement.

He was already a quarter mile down the road before he heard the sirens whooping behind him. First one, then two. That was all right, he thought. That was just dandy, in fact. They didn't know it yet, but the mounties were on their way to Lahaina to throw a net around Komake, and he hadn't had to waste valuable time explaining anything.

The accelerator pedal was already floored, but he pressed it harder anyway. Because he was being chased by more than just the two screaming police cars. Rand felt an icy demon perched between his shoulder blades telling him that he was already too late.

He tried to shake it off, but couldn't get the thought out of his mind. In a withering flash of insight, he realized that he wouldn't want to be part of any world without Alyse and Tommy.

The lights of the outskirts of Lahaina appeared up ahead, along with a set of headlights. A dark vehicle passed him in the opposite lane, then made a skidding U-turn in the middle of the road. Rand watched in the rearview mirror as the vehicle raced up behind him and flashed its bright lights.

When he ignored the signal, the vehicle pulled out to pass, its more powerful engine drowning out the sound of Rand's car as it moved ahead. Suddenly, the driver whipped the car—a black Land Rover—into Rand's lane. The Land Rover's brake lights came on, forcing Rand to hit his own brakes.

Both vehicles went into partially controlled skids, the smell of burning rubber pouring in through the ventilation system. Rand clipped the shoulder, fishtailed back onto the pavement, and then hit the shoulder again before grinding to a halt.

The Land Rover stopped farther down the road and the driver's door flew open. Before Rand could pry his death grip off the steering wheel and react, he saw Eddie Komake trotting toward him. Rand bolted out of his car, barely aware of the police sirens approaching from behind.

"Where's Alyse?" Komake shouted before they had closed half the distance separating them.

Rand stopped, fists knotted at his sides, shaking with rage. Komake halted in the glare of headlights from Rand's car. His bright floral shirt was hiked up on one side, revealing a holstered revolver clipped to the belt of his white pants.

"She's gone to Lahaina to shake some trees, slimeball," Rand snapped, relieved that Alyse apparently hadn't crossed Komake's path. He couldn't seem to take his eyes off the revolver. "What have you done with Tommy?"

Komake ignored his question, as well as the two police cruisers that were screaming to a stop behind Rand, blocking both lanes of the highway.

"I just came from a roadblock between here and town," Komake said, stonefaced. "Alyse hasn't been through it."

Rand raised a fist slowly to his mouth, rubbing the white knuckles across his tight lips. Something was wrong here. He glanced over his shoulder. The officers hadn't left their cruisers. They were just sitting there, watching Rand and Komake.

While he was still trying to figure out what was going on, the passenger door of the Land Rover swung open. Tommy came darting around the front of the black vehicle into the highway, running toward Rand.

Komake took two quick steps to one side and

scooped up the child in one arm. Tommy squirmed in his grasp, his face pale in the harsh wash of headlights.

Rand twisted around again and looked anxiously at the policemen. Why weren't they moving?

Chapter Fifteen

Fear, darkness, and the belated realization that they were speeding in the wrong direction—away from Lahaina—plunged Alyse into a disorienting freefall of confusion. She didn't know where they were until Lyle Eason turned into the sloping driveway leading down to Rand's cottage. This was the last place she had expected Eason to head.

In her surprise, Alyse realized she had reached a kind of emotional plateau. Her senses seemed to come suddenly and sharply into focus. Eason was a powerful and deadly predator. And he had already begun looking at her the way a beast studies its prey. If she were going to escape Conrad's fate, she would have to keep her wits about her.

He killed the headlights and rolled all the way to the head of the driveway, parking beneath the big angel trumpet tree. Opening his door, Eason grabbed Alyse's left wrist and dragged her across the seat after him as he got out.

She stumbled out of the car, fell, then scrambled after the Texan as he jerked her roughly across the driveway. Alyse didn't resist, although everything in her cried out to fight back. But she was afraid that if she struggled, he would notice the pendant clutched in her left hand.

The darkness proved to be an ally. Eason released Alyse's wrist and pushed her ahead of him toward the house. As he prodded her around to the side door, she tucked her left hand back among the folds of her flowing muumuu. She would have given a great deal for a pocket just then.

Eason tried the side door. Undaunted by finding it locked, he simply hauled off and kicked it in.

"What are you doing?" Alyse demanded, surprised by the firmness in her voice.

"Breaking and entering," Eason said coolly.

He marched her through the darkened house to the living room, where he switched on a table lamp. She noticed that Eason hadn't bumped into any furniture before turning on the light.

"You act as if you've been here before."

"Very perceptive, princess. As a matter of fact, I had a look around last night." He patted his jacket pocket. "This time, I came better prepared."

So, it had been Eason whom she had heard roaming the hallway during the wee hours of the morning. Alyse edged toward the couch, keeping her left hand tucked out of sight.

"You were after the Tokugawa box." She made it a statement instead of a question. "Even though you knew Rand was planning to give it to your Japanese partners this evening."

Eason's crooked smile made her blanch. "You still haven't figured it out, have you, princess?"

"I know about the false bottom in the box," she said, drawing a raised eyebrow from Eason.

"And the dragonfly pendant," he said.

Alyse licked her lips before she could stop herself. It was a tiny mistake—a minor slip of body language—but Eason noticed. He didn't say anything. He just stood there smiling at her, his head tilted slightly to one side.

She had a feeling the odious Texan was sizing her up all over again, using the new information she had just provided or rather confirmed. She could almost see that in his cold eyes. She was also just beginning to guess that she had underestimated Eason. He knew a good deal more than she was giving him credit for.

"Why did you murder Conrad—and that other man?" she asked.

"Ah!" Eason grinned, raising one finger. "I see. You know—and yet, you don't know."

He pointed to the couch. Alyse sat down on the edge of the cushion, her body as tense as a coiled spring. Eason took two steps back and bent, tossing aside the section of woven rice straw mat covering Rand's floor safe.

"Turnbull was supposed to have bought the

273

Tokugawa box from Brace," he said, as he knelt to remove the section of flooring beneath the mat. "We had no idea Rand would choose to bypass the middleman by attending the auction himself."

"We?"

"Brace and I, of course." Eason leaned the floor panel against a leg of the piano. "Your late employer was my last surviving partner in crime. When he showed up at the luau in a panic, I decided to play it safe. Frightened men have loose lips, and I couldn't risk that. As for that other slob, well, he just popped out of the bushes at a most inopportune time."

He chuckled at Alyse's expression.

"Brace was supposed to purchase the box at the Bundys auction, remove the pendant and a rare haiku from the hidden compartment, then sell the box to Turnbull," Eason went on conversationally. "But Rand screwed the deal by attending the auction himself. When Brace let the Tokugawa box slip through his hands, I was suspicious. I thought he might be trying to pull a fast one on me—with the help of Rob's lovely widow."

"You keep mentioning Rob," Alyse said. "What does he have to do with any of this?"

"Why, everything." Eason reached into his inside jacket pocket and removed a small foil-wrapped packet, grinning to himself. "Good old Rob arranged the theft of the pendant and died

274

of wounds incurred during a shoot-out with security guards."

"That's a lie!" Alyse protested, her voice faltering slightly as she glimpsed a flat shoulder holster strapped under Eason's jacket. "Rob died of a heart attack. I was officially notified by Japanese authorities."

"I was in Japan at the time," Eason said as if she hadn't spoken. "I provided your husband with a cover story after he died—one that satisfied the *Japanese authorities*. I also sent you an *official* notification of Rob's unfortunate heart attack."

He grinned, shaking his head in wonder at his own cleverness as he unwound the foil from the packet. His movements were measured and efficient, as if he had them all charted out in his head. He even folded the foil neatly and put it in his pocket.

"You see, princess," Eason continued, "Rob's illegal activities in Japan were conducted under an assumed identity. The real Japanese authorities had no idea that anyone by the name of Rob Marlowe was even in their country."

While Alyse sat in mute shock, desperately trying to assimilate the barrage of bombs that had just blown apart her world, Eason examined the material that he had just unwrapped. It appeared to be a chunk of yellowish clay approximately the size and shape of a deck of cards. Reaching down into the floor recess, he quickly molded the substance around the combination lock on the safe.

"Brace and I split the cost of Rob's funeral in Kyoto," Eason said, wedging two thin wires into the malleable substance. "I can assure you, it was all first-class."

He began carefully feeding out a double strand of wire, whistling industriously under his breath as he backed away from the safe toward the couch. Alyse watched him in a daze. Her hands and feet felt numb. She tried to tell herself that this wasn't just a macabre dream and that she hadn't completely lost touch with reality.

"What is that?" she asked in a small voice.

"Ordinary garden-variety plastique explosives, princess," he replied, glancing back toward the safe. "If I had time, I could bring in a specialist and avoid the mess, but I'm a tad rushed tonight. So in another two shakes, I'm going to blow the lock off your lover boy's little vault."

"But why?" she asked as he trailed the wires over the back of the couch. "The Tokugawa box is back at the luau. You know that."

Eason stopped and looked at her, the maddening smile playing at his lips. "I still haven't figured you out, princess. You're either too foxy or too naive for your own good. I'm afraid your pretty little goose is cooked either way.

"You see, I happen to know the hidden compartment in the Tokugawa box is empty. At least, the haiku isn't in it, because I found it in Turnbull's bedroom — among some delightful lingerie, I might add — during my first visit last night." Eason smacked his lips.

"And if the haiku wasn't in the box," he added, "then it stands to reason that the pendant isn't either. Which tells me that Turnbull had an ulterior motive for buying it out from under Brace at the Bundys auction. And maybe you had your own motive for being late for the auction?"

Eason winked at her.

"That's crazy," said Alyse.

His smile died suddenly, leaving a dead, steely-eyed expression. "We'll see about that, won't we," he said, a dangerous edge on his voice. "I'm betting that you and your lover boy have the pendant stashed in his safe."

Eason reached over the back of the couch and grabbed her arm, dragging Alyse roughly around to his side. He leaned close, twisting her arm painfully. His warm breath washed sourly over her face.

"You'd better pray it's in there, princess," he whispered through bared teeth. "Because when I'm crossed, I can be a very difficult man to like."

Eason dropped to his knees behind the couch and jerked her down beside him. The numb feeling returned as Alyse watched him attach the ends of the thin wires to a device the size of a cigarette lighter. Gripping the detonator in one thick fist, his thumb poised over a black button on the end, he hooked his other hand around the back of her neck and shoved her head down toward the floor.

The detonation wasn't as loud as Alyse had expected, but it reverberated across the floor as if the foundation of the cottage had been struck with a giant sledgehammer. Eason got heavily to his feet. He totally lacked Rand's athletic grace and agility, she noticed, even though Rand was much taller and a good twenty pounds heavier.

Alyse rose to her knees. A fine dust hung in the air. Eason coughed wheezily, fanning a hand in front of his face as he circled the couch and shuffled through splintered wood and shredded rice straw matting. The stainless steel knob from the combination lock was embedded sideways in the textured ceiling directly above the floor safe.

She glanced toward the French door leading to the lanai. It was closed, and most certainly locked. She was pretty sure she could make it across the living room before Eason caught up. But by the time she fumbled the little lock around on the brass door handle trying to figure out if it turned left or right, he would be on top of her. As he said, he would be a difficult man to like if he were crossed, and she already liked him not at all.

But what other choice did she have? Eason was bending over the safe right now, pulling at the heavy steel door.

She moved quietly around toward the end of the couch, barely breathing, her gaze riveted on Eason's broad back. He growled in triumph as the safe door swung open.

He stared down into the safe for several seconds, as if he couldn't quite believe what he was seeing. Or, to be more exact, what he wasn't seeing. Then he spun around, his features twisted and reddened with fury. His cold eyes contained a madness that Alyse had not seen before. She momentarily lost track of space and time, as if she were staring her own worst nightmare in the face.

"I warned you, princess," he said, his voice as frosty as his gaze. "You and your lover boy shouldn't try to cheat a crook."

Alyse stood petrified as Eason came toward her. He grabbed her wrist and hauled her back in the direction of the safe. She leaned away from him, resisting his pull in spite of her better judgment.

For once, she didn't give a hang about judgment. She was listening only to her instincts, and they were screaming at her not to fight, but to flee. Only she couldn't. The predator had her in his talons.

He twisted her arm until she had to grit her teeth to keep from crying out. Straddling the splintery hole in the floor, Eason forced her to look down.

"Did you ever see anything as empty as that, princess?" he snarled. "You want to know what it reminds me of? An open grave, that's what."

Her heart surged frighteningly in her chest, and then seemed to flutter. *This is how a rabbit feels,* she thought, and pulled harder against his grip. His hamlike fist rotated her arm, punishing Alyse for her efforts. He was enjoying hurting her.

Then he saw it.

He raised her much smaller fist in front of his rage-contorted face. A fragment of inlaid jade and mother-of-pearl protruded from her tightly clenched fingers. The plaster and paste beads looped around her hand were badly chipped, revealing segments of finely wrought gold chain.

"Oh, you'll pay for this, princess," Eason threatened, his tone changing abruptly, becoming calm, almost pleasant. "You have no idea how much you'll pay."

His cold blue gaze shifted from her hand to her eyes. Alyse strained back still harder, but was no match for his strength.

Push! The thought came to her from the very core of her survival instincts. Alyse braced her feet, shifted her weight, and shoved with all her might. He released her and toppled backward, arms flailing the air, his expression suddenly going stupid with surprise. Before he hit the floor, Alyse took off like a jackrabbit.

Haste makes waste. The homily spun ludicrously through her mind as she reached the French door. But she took her time—a precious extra half second—and the outrageously miniscule locking mechanism on the brass door handle rotated smoothly to the left.

Alyse jerked down on the lever handle and opened the door. Only as she darted out onto the lanai did she permit herself to glance back. Eason had lumbered to his feet and was charging after her. But his shoe caught on an edge of the rice straw matting that had been frayed by the explosion, sending him sprawling on his face. He went down roaring like an enraged bull.

Her soles skidded on the flagstone paving of the lanai. Alyse took another split second to kick out of her pumps, then went racing down the moonlit path to the beach. Her feet barely seemed to touch the ground as she ran. Her arms pumped wildly and the sound of her own heartbeat pounded in her ears.

Rand! Help me!

The words formed a silent scream inside her head. Even as she reached the foot of the path and turned right, however, Alyse realized that Rand was far beyond her reach. And even in the sheer terror of her flight, she felt a bubble of acute sadness rise and burst within her, knowing that she might never see him again.

Out in the open, the wind whipped at her muumuu, trying to slow her. Alyse stole another glance behind her as she sprinted along the beach, keeping to the wet sand where the footing was more firm. *Headlights!* She glimpsed a shadow moving swiftly along the side of the cottage from where a vehicle had just pulled into the driveway in front.

"Please, please, let it be Rand," she prayed on a single exhaled breath.

But she couldn't stop to find out who had come to save her from the mad, deadly, dark hunter of the dragonfly. Because much closer, another indistinct shape was crashing down the beach path after her. *Eason.*

If she so much as slowed, Eason would be on her. Alyse tried to scream. The faint sound that whistled out past her lips was lost in the noise of the pounding surf. So she just kept running, her lungs burning, her mind on fire.

The landscaping lights were off. Rand dodged around the sedan parked under the churning branches of the angel trumpet tree and ran through a tunnel of darkness along the east side of the house toward the lanai. Komake had gone in the opposite direction, toward the door on the west side.

There were three entrances to the cottage, and only two of them. They were both counting on the probability that Eason wouldn't come storming out the front door—not with the Land Rover parked there with its lights blazing. Rand prayed that he wasn't making an enormous mistake in leaving Tommy crouched on the rear floorboard of the Land Rover with the doors securely locked.

There hadn't been time to find a safer place for him. Until they had pulled into the driveway and spotted a car parked close to the house, they hadn't been sure where—or even if—they would find Eason and Alyse. And by then, the police officers who had chased Rand almost to Lahaina were already speeding north to set up another roadblock.

Rand vaulted a shrub and came down hard in the darkness, jamming his knee. He staggered on a few paces until he got his legs back under him, cursing to himself all the way, and limped on. The heat was building up under the lightweight Ballistics Cloth vest that Komake had insisted he borrow from one of the cops. He was sweating heavily by the time he reached the back corner of the house and heard footsteps running across the stone paving of the lanai.

He rounded the corner just as Eason charged off down the beach path out of the wash of light from the open French door. Rand veered to the right, plunging down the rough, brushy slope toward the beach, hoping to cut him off.

His knee slowed him down just enough to enable Eason to reach the sandy shore before him. Eason turned north. As Rand cleared the slope and took off after him, he realized that the Texan didn't seem aware that he was being chased.

Rand suddenly saw why.

Eason's attention was focused on someone else who was running along the beach a dozen yards ahead. *Alyse!* And Eason was rapidly gaining on her!

A stiff wind whipped across the beach, flapping the unfastened straps on the vest against Rand's face. He ignored the sharp, shooting pains in his jammed knee and redoubled his effort, sucking up his reserves as he closed the gap between himself and Eason.

Alyse was losing ground fast. She tried to look back and that was a mistake, because Eason gained a step on her, and then two more when she dodged a driftwood snag half buried in the sand. The Texan reached under his jacket with one hand, and Rand knew with sickening certainty what it was even before he saw the ugly shape of an automatic in the moonlight.

Still unaware that Rand was close behind him, Eason lunged forward with a ferocious bellow. He clawed at Alyse with his left hand, his right hand holding the weapon out to his side. Alyse cried out as he caught her hair and she was dragged to a standstill.

Almost on top of them now, Rand launched

himself at Eason with a savage shout. Eason whirled in alarm. The automatic swept around and fired.

Rand glimpsed a bright flash at the same instant he was hit. The bullet slammed into him with a teeth-jarring impact that drove the wind from his lungs as it picked him up and flipped him backward. He pancaked hard onto the firm, wet sand.

The edge of a wave foamed across his outstretched arm.

He lay still.

Chapter Sixteen

The sound of Rand's voice only a few feet away gave Alyse the strength to wrench her hair from Eason's grasp. A split second later, a gunshot rang out and she turned in time to see Rand hit the ground. He lay dead still.

Rand! She screamed his name in her mind as a horrendous pain tore through her. It was as if the very tapestry of her life were being ripped down the middle.

Alyse reeled away in horror.

"Give it to me, princess," Eason said in a deadly calm voice that was somehow more terrifying than the shriek of any monster. He held the gun down at his side, as if to prove to her that she had indeed reached the end.

She stared at him for a moment, uncomprehending. Her emotions had overloaded and shut down. First, the sense of shock and grief—then, fear itself.

He held out a hand waiting for something. What? Suddenly, she remembered the dragonfly pendant, clasped in her fist so tightly that it was cutting into her flesh. Alyse opened her palm and looked at it.

The dragonfly had unlocked her dreams only to then steal from her the one thing that she had come to hold most precious. She tried to look past Eason at Rand, lying so still on the moonlit wet sand, but tears blurred her vision.

Alyse was left with the agonizing guilt that Rand had given his life trying to save hers. If it was the last thing she ever did, she would make sure Rand's sacrifice wasn't for nothing. And she knew exactly how she would do that.

"I'll throw it into the sea first," she threatened, evenly, closing her fingers around the priceless piece.

Eason froze for a second—just long enough for Alyse to dart out into the water before he belatedly raised the automatic. But by then it was too late. She waded out deeper, swinging the dragonfly tauntingly on its gold chain, confident that he wouldn't risk shooting her now. If he did, if she dropped the pendant in the ocean, it might be lost to him forever.

The surf pounded her roughly from behind as she backed into it up to her waist. The hem of her muumuu floated around her in the receding waves. Alyse wound the chain snugly around her wrist.

"You killed for it," she said, tears streaming down her cheeks, "Now you'll have to swim for it."

287

Eason hesitated, one hand still stretched forward. Then he made a fist, raising it high over his head. He aimed the gun at her again. But Alyse gambled it was an empty threat and ignored him. And then, with a final shriek of rage, he took the bait. Jamming the automatic back into his shoulder holster, he lunged into the Pacific.

Alyse rolled onto her side and threw herself into a foam-crested wave, stroking with all her strength. Eason peeled off his jacket and flung it toward shore, then threw himself headfirst into the same wave. The strong wind caught the jacket, kiting it higher, and finally flipping it far away onto the dry sand of the beach.

As soon as she cleared the surf line, Alyse glanced back. Eason was directly behind, close enough for her to see his labored expression in the moonlight. He was strong, but he swam every bit as clumsily as he ran. Even with the muumuu occasionally binding at her legs, she had no difficulty maintaining the distance separating them.

After a while, she found that she actually had to take care not to stretch her lead too far. She didn't want Eason to lose heart and give up the chase too soon.

Alyse didn't worry about conserving sufficient strength to make it back to shore herself. She was determined to keep going as long and as far as she had to. The sea and Eason's own greed were her best and only weapons against him.

As she tired, the fear began to return, weighing her down in the turbulent darkness. But when Alyse thought of Rand lying on the beach, angry grief renewed her strength. She plowed on through the choppy swells.

Every now and then, she glanced over her shoulder at Eason. And each time, she found that his strokes had grown less energetic, more erratic. She couldn't hear him, but she knew he was gasping for breath, perhaps even beginning to feel the onset of genuine desperation.

Alyse sensed a change in the water—a subtle shift in temperature—almost before she felt the inexorable pull of a rip tide. From deep within her, a cold, quivering vestige of terror surfaced. She responded automatically to her swimmer's instincts, altering the angle of her course from shore, using the lights of the distant cottage as a directional beacon.

She was at the edge of the treacherous, invisible current. In spite of her fatigue, she still had a chance to work herself free if she didn't panic.

Seconds later, she thought she heard a cry of distress. It was probably her imagination. Someone had once told her that sailors couldn't hear thunder. So Alyse doubted very much that she could hear Eason shouting for help.

But he was out there, and he was definitely in trouble. Because he was caught in the rip tide right along with her. And he was tired. And when he finally used up all that rage trying to keep his head above water, he would have nothing left but panic.

Alyse stopped looking back, concentrating instead on breaking free of the sucking undertow, her efforts handicapped by the fist mindlessly clenched around the dragonfly. She kept an eye on the cottage lights and swam diagonally toward shore. Her arms grew heavier, until she was aware of nothing but the stubbornly rhythmic movements that drove her on, on through the moonlit water.

And suddenly, the deadly tug was gone.

She closed her eyes, her muscles and lungs straining and quivering on the edge of total exhaustion as she doggedly continued the slow crawl stroke. Her heartbeat boomed in her ears like an endless, watery cannon salute.

Alyse wept as she swam, her tears mixing with the salty sea, anointing it with her grief. Rand was gone. She felt so alone. So desolate. She opened her hand at last to release the treasure. But the chain was wrapped so tightly around her wrist that it stayed tethered to her, just as Rand would remain forever bound to her heart.

Suddenly, she felt very close to him, almost as if he were at her side, coaxing her on, one arm stroke at a time. A light flared briefly behind her closed eyelids. Then it flared again, only this time it didn't go away.

Through a thick fog of exhaustion, Alyse finally realized that the light was coming from ahead, not from within. She opened her eyes, squinting dazedly at a brilliant beacon, slowly realizing that it was a flashlight beam directed at her from the beach.

The light began bobbing wildly as its holder ran out into the water toward her. Alyse finally stopped moving as she reached Eddie Komake's enveloping arms. She didn't have the strength to worry about whether he was friend or foe. She no longer cared.

"You're safe now, *wahini*," he said, lifting her out of the water. "Everything's okay."

Alyse shook her head. It would be a long, long time, she thought, before anything in her life would be okay again.

"You were out there a long time," Komake said, trudging back along the sand toward the cottage. "We thought we had lost you."

She clung to him weakly, her arms and legs still aching with fatigue. Then she abruptly stiffened. *"We?"*

"Yeah." Komake raised the beam of his flashlight. "I almost had to stake that bone-headed *kanaka* of yours to the beach to keep him from crawling into the ocean after you."

Alyse twisted around in Komake's arms, following the dancing beam of his flashlight. Up ahead, she spotted a shape on the beach—two shapes!—bright splashes of white and blue and hot pink.

Rand and Tommy. Rand *holding* Tommy! She stared in disbelief, the image going dizzily out of focus. She had to be hallucinating. Perhaps she had drowned after all, and this was some kind of out-of-body experience. They couldn't possibly be sitting there on the beach, watching her approach.

"Rand was shot," she whispered.

"Point-blank," Komake chuckled. "The dumb *kanaka* must have thought he was some kind of samurai warrior, the way he charged after Eason. The bullet almost knocked the stuffing out of him."

"He's alive!"

"It was an idiotic stunt," Komake said. "But he says Eason was going to shoot *you.* So, better him than our beautiful and resourceful *wahini* is what I say. And I'll bet the manufacturer of the bulletproof vest will be after him for a testimonial."

"Eddie . . . please . . . shut up!"

Alyse wriggled, and he set her down. She took off running as soon as her feet touched the sand, her exhaustion gone in a rush of adrenaline. Rand shouted her name into the wind and tried to stand up, but sank to his knees with a grimace, Tommy's arms locked around his neck.

She stopped a few feet away, afraid to go closer. *They're just a mirage,* she thought. *If you touch them, they'll disappear.*

A thick, dark blue vest with wide Velcro straps

lay next to Rand. His shirt was pulled away from his chest and right shoulder, where the reddened skin had swollen and a huge bruise was developing. His brimming eyes were as red as his shoulder. He looked stunned with joy, as if he couldn't quite believe that Alyse was real either.

Tommy looked up at her, grinning through his own tears. *Mirages don't cry,* Alyse reasoned. *And they don't bruise.*

She moved closer and knelt beside them. Rand devoured her with his eyes, but seemed unable to raise his right arm. Tommy put a hand in hers. It felt warm and reassuringly real. She kissed his thumb. Rand reached his good arm around Tommy and took her other hand — the one with the dragonfly pendant dangling almost forgotten from the wrist.

No one spoke. Even Tommy remained silent as if he, too, sensed that the time for words would come later. For now, it was enough to simply hold onto each other as they adjusted to the miracle of their survival.

Sirens approached on the highway beyond the cottage. People arrived, hurrying. The beach grew crowded with flashlights and battery-powered searchlights and strange, urgent voices. To Alyse, none of that seemed of her world.

She was still huddled on the sand with Rand and Tommy when Eddie Komake joined them. Now he wore a laminated U.S. Customs Service identification card clipped to the pocket of his damp luau shirt.

"How's the wing, brudda?" he asked, inspecting Rand's shoulder. "You ought to put an ice pack on that, you know."

"I'm fine." Rand squeezed Alyse's hand. "We all are."

"Good." Komake chucked Tommy under the chin. "You were supposed to stay in the car, short stuff."

"You were supposed to take me for an ice cream cone," Tommy shot back.

Komake burst out laughing and ruffled the boy's hair. Alyse looked at him quizzically.

"When the luau started turning homicidal," Komake explained, "I thought I'd better whisk Tommy out of harm's way until we got the villains sorted out. But he ended up right in the thick of things anyway."

"I thought *you* were one of the villains," Alyse told him.

Komake laughed again, this time less boisterously. "I'm afraid there were only two. Conrad Brace and Lyle Eason."

"Speaking of Eason . . ." Rand said, looking sharply at Komake.

The Customs agent shook his head. "He apparently wasn't as good a swimmer as our *wahini u'i*. All we found was his jacket where he'd left it on the beach." He smiled. "The haiku from the Tokugawa Shogun box was in the pocket."

They all looked down at the pendant. The last of the plaster camouflage had dissolved in the water, leaving the jade, mother-of-pearl, and gold fully exposed.

"Where did you get that?" Tommy asked.

The adults laughed and Alyse hugged Tommy. "It's a *very* long story, sweetie. I'll tell it to you over a cup of hot chocolate sometime."

"Come on, brudda," Komake said, picking up the bulletproof vest. "Let's get up to the house. You aren't going to believe the changes Eason made to the decor of your living room."

The night sky outside the window wall had turned a paler shade of black. Alyse sat between Rand and Tommy on the couch, waiting for the dawn, waiting for the last of the police crime scene investigators to leave, waiting for the dust of her past life to settle.

"Have the pain pills taken hold yet?" she asked, toying absently with the dragonfly necklace still around her wrist.

"No. I'm still too wound up, I think." Rand leaned down and kissed the top of her head, where her hair hadn't quite dried yet.

"They'll probably hit you all at once, and you'll go out like a light."

She resettled Tommy's head on her lap. The boy murmured in his sleep, but didn't awaken. They had all changed into dry clothes. Tommy into pajamas, Rand into cutoffs, Alyse into Rand's big terrycloth robe. But nobody had even suggested going to bed.

"Don't worry about me." Rand kissed her temple. "Don't worry about anything."

Alyse turned her face to him and he pressed his lips to hers. She sighed into his gentle kiss, feeling as if she were being welcomed into another life.

"Knock it off, you two," Komake said quietly. "You'll corrupt the morals of my boy."

Rand looked over his shoulder at Eddie, who had just wandered in from the kitchen carrying a cup of coffee. "Since when did Tommy get to be community property?"

"Since he told me you were adopting him." Komake grinned. "I figured the little *keiki* could use all the outside support he can get. I'm his new godfather."

"He already has one. Me."

"Well, a kid can't have too many, can he? Besides, young Tom needs a godfather who can trace his family back to the first King Kamehameha."

"If such a godfather exists," Rand said. "I don't think I'm going to take your word for it, Eddie."

"Amen," said Alyse.

Rand shifted his gaze to her, and she could tell they were thinking the same thing. They both glanced down at Tommy to make sure he was still sleeping soundly. The child had conked out fifteen seconds after his head touched her thigh, and had been totally oblivious to the world ever since.

"The man who was killed with Conrad," Alyse revealed in a half whisper. "Rand thinks he worked for Tommy's grandmother."

Komake raised a finger, as if she had just reminded him of something. "About that clown. He wasn't killed, although he's some the worse for wear after stumbling onto Eason and Brace on the path to the *heiau*. He's blabbering his head off at the hospital."

He took a swig of coffee, squinting over the rim of the cup at Rand. "The grandmother's name wouldn't be Elaine Fielding, by any chance, would it?"

Rand nodded glumly. He glanced at Tommy again, and said in an undertone, "Vampira in the flesh."

"Well, *well*." Eddie pursed his lips and stared thoughtfully at the wall. "That certainly explains a lot. We've been trying to figure out where a sleazy Honolulu private investigator fitted into all this."

When Rand fell silent, Alyse explained how Mrs. Fielding had hired the man to follow Rand, in hopes of coming up with evidence that would prove him to be an unfit guardian for Tommy. Komake frowned as she talked, his gaze shifting from Tommy to Rand and back to Alyse.

"Considering what happened tonight," Rand said, his lips tightening into a hard line, "I can just imagine what kind of report he is going to hand over to the old bag."

Eddie's eyes narrowed, and he made a growling sound in his throat, like a terrier with its hackles raised. "We'll see about that."

"What do you have in mind?" Alyse asked.

"For starters, I'll have a little talk with the folks at the Japanese consulate—who are on their way here to retrieve their national treasures, by the way. Now that the theft ring has been eliminated—with your help—I'm sure they can be persuaded to get out some carefully targeted publicity in your behalf." Komake winked. "Who's going to have the gall to refuse a genuine international hero guardianship of his own nephew?"

"Especially when the genuine international hero plans to marry another genuine international hero," Rand said.

Alyse looked at him in surprise. He gazed at her, his features frozen in a mixed-bag expression of dread, hope, anticipation, and a dozen other emotions all glued together with love. If she hadn't cried herself out hours ago, she would have now. Instead, she slid her hand onto his thigh and smiled at him.

She felt Rand relax against her for the first time since they had sat down together. His hand drifted over to trace the shelllike contours of her

298

left ear. She hoped Komake didn't notice the goose-flesh that erupted on her arms.

She reached up and moved Rand's hand away, trying to make her gesture appear casual. He took her hand and drew feathery little figure eights in her palm with his thumb.

"You're a very devious person, Eddie," she said, pleased that her voice didn't betray the fact that Rand was engaged in a mapping expedition of her erogenous zones.

Komake winked again, fairly blatantly this time, and was about to say something when his attention suddenly veered toward the kitchen door. Kiku came bustling in, shaking out yet another garbage bag. She had already filled three with debris from the living room, since returning to the cottage several hours ago.

She put both fists on her hips and scowled at Tommy. Kiku had changed out of her party kimono. In her house-cleaning garb, she looked less fragile, and more formidable.

"The child should be in bed," she said flatly.

When Komake stepped forward to do the honors, Kiku thrust the garbage bag into his hands and picked up Tommy herself. She carried him around the couch and disappeared down the hallway toward the bedrooms.

Eddie wadded the garbage bag into a tight roll and tossed it onto the piano. "I don't do windows or aftermaths. *Aloha*, for now."

He snapped them a very un-Hawaiian salute,

and left. A moment later, they heard the front door open and close.

The sky outside the window had brightened to a clear, unblemished eggshell blue. A catamaran appeared on the gentle ocean swells. Alyse tensed for an instant before it struck her that the sail colors were a nice, safe combination of alternating light and dark blue stripes.

"I'll make you happy, Alyse," Rand said softly.

She snuggled closer against him. "You don't have to. I'm already as happy as one human being can be."

He reached over and unwound the dragonfly pendant from her wrist, carefully straightened the gold chain, and slipped it around her neck.

"A treasure for a treasure," he said, curling his good arm around her.

She smiled up at him, and he kissed her languidly. Then not so languidly. His finger was tracing her ear again, doing crazy things to her entire body.

He stopped kissing her just long enough to whisper, "Let's go to bed."

Alyse smiled around his lips. "Kiku would have kittens if she caught us in bed together."

She did a little exploring of her own, and found a place on the side of his neck that made him squirm when she brushed it with her tongue. She went to work exacting revenge for her ear, smiling, thinking how much fun Rand was going to be — when she thought at all.

"We could go out on the beach," he suggested in a gravelly voice. "I know a certain coconut palm . . ."

"In broad daylight? Sure."

Rand growled and removed her from his neck. They sat holding each other as she waited to hear his next idea. After a while, he sighed heavily, and Alyse felt him sag slightly,

The pain pills were finally taking hold. He was asleep.

She kissed Rand's slack cheek and took his limp hand in both of hers, holding it under her chin as her gaze drifted out the window toward the great ocean beyond. The prize he had placed around her neck was temporary. Everything else was forever.

In the distance, an ultra-light airplane buzzed like a mechanical insect across the bright infinity of sky. She watched it grow smaller and smaller in the distance. Then for just a fleeting moment, the rising sun caught the pale green-and-gold fabric of its fragile wings, turning them gossamer—like the wings of a dragonfly.

LET ARCHER AND CLEARY
AWAKEN AND CAPTURE YOUR HEART!

CAPTIVE DESIRE (2612, $3.75)
by Jane Archer

Victoria Malone fancied herself a great adventuress and student of life, but being kidnapped by handsome Cord Cordova was too much excitement for even her! Convincing her kidnapper that she had been an innocent bystander when the stagecoach was robbed was futile when he was kissing her until she was senseless!

REBEL SEDUCTION (3249, $4.25)
by Jane Archer

"Stop that train!" came Lacey Whitmore's terrified warning as she rushed toward the locomotive that carried wounded Confederates and her own beloved father. But no one paid heed, least of all the Union spy Clint McCullough, who pinned her to the ground as the train suddenly exploded into flames.

DREAM'S DESIRE (3093, $4.50)
by Gwen Cleary

Desperate to escape an arranged marriage, Antonia Winston y Ortega fled her father's hacienda to the arms of the arrogant Captain Domino. She would spend the night with him and would be free for no gentleman wants a ruined bride. And ruined she would be, for Tonia would never forget his searing kisses!

VICTORIA'S ECSTASY (2906, $4.25)
by Gwen Cleary

Proud Victoria Torrington was short of cash to run her shipping empire, so she traveled to America to meet her partner for the first time. Expecting a withered, ancient cowhand, Victoria didn't know what to do when she met virile, muscular Judge Colston and her body budded with desire.

Available wherever paperbacks are sold, or order direct from the Publisher. Send cover price plus 50¢ per copy for mailing and handling to Zebra Books, Dept. 3839, 475 Park Avenue South, New York, N.Y. 10016. Residents of New York and Tennessee must include sales tax. DO NOT SEND CASH. For a free Zebra/ Pinnacle catalog please write to the above address.

FEEL THE FIRE IN CAROL FINCH'S ROMANCES!

BELOVED BETRAYAL (2346, $3.95)

Sabrina Spencer donned a gray wig and veiled hat before blackmailing rugged Ridge Tanner into guiding her to Fort Canby. But the costume soon became her prison—the beauty had fallen head over heels in love!

LOVE'S HIDDEN TREASURE (2980, $4.50)

Shandra d'Evereux felt her heart throb beneath the stolen map she'd hidden in her bodice when Nolan Elliot swept her out onto the veranda. It was hard to concentrate on her mission with that wily rogue around!

MONTANA MOONFIRE (3263, $4.95)

Just as debutante Victoria Flemming-Cassidy was about to marry an oh-so-suitable mate, the towering preacher, Dru Sullivan flung her over his shoulder and headed West! Suddenly, Tori realized she had been given the best present for a bride: a night of passion with a real man!

THUNDER'S TENDER TOUCH (2809, $4.50)

Refined Piper Malone needed bounty-hunter, Vince Logan to recover her swindled inheritance. She thought she could coolly dismiss him after he did the job, but she never counted on the hot flood of desire she felt whenever he was near!

OFFICIAL ENTRY FORM
Please enter me in the

Lucky in Love

SWEEPSTAKES

Grand Prize choice: _____

Name: _____

Address: _____

City: _____ **State** _____ **Zip** _____

Store name: _____

Address: _____

City: _____ **State** _____ **Zip** _____

MAIL TO: LUCKY IN LOVE
P.O. Box 1022B
Grand Rapids, MN 55730-1022B

Sweepstakes ends: 3/31/93

OFFICIAL RULES
"LUCKY IN LOVE" SWEEPSTAKES

1. To enter complete the official entry form. No purchase necessary. You may enter by hand printing on a 3" x 5" piece of paper, your name, address and the words "Lucky In Love." Mail to: "Lucky In Love" Sweepstakes, P.O. Box 1022B, Grand Rapids, MN 55730-1022-B.

2. Enter as often as you like, but each entry must be mailed separately. Mechanically reproduced entries not accepted. Entries must be received by March 31, 1993.

3. Winners selected in a random drawing on or about April 16, 1993 from among all eligible entries received by Marden-Kane, Inc. an independent judging organization whose decisions are final and binding. Winner may be required to sign an affidavit of eligibility and release which must be returned within 14 days or alternate winner(s) will be selected. Winners permit the use of their name/photograph for publicity/advertising purposes without further compensation. No transfer of prizes permitted. Taxes are the sole responsibility of the prize winners. Only one prize per family or household.

4. Winners agree that the sponsor, its affiliate and their agencies and employees shall not be liable for injury, loss or damage of any kind resulting from participation in this promotion or from the acceptance or use of the prizes awarded.

5. Sweepstakes open to residents of the U.S., except employees of Zebra Books, their affiliates, advertising and promotion agencies and Marden-Kane, Inc. Void where taxed, prohibited or restricted by law. All Federal, State and Local laws and regulations apply. Odds of winning depend upon the total number of eligible entries received. All prizes will be awarded. Not responsible for lost, misdirected mail or printing errors.

6. For the name of the Grand Prize Winner, send a self-addressed stamped envelope to: "Lucky In Love" Winners, P.O. Box 706-B, Sayreville, NJ 08871.